Nora Roberts is the *New York Times* bestselling author of more than one hundred and ninety novels. A born storyteller, she creates a blend of warmth, humour and poignancy that speaks directly to her readers and has earned her almost every award for excellence in her field. The youngest of five children, Nora lives in western Maryland. She has two sons.

Visit her website at www.noraroberts.com

014190589 9

Also available by Nora Roberts

THE MACKADE BROTHERS
The Return of Rafe MacKade
The Pride of Jared MacKade
The Heart of Devin MacKade
The Fall of Shane MacKade

THE O'HURLEYS
The Last Honest Woman
Dance to the Piper
Skin Deep
Without a Trace

THE STANISLASKIS
Taming Natasha
Falling for Rachel
Luring a Lady
Convincing Alex
Waiting for Nick
Considering Kate

THE CALHOUN WOMEN
The Calhoun Sisters
For the Love of Lilah
Suzanna's Surender
Megan's Mate

CORDINA'S ROYAL FAMILY
Affaire Royale
Command Performance
The Playboy Prince
Cordina's Crown Jewel

THE MacGREGORS
Playing the Odds
Tempting Fate
All the Possibilities
One Man's Art
The MacGregor Grooms
The Perfect Neighbour
Rebellion

THE STARS OF MITHRA
Hidden Star
Captive Star
Secret Star

THE DONOVAN LEGACY
Captivated
Entranced
Charmed

NIGHT TALES
Night Shift
Night Shadow
Nightshade
Night Smoke
Night Shield

Reflections
Night Moves
Dance of Dreams
Boundary Lines
Dream Makers
Risky Business
The Welcoming
The Right Path
Partners
The Art of Deception
The Winning Hand
Irish Rebel
The Law is a Lady
Summer Pleasures
Under Summer Skies
California Summer
Hazy Summer Nights
Summer Dreams
Dual Image
Unfinished Business
Mind Over Matter
Best Laid Plans
Lessons Learned
Summer With You
Loving Jack
Summer in the Sun
Catching Snowflakes
Christmas Magic
Mistletoe and Snow
Time Was
Times Change
This Christmas...
Summer Desserts
For Now, Forever

Nora Roberts

Summer Desserts

MILLS & BOON

This edition published in Great Britain 2017
By Mills & Boon, an imprint of HarperCollins*Publishers*
1 London Bridge Street, London, SE1 9GF

Summer Desserts © 1985 Nora Roberts

ISBN: 978-0-263-93138-9

29-0817

Printed and bound
by CPI Group (UK) Ltd, Croydon, CRO 4YY

To Marianne Shock,
for the cheerful and clever last-minute help.

Chapter 1

Her name was Summer. It was a name that conjured visions of hot petaled flowers, sudden storms and long, restless nights. It also brought images of sun-warmed meadows and naps in the shade. It suited her.

As she stood, hands poised, body tensed, eyes alert, there wasn't a sound in the room. No one, absolutely no one, took their eyes off her. She might move slowly, but there wasn't a person there who wanted to chance missing a gesture, a motion. All attention, all concentration, was riveted upon that one slim, solitary figure. Strains of Chopin floated romantically through the air. The light slanted and shot through her neatly bound hair—rich, warm brown with hints and tints of gold. Two emerald studs winked at her ears.

Her skin was a bit flushed so that a rose tinge accented already prominent cheekbones and the elegant bone structure that comes only from breeding. Excitement, intense concentration, deepened the amber flecks that were sprinkled in the hazel of her eyes. The same excitement and concentration had her soft, molded lips forming a pout.

She was all in white, plain, unadorned white, but she drew the eye as irresistibly as a butterfly in full, dazzling flight. She wouldn't speak, yet everyone in the room strained forward as if to catch the slightest sound.

The room was warm, the smells exotic, the atmosphere taut with anticipation.

Summer might have been alone for all the attention she paid to those around her. There was only one goal, one end. Perfection. She'd never settled for less.

With infinite care she lifted the final diamond-shape and pressed the angelica onto the Savarin to complete the design she'd created. The hours she'd already spent preparing and baking the huge, elaborate dessert were forgotten, as was the heat, the tired leg muscles, the aching arms. The final touch, the *appearance* of a Summer Lyndon creation, was of the utmost importance. Yes, it would taste perfect, smell perfect, even slice perfectly. But if it didn't look perfect, none of that mattered.

With the care of an artist completing a masterpiece, she lifted her brush to give the fruits and almonds a light, delicate coating of apricot glaze.

Still, no one spoke.

Asking no assistance—indeed, she wouldn't have tolerated any—Summer began to fill the center of the Savarin with the rich cream whose recipe she guarded jealously.

Hands steady, head erect, Summer stepped back to give her creation one last critical study. This was the ultimate test, for her eye was keener than any other's when it came to her own work. She folded her arms across her body. Her face was without expression. In the huge kitchen, the ping of a pin dropped on the tile would have reverberated like a gunshot.

Slowly her lips curved, her eyes glittered. Success. Summer lifted one arm and gestured rather dramatically. "Take it away," she ordered.

As two assistants began to roll the glittering concoction from the room, applause broke out.

Summer accepted the accolade as her due. There was a place for modesty, she knew, and she knew it didn't apply to her Savarin. It was, to put it mildly, magnificent. Magnificence was what the Italian duke had wanted for his daughter's engagement party, and magnificence was what he'd paid for. Summer had simply delivered.

"Mademoiselle." Foulfount, the Frenchman whose specialty was shellfish, took Summer by both shoulders. His eyes were round and damp with appreciation. *"Incroyable."* Enthusiastically, he kissed both her cheeks while his thick, clever fingers squeezed her skin as they might a fresh-baked loaf of bread. Summer broke out in her first grin in hours.

"Merci." Someone had opened a celebratory bottle of wine. Summer took two glasses, handing one to the French chef. "To the next time we work together, *mon ami.*"

She tossed back the wine, took off her chef's hat, then breezed out of the kitchen. In the enormous marble-floored, chandeliered dining room, her Savarin was even now being served and admired. Her last thought before leaving was—thank God someone else had to clean up the mess.

Two hours later, she had her shoes off and her eyes closed. A gruesome murder mystery lay open on her lap as her plane cruised over the Atlantic. She was going home. She'd spent almost three full days in Milan for the sole purpose of creating that one dish. It wasn't an unusual experience for her. Summer had baked *Charlotte Malakoff* in Madrid, flamed *Crêpes Fourée* in Athens and molded *île Flottante* in Istanbul. For her expenses, and a stunning fee, Summer Lyndon would create a dessert that would live in the memory long after the last bite, drop or crumb was consumed.

Have wisk, will travel, she thought vaguely and smiled through a yawn.

She considered herself a specialist, not unlike a skilled surgeon. Indeed, she'd studied, apprenticed and practiced as long as many respected members of the medical profession. Five years after passing the stringent requirements to become a Cordon Bleu chef in Paris, the city where cooking is its own art, Summer had a reputation for being as temperamental as any artist, for having the mind of a computer when it came to remembering recipes and for having the hands of an angel.

Summer half dozed in her first-class seat and fought off a desperate craving for a slice of pepperoni pizza.

She knew the flight time would go faster if she could read or sleep her way through it. She decided to mix the two, taking the light nap first. Summer was a woman who prized her sleep almost as highly as she prized her recipe for chocolate mousse.

On her return to Philadelphia, her schedule would be hectic at best. There was the bombe to prepare for the governor's charity banquet, the annual meeting of the Gourmet Society, the demonstration she'd agreed to do for public television…and that meeting, she remembered drowsily.

What had that bird-voiced woman said over the phone? Summer wondered. Drake—no, Blake—Cocharan. Blake Cocharan III of the Cocharan hotel chain. Excellent hotels, Summer thought without any real interest. She'd patronized a number of them in various corners of the world. Mr. Cocharan the Third had a business proposition for her.

Summer assumed that he wanted her to create some special dessert exclusively for his chain of hotels, something they could attach the Cocharan name to. She wasn't averse to the notion—under the proper circumstances. And for the proper fee. Naturally she'd have to investigate the entire Cocharan enterprise carefully before she agreed to involve her skill or her name with it. If any one of their hotels was of inferior quality...

With a yawn, Summer decided to think about it later—after she'd met with The Third personality. Blake Cocharan III, she thought again with a sleepily amused smile. Plump, balding, probably dyspeptic. Italian shoes, Swiss watch, French shirts, German car—and no doubt he'd consider himself unflaggingly American. The image she created hung in her mind a moment, and, bored with it, she yawned again—then sighed as the idea of pizza once again invaded her thoughts. Summer tilted her seat back farther and determinedly willed herself to sleep.

Blake Cocharan III sat in the plush rear seat of the gunmetal-gray limo and meticulously went over the report on the newest Cocharan House being constructed in Saint Croix. He was a man who could scoop us a mess of scattered details and align them in perfect, systematic order. Chaos was simply a form of order waiting to be unjumbled with logic. Blake was a very logical man. Point A invariably led to point B, and from there to C. No matter how confused the maze, with patience and logic, one could find the route.

Because of his talent for doing just that, Blake, at thirty-five, had almost complete control of the Cocharan empire. He'd inherited his wealth and, as a result, rarely thought of it. But he'd earned his position, and valued it. Quality was a Cocharan tradition. Nothing but the finest would do for any Cocharan House, from the linen on the beds to the mortar in the foundations.

His report on Summer Lyndon told him she was the best.

Setting aside the Saint Croix packet, Blake slipped another file from the slim briefcase by his feet. A single ring, oval-faced, gold and scrolled, gleamed dully on his hand. Summer Lyndon, he mused, flipping the file open...

Twenty-eight, graduate Sorbonne, certified Cordon Bleu chef. Father, Rothschild Lyndon, respected member of British Parliament. Mother, Monique Dubois Lyndon, former star of the French cinema. Parents amicably divorced for twenty-three years. Summer Lyndon had spent her formative years between London and Paris before her mother had married an American hardware tycoon, based in Philadelphia. Summer had then returned to Paris to complete her education and currently had living quarters both there and in Philadelphia. Her mother had since married a third time, a paper baron on this round, and her father was separated from his second wife, a successful barrister.

All of Blake's probing had produced the same basic answer. Summer Lyndon was the best dessert chef on either side of the Atlantic. She was also a superb all-around chef with an instinctive knowledge of quality, a flair for creativity and the ability to improvise in a crisis. On the other hand, she was reputed to be dictatorial, temperamental and brutally frank. These qualities, however, hadn't alienated her from heads of state, aristocracy or celebrities.

She might insist on having Chopin piped into the kitchen while she cooked, or summarily refuse to work at all if the lighting wasn't to her liking, but her mousse alone was enough to make a strong man beg to grant her slightest wish.

Blake wasn't a man to beg for anything…but he wanted Summer Lyndon for Cocharan House. He never doubted he could persuade her to agree to precisely what he had in mind.

A formidable woman, he imagined, respecting that. He had no patience with weak wills or soft brains— particularly in people who worked for him. Not many women had risen to the position, or the reputation, that Summer Lyndon held. Women might traditionally be cooks, but men were traditionally chefs.

He imagined her thick waisted from sampling her own creations. Strong hands, he thought idly. Her skin was probably a bit pasty from all those hours indoors in kitchens. A no-nonsense woman, he was sure, with an uncompromising view on what was edible and why. Organized, logical and cultured—perhaps a bit plain due to her preoccupation with food rather than fashion. Blake imagined that they would deal with each other very well. With a glance at his watch, Blake noted with satisfaction that he was right on time for the meeting.

The limo cruised to a halt beside the curb. "I'll be no more than an hour," Blake told the driver as he climbed out.

"Yes, sir." The driver checked his watch. When Mr. Cocharan said an hour, you could depend on it.

Blake glanced up at the fourth floor as he crossed to the well-kept old building. The windows were open, he noted. Warm spring air poured in, while music— a melody he couldn't quite catch over the sounds of traffic—poured out. When Blake went in, he learned that the single elevator was out of order. He walked up four flights.

After Blake knocked, the door was opened by a small woman with a stunning face who was dressed in a T-shirt and slim black jeans. The maid on her way out for a day off? Blake wondered idly. She didn't look strong enough to scrub a floor. And if she was going out, she was going out without her shoes.

After the brief, objective glance, his gaze was drawn irresistibly back to her face. Classic, naked and undeniably sensuous. The mouth alone would make a man's blood move. Blake ignored what he considered an automatic sexual pull.

"Blake Cocharan to see Ms. Lyndon."

Summer's left brow rose—a sign of surprise. Then her lips curved slightly—a sign of pleasure.

Plump, he wasn't, she observed. Hard and lean—racketball, tennis, swimming. He was obviously a man more prone to these than lingering over executive lunches. Balding, no. His hair was rich black and thick. It was styled well, with slight natural waves that added to the attractiveness of a cool, sensual face. A sweep of cheekbones, a firm line of chin. She liked the look of the former that spoke of strength, and the latter, just barely cleft, that spoke of charm. Black brows were almost straight over clear, water-blue eyes. His mouth was a bit long but beautifully shaped. His nose was very straight—the sort she'd always thought was made to be looked down. Perhaps she'd been right about the outward trimmings—the Italian shoes, and so forth—but, Summer admitted, she'd been off the mark with the man.

The assessment didn't take her long—three, perhaps four, seconds. But her mouth curved more. Blake couldn't take his eyes off it. It was a mouth a man, if he breathed, wanted to taste. "Please come in, Mr. Cocharan." Summer stepped back, swinging the door wider in invitation. "It's very considerate of you to agree to meet here. Please have a seat. I'm afraid I'm in the middle of something in the kitchen." She smiled, gestured and disappeared.

Blake opened his mouth—he wasn't used to being brushed off by servants—then closed it again. He had enough time to be tolerant. As he set down his briefcase he glanced around the room. There were fringed lamps, a curved sofa in plush blue velvet, a fussily carved cherrywood table. Aubusson carpets—two—softly faded in blues and grays—were spread over the floors. A Ming vase. Potpourri in what was certainly a Dresden compote.

The room had no order; it was a mix of European periods and styles that should never have suited, but was instantly attractive. He saw that a pedestal table at the far end of the room was covered with jumbled typewritten pages and handwritten notes. Street sounds drifted in through the window. Chopin floated from the stereo.

As he stood there, drawing it in, he was abruptly certain there was no one in the apartment but himself and the woman who had opened the door. Summer Lyndon? Fascinated with the idea, and with the aroma creeping from the kitchen, Blake crossed the room.

Six pastry shells, just touched with gold and moisture, sat on a rack. One by one Summer filled them to overflowing with what appeared to be some rich white cream. When Blake glanced at her face he saw the concentration, the seriousness and intensity he might have associated with a brain surgeon. It should have amused him. Yet somehow, with the strains of Chopin pouring through the kitchen speakers, with those delicate, slim-fingered hands arranging the cream in mounds, he was fascinated.

She dipped a fork in a pan and dribbled what he guessed was warmed caramel over the cream. It ran lavishly down the sides and gelled. He doubted that it was humanly possible not to lust after just one taste. Again, one by one, she scooped up the tarts and placed them on a plate lined with a lacy paper doily. When the last one was arranged, she looked up at Blake.

"Would you like some coffee?" She smiled and the line of concentration between her brows disappeared. The intensity that had seemed to darken her irises lightened.

Blake glanced at the dessert plate and wondered how her waist could be hand-spannable. "Yes, I would."

"It's hot," she told him as she lifted the plate. "Help yourself. I have to run these next door." She was past him and to the doorway of the kitchen before she turned around. "Oh, there're some cookies in the jar, if you like. I'll be right back."

She was gone, and the pastries with her. With a shrug, he turned back to the kitchen, which was a shambles. Summer Lyndon might be a great cook, but she was obviously not a neat one. Still if the scent and look of the pastries had been any indication...

He started to root in the cupboards for a cup, then gave in to temptation. Standing in his Saville Row suit, Blake ran his finger along the edge of the bowl that had held the cream. He laid it on his tongue. With a sigh, his eyes closed. Rich, thick and very French.

He'd dined in the most exclusive restaurants, in some of the wealthiest homes, in dozens of countries all over the world. Logically, practically, honestly, he couldn't say he'd ever tasted better than what he now scooped from the bowl in this woman's kitchen. In deciding to specialize in desserts and pastries, Summer Lyndon had chosen well, he concluded. He felt a momentary regret that she'd taken those rich, fat tarts to someone else. This time when Blake started his search for a cup, he spotted the ceramic cookie jar shaped like a panda.

Normally he wouldn't have been interested. He wasn't a man with a particularly active sweet tooth. But the flavor of the cream lingered on his tongue. What sort of cookie did a woman who created the finest of haute cuisine make? With a cup of English bone china in one hand, Blake lifted off the top of the panda's head. Setting it down, he pulled out a cookie and stared in simple wonder.

No American could mistake that particular munchie. A classic? he mused. A tradition? An Oreo. Blake continued to stare at the chocolate sandwich cookie with its double dose of white center. He turned it over in his hand. The brand was unmistakably stamped into both sides. This from a woman who baked and whipped and glazed for royalty?

A laugh broke from him as he dropped the Oreo back into the panda. Throughout his career he'd had to deal with more than his share of eccentrics. Running a chain of hotels wasn't just a matter of who checked in and who checked out. There were designers, artists, architects, decorators, chefs, musicians, union representatives. Blake considered himself knowledgeable of people. It wouldn't take him long to learn what made Summer tick.

She dashed back into the kitchen just as he was finally pouring the coffee. "I'm sorry to have kept you waiting, Mr. Cocharan. I know it was rude." She smiled, as if she had no doubt she'd be forgiven, as she poured her own coffee. "I had to get those pastries finished for my neighbor. She's having a small engagement tea this afternoon—with prospective in-laws." Her smile turned to a grin and, sipping her black coffee, she plucked the top from the panda. "Did you want a cookie?"

"No. Please, you go ahead."

Taking him at his word, Summer chose one and nibbled. "You know," she said thoughtfully, "these are uniformly excellent for their kind." She gestured with the half cookie she had left. "Shall we go sit down and discuss your proposition?"

She moved fast, he mused with approval. Perhaps he'd at least been on the mark about the no-nonsense attitude. With a nod of acknowledgment, Blake followed her. He was successful in his profession, not because he was a third-generation Cocharan, but because he had a quick and analytical mind. Problems were systematically solved. At the moment, he had to decide just how to approach a woman like Summer Lyndon.

She had a face that belonged in the shade of a tree on the Bois de Boulogne. Very French, very elegant. Her voice had the round, clear tones that spoke unmistakably of European education and upbringing—a wisp of France again but with the discipline of Britain. Her hair was pinned up, a concession to the heat and humidity, he imagined—though she had the windows open, ignoring the available air-conditioning. The studs in her ears were emeralds, round and flawless. There was a good-sized tear in the sleeve of her T-shirt.

Sitting on the couch, she folded her legs under her. Her bare toes were painted with a wild rose enamel, but her fingernails were short and unvarnished. He caught the allure of her scent—a touch of the caramel from the pastries, but under it something unmistakably French, unapologetically sexual.

How did one approach such a woman? Blake reflected. Did he use charm, flattery or figures? She was reputed to be a perfectionist and occasionally a firebrand. She'd refused to cook for an important political figure because he wouldn't fly her personal kitchen equipment to his country. She'd charged a Hollywood celebrity a small fortune to create a twenty-tiered wedding cake extravaganza. And she'd just hand-baked and hand-delivered a plate of pastries to a neighbor for a tea. Blake would much prefer to have the key to her before he made his offer. He knew the advantages of taking a circular route. Indeed some might call it stalking.

"I'm acquainted with your mother," Blake began easily as he continued to gauge the woman beside him.

"Really?" He caught both amusement and affection in the word. "I shouldn't be surprised," she said as she nibbled on the cookie again. "My mother always patronized a Cocharan House when we traveled. I believe I had dinner with your grandfather when I was six or seven." The amusement didn't fade as she sipped at her coffee. "Small world."

An excellent suit, Summer decided, relaxing against the back of the sofa. It was well cut and conservative enough to have gained her father's approval. The form it was molded to was well built and lean enough to have gained her mother's. It was perhaps the combination of the two that drew her interest.

Good God, he is attractive, she thought as she took another considering survey of his face. Not quite smooth, not quite rugged, his power sat well on him. That was something she recognized—in herself and in others. She respected someone who sought and got his own way, as she judged Blake did. She respected herself for the same reason. Attractive, she thought again—but she felt that a man like Blake would be so, regardless of physical appearance.

Her mother would have called him *séduisant,* and accurately so. Summer would have called him dangerous. A difficult combination to resist. She shifted, perhaps unconsciously, to put more distance between them. Business, after all, was business.

"You're familiar then with the standards of a Cocharan House," Blake began. Quite suddenly he wished her scent weren't so alluring or her mouth so tempting. He didn't care to have business muddled with attraction, no matter how pleasant.

"Of course." Summer set down her coffee because drinking it only seemed to accentuate the odd little flutter in her stomach. "I invariably stay at them myself."

"I've been told your standards of quality are equally high."

This time when Summer smiled there was a hint of arrogance to it. "I'm the very best at what I do because I have no intention of being otherwise."

The first key, Blake decided with satisfaction. Professional vanity. "So my information tells me, Ms. Lyndon. The very best is all that interests me."

"So." Summer propped an elbow on the back of the sofa then rested her head on the palm. "How exactly do I interest you, Mr. Cocharan?" She knew the question was loaded, but couldn't resist. When a woman was constantly taking risks and making experiments in her professional life, the habit often leaked through.

Six separate answers skimmed through his mind, none of which had any bearing on his purpose for being there. Blake set down his coffee. "The restaurants at the Cocharan Houses are renowned for their quality and service. However, recently the restaurant here in our Philadelphia complex seems to be suffering from a lack of both. Frankly, Ms. Lyndon, it's my opinion that the food has become too pedestrian—too boring. I plan to do some remodeling, both in physical structure and in staff."

"Wise. Restaurants, like people, often become too complacent."

"I want the best head chef available." He aimed a level look. "My research tells me that's you."

Summer lifted a brow, not in surprise this time but in consideration. "That's flattering, but I freelance, Mr. Cocharan. And I specialize."

"Specialize, yes, but you do have both experience and knowledge in all areas of haute cuisine. As for the freelancing, you'd be free to continue that to a large extent, at least after the first few months. You'd need to establish your own staff and create your own menu. I don't believe in hiring an expert, then interfering."

She was frowning again—concentration, not annoyance. It was tempting, very tempting. Perhaps it was just the travel weariness from her trip back from Italy, but she'd begun to grow a bit tired—bored?—with the constant demands of flying to any given country to make that one dish. It seemed he'd hit her at the right moment to stir her interest in concentrating on one place, and one kitchen, for a span of time.

It would be interesting work—if he were being truthful about the free hand she'd have—redoing a kitchen and the menu in an old, established and respected hotel. It would take her perhaps six months of intense effort, and then… It was the "and then" that made her hesitate again. If she gave that much time and effort to a full-time job, would she still retain her flair for the spectacular? That, too, was something to consider.

She'd always had a firm policy against committing herself to any one establishment—a wariness of commitments ribboned through all areas of her life. If you locked yourself into something, to someone, you opened yourself to all manner of complications.

Besides, Summer reasoned, if she wanted to affiliate herself with a restaurant, she could open and run her own. She hadn't done it yet because it would tie her too long to one place, attach her too closely to one project. She preferred traveling, creating one superb dish at a time, then moving on. The next country, the next dish. That was her style. Why should she consider altering it now?

"A very flattering offer, Mr. Cocharan—"

"A mutually advantageous one," he interrupted, perceptive enough to catch the beginning of a refusal. With deliberate ease, he tossed out a six-digit annual salary that rendered Summer momentarily speechless—not a simple task.

"And generous," she said when she found her voice again.

"One doesn't get the best unless one's willing to pay for it. I'd like you to think about this, Ms. Lyndon." He reached in his briefcase and pulled out a sheaf of papers. "This is a draft of an agreement. You might like to have your attorney look it over, and of course, points can be negotiated."

She didn't want to look at the damn contract because she could feel, quite tangibly, that she was being maneuvered into a corner—a very plush one. "Mr. Cocharan, I do appreciate your interest, but—"

"After you've thought it over, I'd like to discuss it with you again, perhaps over dinner. Say, Friday?"

Summer narrowed her eyes. The man was a steamroller, she decided. A very attractive, very sleek steamroller. No matter how elegant the machinery, you still got flattened if you were in the path. Haughtiness emanated from her. "I'm sorry, I'm working Friday evening—the governor's charity affair."

"Ah, yes." He smiled, though his stomach had tightened. He had a suddenly vivid, completely wild image of making love to her on the ground of some moist, shadowy forest. That alone nearly made him consider accepting her refusal. And that alone made him all the more determined not to. "I can pick you up there. We can have a late supper."

"Mr. Cocharan," Summer said in a frigid voice, "you're going to have to learn to take no for an answer."

Like hell, he thought grimly, but gave her a rather rueful, rather charming smile. "My apologies, Ms. Lyndon, if I seem to be pressuring you. You were my first choice, you see, and I tend to go with my instincts. However…" Seemingly reluctant, he rose. The knot of tension and anger in Summer's stomach began to loosen. "If your mind's made up…" He plucked the contract from the table and started to slip it into his briefcase. "Perhaps you can give me your opinion on Louis LaPointe."

"LaPointe?" The word whispered through Summer's lips like venom. Very slowly she uncurled from the sofa, then rose, her whole body stiff. "You ask me of LaPointe?" In anger, her French ancestry became more pronounced in her speech.

"I'd appreciate anything you could tell me," Blake went on amiably, knowing full well he'd scored his first real point off her. "Seeing that you and he are associates and—"

With a toss of her head, Summer said something short, rude and to the point in her mother's tongue. The gold flecks in her eyes glimmered. Sherlock Holmes had Professor Moriarty. Superman had Lex Luthor. Summer Lyndon had Louis LaPointe.

"Slimy pig," she grated, reverting to English. "He has the mind of a peanut and the hands of a lumberjack. You want to know about LaPointe?" She snatched a cigarette from the case on the table, lighting it as she did only when extremely agitated. "He's a peasant. What else is there to know?"

"According to my information, he's one of the five top chefs in Paris." Blake pressed because a good pressure point was an invaluable weapon. "His *Canard en Croûte* is said to be unsurpassable."

"Shoe leather." She all but spat out the words, and Blake had to school every facial muscle to prevent the grin. Professional vanity, he thought again. She had her share. Then as she drew in a deep breath, he had to school the rest of his muscles to hold off a fierce surge of desire. Sensuality—perhaps she had more than her share. "Why are you asking me about LaPointe?"

"I'm flying to Paris next week to meet with him. Since you're refusing my offer—"

"You'll offer this—" she wagged a finger at the contract still in Blake's hand "—to him?"

"Admittedly he's my second choice, but there are those on the board who feel Louis LaPointe is more qualified for the position."

"Is that so?" Her eyes were slits now behind a screen of smoke. She plucked the contract from his hand, then dropped it beside her cooling coffee. "The members of your board are perhaps ignorant?"

"They are," he managed, "perhaps mistaken."

"Indeed." Summer took a drag of her cigarette, then released smoke in a quick stream. She detested the taste. "You can pick me up at nine o'clock on Friday at the governor's kitchen, Mr. Cocharan. We'll discuss this matter further."

"My pleasure, Ms. Lyndon." He inclined his head, careful to keep his face expressionless until he'd closed the front door behind him. He laughed his way down four flights of steps.

Chapter 2

Making a good dessert from scratch isn't a simple matter. Creating a masterpiece from flour, eggs and sugar is something else again. Whenever Summer picked up a bowl or a whisk or beater, she felt it her duty to create a masterpiece. Adequate, as an adjective in conjunction with her work, was the ultimate insult. Adequate, to Summer, was the result achieved by a newlywed with a cookbook first opened the day after the honeymoon. She didn't simply bake, mix or freeze—she conceived, developed and achieved. An architect, an engineer, a scientist did no more, no less. When she'd chosen to study the art of haute cuisine, she hadn't done so lightly, and she hadn't done so without the goal of perfection in mind. Perfection was still what she sought whenever she lifted a spoon.

She'd already spent the better part of her day in the kitchen of the governor's mansion. Other chefs fussed with soups and sauces—or each other. All of Summer's talent was focused on the creation of the finale, the exquisite mix of tastes and textures, the overall aesthetic beauty of the bombe.

The mold was already lined with the moist cake she'd baked, then systematically sliced into a pattern. This had been done with templates as meticulously as when an engineer designs a bridge. The mousse, a paradise of chocolate and cream, was already inside the dessert's dome. This deceptively simple element had been chilling since early morning. Between the preparations, the mixing, making and building, Summer had been on her feet essentially that long.

Now, she had the beginnings of her bombe on a waist-high table, with a large stainless steel bowl of crushed berries at her elbow. At her firm instructions, Chopin drifted through the kitchen speakers. The first course was already being enjoyed in the dining room. She could ignore the confusion reigning around her. She could shrug off the pressure of having her part of the meal complete and perfect at precisely the right moment. That was all routine. But as she stood there, prepared to begin the next step, her concentration was scattered.

LaPointe, she thought with gritted teeth. Naturally it was anger that had kept her attention from being fully focused all day, the idea of having Louis LaPointe tossed in her face. It hadn't taken Summer long to realize that Blake Cocharan had used the name on purpose. Knowing it, however, didn't make the least bit of difference to her reaction…except perhaps that her venom was spread over two men rather than one.

Oh, he thinks he's very clever, Summer decided, thinking of Blake—as she had too often that week. She took three cleansing breaths as she studied the golden dome in front of her. Asking me, *me,* to give LaPointe a reference. Despicable French swine, she muttered silently, referring to LaPointe. As she scooped up the first berries she decided that Blake must be an equal swine even to be considering dealing with the Frenchman.

She could remember every frustrating, annoying contact she'd had with the beady-eyed, undersized LaPointe. As she carefully coated the outside of the cake with crushed berries, Summer considered giving him a glowing recommendation. It would teach that sneaky American a lesson to find himself stuck with a pompous ass like LaPointe. While her thoughts raged, her hands were delicately smoothing the berries, rounding out and firming the shape.

Behind her one of the assistants dropped a pan with a clatter and a bang and suffered a torrent of abuse. Neither Summer's thoughts nor her hands faltered.

Smug, self-assured jerk, she thought grimly of Blake. In a steady flow, she began layering rich French cream over the berries. Her face, though set in concentration, betrayed anger in the flash in her eyes. A man like him delighted in maneuvering and outmaneuvering. It showed, she thought, in that oh-so-smooth delivery, in that gloss of sophistication. She gave a disdainful little snort as she began to smooth out the cream.

She'd rather have a man with a few rough edges than one so polished that he gleamed. She'd rather have a man who knew how to sweat and bend his back than one with manicured nails and five-hundred-dollar suits. She'd rather have a man who…

Summer stopped smoothing the cream while her thoughts caught up with her consciousness. Since when had she considered having any man, and why, for God's sake, was she using Blake for comparisons? Ridiculous.

The bombe was now a smooth white dome waiting for its coating of rich chocolate. Summer frowned at it as an assistant whisked empty bowls out of her way. She began to blend the frosting in a large mixer as two cooks argued over the thickness of the sauce for the entrée.

For that matter, her thoughts ran on, it was ridiculous how often she'd thought of him the past few days, remembering foolish details… His eyes were almost precisely the shade of the water in the lake on her grandfather's estate in Devon. How pleasant his voice was, deep, with that faint but unmistakable inflection of the American Northeast. How his mouth curved in one fashion when he was amused, and another when he smiled politely.

It was difficult to explain why she'd noticed those things, much less why she'd continued to think of them days afterward. As a rule, she didn't think of a man unless she was with him—and even then she only allowed him a carefully regulated portion of her concentration.

Now, Summer reminded herself as she began to layer on frosting, wasn't the time to think of anything but the bombe. She'd think of Blake when her job was finished, and she'd deal with him over the late supper she'd agreed to. Oh, yes—her mouth set—she'd deal with him.

Blake arrived early deliberately. He wanted to see her work. That was reasonable, even logical. After all, if he were to contract Summer to Cocharan House for a year, he should see firsthand what she was capable of, and how she went about it. It wasn't at all unusual for him to check out potential employees or associates on their own turf. If anything, it was characteristic of him. Good business sense.

He continued to tell himself so, over and over, because there was a lingering doubt as to his own motivations. Perhaps he had left her apartment in high good spirits knowing he'd outmaneuvered her in the first round. Her face, at the mention of her rival LaPointe, had been priceless. And it was her face that he hadn't been able to push out of his mind for nearly a week.

Uncomfortable, he decided as he stepped into the huge, echoing kitchen. The woman made him uncomfortable. He'd like to know the reason why. Knowing the reasons and motivations was essential to him. With them neatly listed, the answer to any problem would eventually follow.

He appreciated beauty—in art, in architecture and certainly in the female form. Summer Lyndon was beautiful. That shouldn't have made him uncomfortable. Intelligence was something he not only appreciated but invariably demanded in anyone he associated with. She was undoubtedly intelligent. No reason for discomfort there. Style was something else he looked for—he'd certainly found it in her.

What was it about her…the eyes? he wondered as he passed two cooks in a heated argument over pressed duck. That odd hazel that wasn't precisely a definable color—those gold flecks that deepened or lightened according to her mood. Very direct, very frank eyes, he mused. Blake respected that. Yet the contrast of moody color that wasn't really a color intrigued him. Perhaps too much.

Sexuality? It was a foolish man who was wary because of a natural feminine sexuality and he'd never considered himself a foolish man. Nor a particularly susceptible one. Yet the first time he'd seen her he'd felt that instant curl of desire, that immediate pull of man for woman. Unusual, he thought dispassionately.

Something he'd have to consider carefully—then dispose of. There wasn't room for desire between business associates.

And they would be that, he thought as his lips curved. Blake counted on his own powers of persuasion, and his casual mention of LaPointe to turn Summer Lyndon his way. She was already turning that way, and after tonight, he reflected, then stopped dead. For a moment it felt as though someone had delivered him a very quick, very stunning blow to the base of the spine. He'd only had to look at her.

She was half-hidden by the dessert she worked on. Her face was set, intent. He saw the faint line that might've been temper or concentration run down between her brows. Her eyes were narrowed, the lashes swept down so that the expression was unreadable. Her mouth, that soft, molded mouth that she seemed never to paint, was forming a pout. It was utterly kissable.

She should have looked plain and efficient, all in white. The chef's hat over her neatly bound hair could have given an almost comic touch. Instead she looked outrageously beautiful. Standing there, Blake could hear the Chopin that was her trademark, smell the exotic pungent scents of cooking, feel the tension in the air as temperamental cooks fussed and labored over their creations. All he could think, and think quite clearly, was how she would look naked, in his bed, with only candles to vie with the dark.

Catching himself, Blake shook his head. *Stop it,* he thought with grim amusement. *When you mix business and pleasure, one or both suffers.* That was something Blake invariably avoided without effort. He held the position he did because he could recognize, weigh and dismiss errors before they were ever made. And he could do so with a cold-blooded ruthlessness that was as clean as his looks.

The woman might be as delectable as the concoction she was creating, but that wasn't what he wanted—correction, what he could afford to want—from her. He needed her skill, her name and her brain. That was all. For now, he comforted himself with that thought as he fought back waves of a more insistent and much more basic need.

As he stood, as far outside of the melee as possible, Blake watched her patiently, methodically apply and smooth on layer after layer. There was no hesitation in her hands—something he noticed with approval even as he noted the fine-boned elegant shape of them. There was no lack of confidence in her stance. Looking on, Blake realized that she might have been alone for all the noise and confusion around her mattered.

The woman, he decided, could build her spectacular bombe on the Ben Franklin Parkway at rush hour and never miss a step. Good. He couldn't use some hysterical female who folded under pressure.

Patiently he waited as she completed her work. By

the time Summer had the pastry bag filled with white icing and had begun the final decorating, most of the kitchen staff were on hand to watch. The rest of the meal was a fait accompli. There was only the finale now.

On the last swirl, she stepped back. There was a communal sigh of appreciation. Still, she didn't smile as she walked completely around the bombe, checking, rechecking. Perfection. Nothing less was acceptable.

Then Blake saw her eyes clear, her lips curve. At the scattered applause, she grinned and was more than beautiful—she was approachable. He found that disturbed him even more.

"Take it in." With a laugh, she stretched her arms high to work out a dozen stiffened muscles. She decided she could sleep for a week.

"Very impressive."

Arms still high, Summer turned slowly to find herself facing Blake. "Thank you." Her voice was very cool, her eyes wary. Sometime between the berries and the frosting, she'd decided to be very, very careful with Blake Cocharan III. "It's meant to be."

"In looks," he agreed. Glancing down, he saw the large bowl of chocolate frosting that had yet to be removed. He ran his finger around the edge, then licked it off. The taste was enough to melt the hardest hearts. "Fantastic."

She couldn't have prevented the smile—a little boy's

trick from a man in an exquisite suit and silk tie. "Naturally," she told him with a little toss of her head. "I only make the fantastic. Which is why you want me—correct, Mr. Cocharan?"

"Mmm." The sound might have been agreement, or it might have been something else. Wisely, both left it at that. "You must be tired, after being on your feet for so long."

"A perceptive man," she murmured, pulling off the chef's hat.

"If you'd like, we'll have supper at my penthouse. It's private, quiet. You'd be comfortable."

She lifted a brow, then sent a quick, distrustful look over his face. Intimate suppers were something to be considered carefully. She might be tired, Summer mused, but she could still hold her own with any man—particularly an American businessman. With a shrug, she pulled off her stained apron. "That's fine. It'll only take me a minute to change."

She left him without a backward glance, but as he watched, she was waylaid by a small man with a dark moustache who grabbed her hand and pressed it dramatically to his lips. Blake didn't have to overhear the words to gauge the intent. He felt a twist of annoyance that, with some effort, he forced into amusement.

The man was speaking rapidly while working his way up Summer's arm. She laughed, shook her head and gently nudged him away. Blake watched the man gaze after her like a forlorn puppy before he clutched his own chef's hat to his heart.

Quite an effect she has on the male of the species, Blake mused. Again dispassionately, he reflected that there was a certain type of woman who drew men without any visible effort. It was an innate...skill, he supposed was the correct term. A skill he didn't admire or condemn, but simply mistrusted. A woman like that could manipulate with the flick of the wrist. On a personal level, he preferred women who were more obvious in their gifts.

He positioned himself well out of the way while the cacophony and confusion of cleaning up began. It was a skill he figured wouldn't hurt in her position as head chef of his Philadelphia Cocharan House.

In nine more than the minute she'd claimed she'd be, Summer strolled back into the kitchen. She'd chosen the thin poppy-colored silk because it was perfectly simple—so simple it had a tendency to cling to every curve and draw every eye. Her arms were bare but for one ornately carved gold bracelet she wore just above the elbow. Drop spiral earrings fell almost to her shoulders. Unbound now, her hair curled a bit around her face from the heat and humidity of the kitchen.

She knew the result was part eccentric, part exotic. Just as she knew it transmitted a primal sexuality. She dressed as she did—from jeans to silks—for her own pleasure and at her own whim. But when she saw the fire, quickly banked, in Blake's eyes she was perversely satisfied.

No iceman, she mused—of course she wasn't interested in him in any personal way. She simply wanted to establish herself as a person, an individual, rather than a name he wanted neatly signed on a contract. Her work clothes were jumbled into a canvas tote she carried in one hand, while over her other shoulder hung a tiny exquisitely beaded purse. In a rather regal gesture, she offered Blake her hand.

"Ready?"

"Of course." Her hand was cool, small and smooth. He thought of streaming sunlight and wet, fragrant grass. Because of it, his voice became cool and pragmatic. "You're lovely."

She couldn't resist. Humor leaped into her eyes. "Of course." For the first time she saw him grin—fast, appealing. Dangerous. In that moment she wasn't quite certain who held the upper hand.

"My driver's waiting outside," Blake told her smoothly. Together they walked from the brightly lit, noisy kitchen out into the moonlit street. "I take it you were satisified with your part of the governor's meal. You didn't choose to stay for the criticism or compliments."

As she stepped into the back of the limo, Summer sent him an incredulous look. "Criticism? The bombe is my specialty, Mr. Cocharan. It's always superb. I need no one to tell me that." She got in the car, smoothed her skirt and crossed her legs.

"Of course," Blake murmured, sliding beside her, "it's a complicated dish." He went on conversationally, "If my memory serves me, it takes hours to prepare properly."

She watched him remove a bottle of champagne from ice and open it with only a muffled pop. "There's very little that can be superb in a short amount of time."

"Very true." Blake poured champagne into two tulip glasses and, handing Summer one, smiled. "To a lengthy association."

Summer gave him a frank look as the streetlights flickered into the car and over his face. A bit Scottish warrior, a bit English aristocrat, she decided. Not a simple combination. Then again, simplicity wasn't always what she looked for. With only a brief hesitation, she touched her glass to his. "Perhaps," she said. "You enjoy your work, Mr. Cocharan?" She sipped, and without looking at the label, identified the vintage of the wine she drank.

"Very much." He watched her as he drank, noting that she'd done no more than sweep some mascara over her lashes when she'd changed. For an instant he was distracted by the speculation of what her skin would feel like under his fingers. "It's obvious by what I caught of that session in there that you enjoy yours."

"Yes." She smiled, appreciating him and what she

thought would be an interesting struggle for power. "I make it a policy to do only what I enjoy. Unless I'm very much mistaken, you have the same policy."

He nodded, knowing he was being baited. "You're very perceptive, Ms. Lyndon."

"Yes." She held her glass out for a refill. "You have excellent taste in wines. Does that extend to other areas?"

His eyes locked on hers as he filled her glass. "All other areas?"

Her mouth curved slowly as she brought the champagne to it. Summer enjoyed the effervescence she could feel just before she tasted it. "Of course. Would it be accurate to say that you're a discriminating man?"

What the hell was she getting at? "If you like," Blake returned smoothly.

"A businessman," she went on. "An executive. Tell me, don't executives...delegate?"

"Often."

"And you? Don't you delegate?"

"That depends."

"I wondered why Blake Cocharan III himself would take the time and trouble to woo a chef into his organization."

He was certain she was laughing at him. More, he was certain she wanted him to know it. With an effort, he suppressed his annoyance. "This project is a personal pet of mine. Since I want only the best for it, I take the time and trouble to acquire the best personally."

"I see." The limo glided smoothly to the curb. Summer handed Blake her empty glass as the driver opened her door. "Then how strange that you would even mention LaPointe if only the best will serve you." With the haughty grace a woman can only be born with, Summer alighted. That, she thought smugly, should poke a few holes in his arrogance.

The Cocharan House of Philadelphia stood only twelve stories and had a weathered brick facade. It had been built to blend and accent the colonial architecture that was the heart of the city. Other buildings might zoom higher, might gleam with modernity, but Blake Cocharan had known what he'd wanted. Elegance, style and discretion. That was Cocharan House. Summer was forced to approve. In a great many things, she preferred the old world to the new.

The lobby was quiet, and if the gold was a bit dull, the rugs a bit soft and faded looking, it was a deliberate and canny choice. Old, established wealth was the ambience. No amount of gloss, gleam or gilt would have been more effective.

Taking Summer's arm, Blake passed through with only a nod here and there to the many "Good evening, Mr. Cocharans" he received. After inserting a key into a private elevator, he led her inside. They were enveloped by silence and smoked glass.

"A lovely place," Summer commented. "It's been years since I've been inside. I'd forgotten." She glanced around the elevator and saw their reflections trapped deep in gray glass. "But don't you find it confining to live in a hotel—to live, that is, where you work?"

"No. Convenient."

A pity, Summer mused. When she wasn't working, she wanted to remove herself from the kitchens and timers. She'd never been one—as her mother and father had been—to bring her work home with her.

The elevator stopped so smoothly that the change was hardly noticeable. The doors slid open silently. "Do you have the entire floor to yourself?"

"There're three guest suites as well as my penthouse," Blake explained as they walked down the hall. "None of them are occupied at the moment." He inserted a key into a single panel of a double oak door then gestured her inside.

The lights were already dimmed. He'd chosen his colors well, she thought as she stepped onto the thick pewter-toned carpet. Grays from silvery pale to smoky dominated in the low, spreading sofa, the chairs, the walls. With the lights low it had a dreamlike effect that was both sensuous and soothing.

It might have been dull, even bland, but there were splashes of color cleverly interspersed. The deep midnight blue of the drapes, the pearl-like tones of the army of cushions lining the sofa, the rich, primal green of an ivy tangling down the rungs of a breakfront. Then there were the glowing colors of the one painting, a French Impressionist that dominated one wall.

There was none of the clutter she would have chosen for herself, but a sense of style she admired immediately. "Unusual, Mr. Cocharan," Summer complimented as she automatically stepped out of her shoes. "And effective."

"Thank you. Another drink, Ms. Lyndon? The bar's fully stocked, or there's champagne if you prefer."

Still determined to come out of the evening on top, Summer strolled to the sofa and sat. She sent him a cool, easy smile. "I always prefer champagne."

While Blake dealt with the bottle and cork, she took an extra moment to study the room again. Not an ordinary man, she decided. Too often ordinary was synonymous with boring. Summer was forced to admit that because she'd associated herself with the bohemian, the eccentric, the creative for most of her life, she'd always thought of people in business as innately boring.

No, Blake Cocharan wouldn't be dull. She almost regretted it. A dull man, no matter how attractive, could be handled with the minimum of effort. Blake was going to be difficult. Particularly since she'd yet to come to a firm decision on his proposition.

"Your champagne, Ms. Lyndon." When she lifted her eyes to his, Blake had to fight back a frown. The look was too measuring, too damn calculating. Just what was the woman up to now? And why in God's name did she look so right, so temptingly right, curled on his sofa with pillows at her back? "You must be hungry," he said, astonished that he needed the defense of words. "If you'd tell me what you'd like, the kitchen will prepare it. Or I can get you a menu, if you'd prefer."

"A menu won't be necessary." She sipped more cold, frothy French champagne. "I'd like a cheeseburger."

Blake watched the silk shift as she nestled into the corner of the sofa. "A what?"

"Cheeseburger," Summer repeated. "With a side order of fries, shoestring." She lifted her glass to examine the color of the liquid. "Do you know, this was a truly exceptional year."

"Ms. Lyndon…" With strained patience, Blake dipped his hands in his pockets and kept his voice even. "Exactly what game are you playing?"

She sipped slowly, savoring. "Game?"

"Do you seriously want me to believe that you, a gourmet, a Cordon Bleu chef, want to eat a cheeseburger and shoestring fries?"

"I wouldn't have said so otherwise." When her glass was empty, Summer rose to refill it herself. She moved, he noted, lazily, with none of that sharp, almost military motion she'd used when cooking. "Your kitchen does have lean prime beef, doesn't it?"

"Of course." Certain she was trying to annoy him,

or make a fool of him, Blake took her arm and turned her to face him. "Why do you want a cheeseburger?"

"Because I like them," she said simply. "I also like tacos and pizza and fried chicken—particularly when someone else is cooking them. That sort of thing is quick, tasty and convenient." She grinned, relaxed by the wine, amused by his reaction. "Do you have a moral objection to junk food, Mr. Cocharan?"

"No, but I'd think you would."

"Ah, I've shattered your image of a gastronomic snob." She laughed, a very appealing, purely feminine sound. "As a chef, I can tell you that rich sauces and heavy creams aren't easy on the digestion either. Besides that, I cook professionally. For long periods of time I'm surrounded by the finest of haute cuisine. Delicacies, foods that have to be prepared with absolute perfection, split-second timing. When I'm not working, I like to relax." She drank champagne again. "I'd prefer a cheeseburger, medium rare, to *Filet aux Champignons* at the moment, if you don't mind."

"Your choice," he muttered and moved the phone to order. Her explanation had been reasonable, even logical. There was nothing that annoyed him more than having his own style of manuevering used against him.

With her glass in hand, Summer wandered to the window. She liked the looks of a city at night. The buildings rose and spread in the distance and traffic wound its way silently on the intersecting roads. Lights, darkness, shadows.

She couldn't have counted the number of cities she'd been in or viewed from a similar spot, but her favorite remained Paris. Yet she'd chosen to live for long lengths of time in the States—she liked the contrast of people and cultures and attitudes. She liked the ambition and enthusiasm of Americans, which she saw typified in her mother's second husband.

Ambition was something she understood. She had a lot of her own. She understood this to be the reason she looked for men with more creative ability than ambition in her personal relationships. Two competitive, career-oriented people made an uneasy couple. She'd learned that early on watching her own parents with each other, and their subsequent spouses. When she chose permanence in a relationship—something Summer considered was at least a decade away—she wanted someone who understood that her career came first. Any cook, from a child making a peanut butter sandwich to a master chef, had to understand priorities. Summer had understood her own all of her life.

"You like the view?" Blake stood behind her, where he'd been studying her for a full five minutes. Why should she seem different from any other woman he'd ever brought to his home? Why should she seem more elusive, more alluring? And why should her presence alone make it so difficult for him to keep his mind on the business he'd brought her there for?

"Yes." She didn't turn because she realized abruptly just how close he was. It was something she should have sensed before, Summer thought with a slight frown. If she turned, they'd be face-to-face. There'd be a brush of bodies, a meeting of eyes. The quick scramble of nerves made her sip the champagne again. Ridiculous, she told herself. No man made her nervous.

"You've lived here long enough to recognize the points of interest," Blake said easily, while his thoughts centered on how the curve of her neck would taste, would feel under the brush of his lips.

"Of course. I consider myself a Philadelphian when I'm in Philadelphia. I'm told by some of my associates that I've become quite Americanized."

Blake listened to the flow of the European accented voice, drew in the subtle, sexy scent of Paris that was her perfume. The dim light touched on the gold scattered through her hair. Like her eyes, he thought. He had only to turn her around and look at her face to see her sculptured, exotic look. And he wanted, overwhelmingly, to see that face.

"Americanized," Blake murmured. His hands were on her shoulders before he could stop them. The silk slid cool under his palms as he turned her. "No..." His gaze flicked down, over her hair and eyes, and lingered on her mouth. "I think your associates are very much mistaken."

"Do you?" Her fingers had tightened on the stem of her glass, her mouth had heated. Willpower alone kept her voice steady. Her body brushed his once, then twice as he began to draw her closer. Needs, tightly controlled, began to smolder. While her mind raced with the possibilities, Summer tilted her head back and spoke calmly. "What about the business we're here to discuss, Mr. Cocharan?"

"We haven't started on business yet." His mouth hovered over hers for a moment before he shifted to whisper a kiss just under one eyebrow. "And before we do, it might be wise to settle this one point."

Her breathing was clogging, backing up in her lungs. Drawing away was still possible, but she began to wonder why she should consider it. "Point?"

"Your lips—will they taste as exciting as they look?"

Her lashes were fluttering down, her body softening. "Interesting point," she murmured, then tilted her head back in invitation.

Their lips were only a breath apart when the sharp knock sounded at the door. Something cleared in Summer's brain—reason—while her body continued to hum. She smiled, concentrating hard on that one slice of sanity.

"The service in a Cocharan House is invariably excellent."

"Tomorrow," Blake said as he drew reluctantly away, "I'm going to fire my room service manager."

Summer laughed, but took a shaky sip of wine when he left her to answer the door. Close, she thought, letting out a long, steadying breath. Much too close. It was time to steer the evening into business channels and keep it there. She gave herself a moment while the waiter set up the meal on the table.

"Smells wonderful," Summer commented, crossing the room as Blake tipped and dismissed the waiter. Before sitting, she glanced at his meal. Steak, rare, a steaming potato popping out of its skin, buttered asparagus. "Very sensible." She shot him a teasing grin over her shoulder as he held out her chair.

"We can order dessert later."

"Never touch them," she said, tongue in cheek. With a generous hand she spread mustard over her bun. "I read over your contract."

"Did you?" He watched as she cut the burger neatly in two then lifted a half. It shouldn't surprise him, Blake mused. She did, after all, keep Oreos in her cookie jar.

"So did my attorney."

Blake added some ground pepper to his steak before cutting into it. "And?"

"And it seems to be very much in order. Except..." She allowed the word to hang while she took the first bite. Closing her eyes, Summer simply enjoyed.

"Except?" Blake prompted.

"*If* I were to consider such an offer, I'd need considerably more room."

Blake ignored the *if.* She was considering it, and they both knew it. "In what area?"

"Certainly you're aware that I do quite a bit of traveling." Summer dashed salt on the French fries, tasted and approved. "Often it's a matter of two or three days when I go to, say, Venice and prepare a *Gâteau St. Honoré.* Some of my clients book me months in advance. On the other hand, there are some that deal more spontaneously. A few of these—" Summer bit into the cheeseburger again "—I'll accommodate because of personal affection or professional challenge."

"In other words you'd want to fly to Venice or wherever when you felt it necessary." However incongruous he felt the combination was, Blake poured more champagne into her glass while she ate.

"Precisely. Though your offer does have some slight interest for me, it would be impossible, even, I feel, unethical, to turn my back on established clients."

"Understood." She was crafty, Blake thought, but so was he. "I should think a reasonable arrangement could be worked out. You and I could go over your current schedule."

Summer nibbled on a fry, then dusted her fingers on a white linen napkin. "You and I?"

"That would keep it simpler. Then if we agreed to discuss whatever other occasions might crop up during the year on an individual basis…" He smiled as she picked up the second half of her cheeseburger. "I like to think I'm a reasonable man, Ms. Lyndon. And, to be frank, I personally would prefer signing you with my hotel. At the moment, the board's leaning toward LaPointe, but—"

"Why?" The word was a demand and an accusation. Nothing could have pleased Blake more.

"Characteristically, the great chefs are men." She cursed, bluntly and brutally in French. Blake merely nodded. "Yes, exactly. And, through some discreet questioning, we've learned that Monsieur LaPointe is very interested in the position."

"The swine would scramble at a chance to roast chestnuts on a street corner if only to have his picture in the paper." Tossing down her napkin, she rose. "You think perhaps I don't understand your strategy, Mr. Cocharan." The regal lifting of her head accentuated her long, slender neck. Blake remembered quite vividly how that skin had felt under his fingers. "You throw LaPointe in my face thinking that I'll grab your offer as a matter of ego, of pride."

He grinned because she looked magnificent. "Did it work?"

Her eyes narrowed, but her lips wanted badly to curve. "LaPointe is a philistine. *I* am an artist."

"And?"

She knew better than to agree to anything in anger.

Knew better, but… "You accommodate my schedule, Mr. Cocharan the Third, and I'll make your restaurant the finest establishment of its kind on the East Coast." And damn it, she could do it. She found she wanted to do it to prove it to both of them.

Blake rose, lifting both glasses. "To your art, mademoiselle." He handed her a glass. "And to my business. May it be a profitable union for both of us."

"To success," she amended, clinking glass to glass. "Which, in the end, is what we both look for."

Chapter 3

Well, I've done it, Summer thought, scowling. She swept back her hair and secured it with two mother-of-pearl combs. Critically she studied her face in the mirror to check her makeup. She'd learned the trick of accenting her best features from her mother. When the occasion called for it, and she was in the mood, Summer exploited the art. Although she felt the face that was reflected at her would do, she frowned anyway.

Whether it had been anger or ego or just plain cussedness, she'd agreed to tie herself to the Cocharan House, and Blake, for the next year. Maybe she did want the challenge of it, but already she was uncomfortable with the long-term commitment and the obligations that went with it.

Three hundred sixty-five days. No, that was too overwhelming, she decided. Fifty-two weeks was hardly a better image. Twelve months. Well, she'd just have to live with it. No, she'd have to do better than that, Summer decided as she wandered back into the studio where she'd be taping a demonstration for public TV. She had to live up to her vow to give the Philadelphia Cocharan House the finest restaurant on the East Coast.

And so she would, she told herself with a flick of her hair over her shoulder. So she damn well would. Then she'd thumb her nose at Blake Cocharan III. The sneak.

He'd manipulated her. Twice, he'd manipulated her. Even though she'd been perfectly aware of it the second time, she'd strolled down the garden path anyway. Why? Summer ran her tongue over her teeth and watched the television crew set up for the taping.

The challenge, she decided, twisting her braided gold chain around one slim finger. It would be a challenge to work with him and stay on top. Competing was her greatest weakness, after all. That was one reason she'd chosen to excel in a career that was characteristically male-dominated. Oh, yes, she liked to compete. Best of all, she liked to win.

Then there was that ripe masculinity of his. Polished manners couldn't hide it. Tailored clothes couldn't cloak it. If she were honest—and she decided she would be for the moment—Summer had to admit she'd enjoy exploring it.

She knew her effect on men. A genetic gift, she'd

always thought, from her mother. It was rare that she paid much attention to her own sexuality. Her life was too full of the pressures of her work and the complete relaxation she demanded between clients. But it might be time, Summer mused now, to alter things a bit.

Blake Cocharan III represented a definite challenge. And how she'd love to shake up that smug male arrogance. How she'd like to pay him back for maneuvering her to precisely where he'd wanted her. As she considered varied ways and means to do just that, Summer idly watched the studio audience file in.

They had the capacity for about fifty, and apparently they'd have a full house this morning. People were talking in undertones, the mumbles and shuffles associated with theaters and churches. The director, a small, excitable man whom Summer had worked with before, hustled from grip to gaffer, light to camera, tossing his arms in gestures that signaled pleasure or dread. Only extremes. When he came over to her, Summer listened to his quick nervous instructions with half an ear. She wasn't thinking of him, nor was she thinking of the vacherin she was to prepare on camera. She was still thinking of the best way to handle Blake Cocharan.

Perhaps she should pursue him, subtly—but not so subtly that he wouldn't notice. Then when his ego was inflated, she'd...she'd totally ignore him. A fascinating idea.

"The first baked shell is in the center storage cabinet."

"Yes, Simon, I know." Summer patted the director's hand while she went over the plan for flaws. It had a big one. She could remember all too clearly that giddy sensation that had swept over her when he'd nearly— just barely—kissed her a few evenings before. If she played the game that way, she just might find herself muddling the rules. So…

"The second is right beneath it."

"Yes, I know." Hadn't she put it there herself to cool after baking? Summer gave the frantic director an absent smile. She could ignore Blake right from the start. Treat him—not with contempt, but with disinterest. The smile became a bit menacing. Her eyes glinted. That should drive him crazy.

"All the ingredients and equipment are exactly where you put them."

"Simon," Summer began kindly, "stop worrying. I can build a vacherin in my sleep."

"We roll tape in five minutes—"

"Where is she!"

Both Summer and Simon looked around at the bellowing voice. Her grin was already forming before she saw its owner. "Carlo!"

"Aha." Dark and wiry and as supple as a snake, Carlo Franconi wound his way around people and over cable to grab Summer and pull her jarringly against his chest. "My little French pastry." Fondly he patted her bottom.

Laughing, she returned the favor. "Carlo, what're

you doing in downtown Philadelphia on a Wednesday morning?"

"I was in New York promoting my new book, *Pasta by the Master.*" He drew back enough to wiggle his eyebrows at her. "And I said, Carlo, you are just around the corner from the sexiest woman who ever held a pastry bag. So I come."

"Just around the corner," Summer repeated. It was typical of him. If he'd been in Los Angeles, he'd have done the same thing. They'd studied together, cooked together, and perhaps if their friendship had not become so solid and important, they might have slept together. "Let me look at you."

Obligingly, Carlo stepped back to pose. He wore straight, tight jeans that flattered narrow hips, a salmon-colored silk shirt and a cloth fedora that was tilted rakishly over his dark, almond-shaped eyes. An outrageous diamond glinted on his finger. As always, he was beautiful, male and aware of it.

"You look fantastic, Carlo. *Fantastico.*"

"But of course." He ran a finger down the brim of his hat. "And you, my delectable puff pastry—" he took her hands and pressed each palm to his lips "—*esquisita.*"

"But of course." Laughing again, she kissed him full on the mouth. She knew hundreds of people, professionally, socially, but if she'd been asked to name a friend, it would have been Carlo Franconi who'd have come to her mind. "It's good to see you, Carlo. What's it been? Four months? Five? You were in Belgium the last time I was in Italy?"

"Four months and twelve days," he said easily. "But who counts? It's only that I lusted for your Napoleons, your eclairs, your—" he grabbed her again and nibbled on her fingers "—chocolate cake."

"It's vacherin this morning," she said dryly, "and you're welcome to some when the show's over."

"Ah, your meringue. To die for." He grinned wickedly. "I will sit in the front row and cross my eyes at you."

Summer pinched his cheek. "Try to lighten up, Carlo. You're so stuffy."

"Ms. Lyndon, please."

Summer glanced at Simon, whose breathing was becoming shallower as the countdown began. "It's all right, Simon, I'm ready. Get your seat, Carlo, and watch carefully. You might learn something this time."

He said something short and rude and easily translated as they went their separate ways. Relaxed, Summer stood behind her work surface and watched the floor director count off the seconds. Easily ignoring the face Carlo made at her, Summer began the show, talking directly to the camera.

She took this part of her profession as seriously as she took creating the royal wedding cake for a European princess. If she were to teach the average person how to make something elaborate and exciting, she would do it well.

She did look exquisite, Carlo thought. Then she always did. And confident, competent, cool. On one hand, he was glad to find it true, for he was a man who disliked things or people who changed too quickly—particularly if he had nothing to do with it. On the other hand, he worried about her.

As long as he'd known Summer—good God, had it been ten years?—she'd never allowed herself a personal involvement. It was difficult for a volatile, emotional man like himself to fully understand her quality of reserve, her apparent disinterest in romantic encounters. She had passion. He'd seen it explode in temper, in joy, but never had he seen it directed toward a man.

A pity, he thought as he watched her build the meringue rings. A woman, he felt, was wasted without a man—just as a man was wasted without a woman. He'd shared himself with many.

Once over kirsch cake and Chablis, she'd loosened up enough to tell him that she didn't think that men and women were meant for permanent relationships. Marriage was an institution too easily dissolved and, therefore, not an institution at all but a hypocrisy perpetuated by people who wanted to pretend they could make commitments. Love was a fickle emotion and, therefore, untrustworthy. It was something exploited by people as an excuse to act foolishly or unwisely. If she wanted to act foolish, she'd do so without excuses.

At the time, because he'd been on the down end of an affair with a Greek heiress, Carlo had agreed with her. Later, he'd realized that while his agreement had been the temporary result of sour grapes, Summer had meant precisely what she'd said.

A pity, he thought again as Summer took out the previously baked rings from beneath the counter and began to build the shell. If he didn't feel about her as he would about a sister, it would be a pleasure to show her the...appealing side of the man/woman mystique. Ah, well—he settled back—that was for someone else.

Keeping an easy monologue with the camera and the studio audience, Summer went through the stages of the dessert. The completed shell, decorated with strips of more meringue and dotted with candied violets, was popped into an oven. The one that she'd baked and cooled earlier was brought out to complete the final stage. She filled it, arranged the fruit, covered it all with rich raspberry sauce and whipped cream to the murmured approval of her audience. The camera came in for a close-up.

"Brava!" Carlo stood, applauding as the dessert sat tempting and complete on the counter. *"Bravissima!"*

Summer grinned and, pastry bag in hand, took a deep bow as the camera clicked off.

"Brilliant, Ms. Lyndon." Simon rushed up to her,

whipping off his earphones as he came. "Just brilliant. And, as always, perfect."

"Thank you, Simon. Shall we serve this to the audience and crew?"

"Yes, yes, good idea." He snapped his fingers at his assistant. "Get some plates and pass this out before we have to clear for the next show. Aerobic dancing," he muttered and dashed off again.

"Beautiful, *cara,*" Carlo told her as he dipped a finger into the whipped cream. "A masterpiece." He took a spoon from the counter and took a hefty serving directly from the vacherin. "Now, I will take you to lunch and you can fill me in on your life. Mine—" he shrugged, still eating "—is so exciting it would take days. Maybe weeks."

"We can grab a slice of pizza around the corner." Summer pulled off her apron and tossed it on the counter. "As it happens, there's something I'd like your advice about."

"Advice?" Though the idea of Summer's asking advice of him, of anyone, stunned him, Carlo only lifted a brow. "Naturally," he said with a silky smile as he drew her along. "Who else would an intelligent woman come to for advice—or for anything—but Carlo?"

"You're such a pig, darling."

"Careful." He slipped on dark glasses and adjusted his hat. "Or you pay for the pizza."

Within moments, Summer was taking her first bite

and bracing herself as Carlo zoomed his rented Ferrari into Philadelphia traffic. Carlo managed to steer and eat and shift gears with maniacal skill. "So tell me," he shouted over the boom of the radio, "what's on your mind?"

"I've taken a job," Summer yelled back at him. Her hair whipped across her face and she tossed it back again.

"A job? So, you take lots of jobs?"

"This is different." She shifted, crossing her legs beneath her and turning sideways as she took the next bite. "I've agreed to revamp and manage a hotel restaurant for the next year."

"Hotel restaurant?" Carlo frowned over his slice of pizza as he cut off a station wagon. "What hotel?"

She took a deep sip of soda through a straw. "The Cocharan House here in Philadelphia."

"Ah." His expression cleared. "First class, *cara*. I should never have doubted you."

"A year, Carlo."

"Goes quickly when one has one's health," he finished blithely.

She let the grin come first. "Damn it, Carlo, I painted myself into a corner because, well, I just couldn't resist the idea of trying it and this—this American steamroller tossed LaPointe in my face."

"LaPointe?" Carlo snarled as only an Italian can. "What does that Gallic slug have to do with this?"

Summer licked sauce from her thumb. "I was going to turn down the offer at first, then Blake—that's the steamroller—asked me for my opinion on LaPointe, since he was also being considered for the position."

"And did you give it to him?" Carlo asked with relish.

"I did, and I kept the contract to look it over. The next hitch was that it was a tremendous offer. With the budget I have, I could turn a two-room slum into a gourmet palace." She frowned, not noticing when Carlo zoomed around a compact with little more than wind between metal. "In addition to that, there's Blake himself."

"The steamroller."

"Yes. I can't control the need to get the best of him. He's smart, he's smug and, damn it, he's sexy as hell."

"Oh, yes?"

"I have this tremendous urge to put him in his place."

Carlo breezed through a yellow light as it was turning red. "Which is?"

"Under my thumb." With a laugh, Summer polished off her pizza. "So because of those things, I've locked myself into a year-long commitment. Are you going to eat the rest of that?"

Carlo glanced down to the remains of his pizza, then took a healthy bite. "Yes. And the advice you wanted?"

After drawing through the straw again, Summer discovered she'd hit bottom. "If I'm going to stay sane while locked into a project for a year, I need a diversion." Grinning, she stretched her arms to the sky. "What's the most foolproof way to make Blake Cocharan III crawl?"

"Heartless woman," Carlo said with a smirk. "You don't need my advice for that. You already have men crawling in twenty countries."

"No, I don't."

"You simply don't look behind you, *cara mia*."

Summer frowned, not certain she liked the idea after all. "Turn left at the corner, Carlo, we'll drop in on my new kitchen."

The sights and smells were familiar enough, but within moments, Summer saw a dozen changes she'd make. The lighting was good, she mused as she walked arm-in-arm with Carlo. And the space. But they'd need an eye-level wall-oven there—brick lined. A replacement for the electric oven, and certainly more kitchen help. She glanced around, checking the corners of the ceiling for speakers. None. That, too, would change.

"Not bad, my love." Carlo took down a large chef's knife and checked it for weight and balance. "You have the rudiments here. It's a bit like getting a new toy for Christmas and having to assemble it, *si*?"

"Hmmm." Absently she picked up a skillet. Stainless steel, she noted and set it down again. The pans would have to be replaced with copper washed with tin. She turned and thudded firmly into Blake's chest.

There was a fraction of a second when she softened, enjoying the sensation of body against body. His scent, sophisticated, slightly aloof, pleased her. Then came the annoyance that she hadn't sensed him behind her as she felt she should have. "Mr. Cocharan." She drew away, masking both the attraction and the annoyance with a polite smile. "Somehow I didn't think to find you here."

"My staff keeps me well informed, Ms. Lyndon. I was told you were here."

The idea of being reported on might have grated, but Summer only nodded. "This is Carlo Franconi," she began. "One of the finest chefs in Italy."

"*The* finest chef in Italy," Carlo corrected, extending his hand. "A pleasure to meet you, Mr. Cocharan. I've often enjoyed the hospitality of your hotels. Your restaurant in Milan makes a very passable linguini."

"Very passable is a great compliment from Carlo," Summer explained. "He doesn't think anyone can make an Italian dish but himself."

"Not think, know." Carlo lifted the lid on a steaming pot and sniffed. "Summer tells me she'll be associated with your restaurant here. You're a fortunate man."

Blake looked down at Summer, glancing at the lean, tanned hand Carlo had placed on her shoulder. Jealousy is a sensation that can be recognized even if it has never been experienced before. Blake didn't care for it, or the cause. "Yes, I am. Since you're here, Ms. Lyndon, you might like to sign the final contract. It would save us both a meeting later."

"All right. Carlo?"

"Go, do your business. They do a rack of lamb over there—it interests me." Without a backward glance, he went to add his two cents.

"Well, he's happy," Summer commented as she walked through the kitchen with Blake.

"Is he in town on business?"

"No, he just wanted to see me."

It was said carelessly, and truthfully, and had the effect of knotting Blake's stomach muscles. So she liked slick Italians, he thought grimly, and slipped a proprietary hand over her arm without being aware of it. That was certainly her business. His was to get her into the kitchens as quickly as possible.

In silence he led her though the lobby and into the hotel offices. Quiet and efficient. Those were brief impressions before she was led into a large, private room that was obviously Blake's.

The colors were bones and creams and browns, the decor a bit more modern than his apartment, but she could recognize his stamp on it. Without being asked, Summer walked over and took a chair. It was hardly past noon, but it occurred to her that she'd been on her feet for almost six consecutive hours.

"Handy that I happened to drop by when you were around," she began, sliding her toes out of her shoes. "It simplifies this contract business. Since I've agreed to do it, we might as well get started." *Then there will be only three hundred and sixty-four days,* she added silently, and sighed.

He didn't like her careless attitude about the contract any more than he liked her careless affection toward the Italian. Blake walked over to his desk and lifted a packet of papers. When he looked back at her, some of his anger drained. "You look tired, Summer."

The lids she allowed to droop lifted again. His first, his only, use of her given name intrigued her. He said it as though he was thinking of the heat and the storms. She felt her chest tighten and blamed it on fatigue. "I am. I was baking meringue at seven o'clock this morning."

"Coffee?"

"No, thanks. I'm afraid I've overdone that already today." She glanced at the papers he held, then smiled with a trace of self-satisfaction. "Before I sign those, I should warn you I'm going to order some extensive changes in the kitchen."

"One of the essential reasons you're to sign them."

She nodded and held out her hand. "You might not be so amiable when you get the bill."

Taking a pen from a holder on his desk, Blake gave it to her. "I think we're both after the same thing, and would both agree cost is secondary."

"I might think so." With a flourish, she looped her name on the line. "But I'm not signing the checks.

So—" she passed the contract back to him "—it's official."

"Yes." He didn't even glance at her signature before he dropped the paper on his desk. "I'd like to take you to dinner tonight."

She rose, though she found her legs a bit reluctant to hold weight again. "We'll have to put the seal on our bargain another time. I'll be entertaining Carlo." Smiling, she held out her hand. "Of course, you're welcome to join us."

"It has nothing to do with business." Blake took her hand, then surprised them both by taking her other one. "And I want to see you alone."

She wasn't ready for this, Summer realized. She was supposed to begin the maneuvers, in her own time, on her own turf. Now she was forced to realign her strategy and to deal with the blood warming just under her skin. Determined not to be outflanked this time, she tilted her head and smiled. "We are alone."

His brow lifted. Was that a challenge, or was she plainly mocking him? Either way, this time, he wasn't going to let it go. Deliberately he drew her into his arms. She fit there smoothly. It was something each of them noticed, something they both found disturbing.

Her eyes were level on his, but he saw, fascinated, that the gold flecks had deepened. Amber now, they seemed to glow against the cloudy, changeable hazel of her irises. Hardly aware of what he did, Blake brushed the hair away from her cheek in a gesture that was as sweet and as intimate as it was uncharacteristic.

Summer fought not to be affected by something so casual. A hundred men had touched her, in greeting, in friendship, in anger and in longing. There was no reason why the mere brush of a fingertip over her skin should have her head spinning. An effort of will kept her from melting into his arms or from jerking away. She remained still, watching him. Waiting.

When his mouth lowered toward hers, she knew she was prepared. The kiss would be different, naturally, because he was different. It would be new because he was new. But that was all. It was still a basic form of communication between man and woman. A touch of lips, a pressure, a testing of another's taste; it was no different from the kiss of the first couple, and so it went through culture and time.

And the moment she experienced that touch of lips, that pressure, that taste, she knew she was mistaken. Different? New? Those words were much too mild. The brush of lips, for it was no more at first, changed the fabric of everything. Her thoughts veered off into a chaos that seemed somehow right. Her body grew hot, from within and without, in the space of a heartbeat. The woman who'd thought she knew exactly what to expect, sighed with the unexpected. And reached out.

"Again," she murmured when his lips hovered a breath from hers. With her hands on either side of his face, she drew him to her, through the smoke and into the fire.

He'd thought she'd be cool and smooth and fragrant. He'd been so sure of it. Perhaps that was why the flare of heat had knocked him back on his heels. Smooth she was. Her skin was like silk when he ran his hands up her back to cup her neck. Fragrant. She had a scent that he would, from that moment on, always associate with woman. But not cool. There was nothing cool about the mouth that clung to his, or the breath that mixed with his as two pairs of lips parted. There was something mindless here. He couldn't grip it, couldn't analyze it, could only experience it.

With a deep, almost feline sound of pleasure, she ran her hands through his hair. God, she'd thought there wasn't a taste she hadn't already known, a texture she hadn't already felt. But his, his was beyond her scope and now, just now, within her reach. Summer wallowed in it and let her lips and tongue draw in the sweetness.

More. She'd never known greed. She'd grown up in a world of affluence where enough was always available. For the first time in her life, Summer knew true hunger, true need. Those things brought pain, she discovered. A deep well of it that spread from the core. *More.* The thought ran through her mind again with the knowledge that the more she took, the more she would ache for.

Blake felt her stiffen. Not knowing the cause, he

tightened his hold. He wanted her now, at once, more than he'd ever wanted or had conceived of wanting any woman. She shifted in his arms, resisting for the first time since he'd drawn her here. Throwing her head back, she looked up into the passion and impatience of Blake's eyes.

"Enough."

"No." His hand was still tangled possessively in her hair. "No, it's not."

"No," she agreed on an unsteady breath. "That's why you have to let me go."

He released her, but didn't back away. "You'll have to explain that."

She had more control now—barely, Summer realized shakily, but it was better than none. It was time to establish the rules—her rules—quickly and precisely. "Blake, you're a businessman, I'm an artist. Each of us has priorities. This—" she took a step back and stood straight "—can't be one of them."

"Want to bet?"

Her eyes narrowed more in surprise than annoyance. Odd that she'd missed the ruthlessness in him. It would be best if she considered that later, when there was some distance between them. "We'll be working together for a specific purpose," she went on smoothly. "But we're two different people with two very different outlooks. You're interested in a profit, naturally, and in the reputation of your company. I'm interested in creating the proper showcase for my art, and my own reputation. We both want to be successful. Let's not cloud the issue."

"That issue's perfectly clear," Blake countered. "So's this one. I want you."

"Ah." The sound came out slowly. Deliberately she reached for her neglected purse. "Straight and to the point."

"It would be a bit ridiculous to take a more circular route at the moment." Amusement was overtaking frustration. He was grateful for that because it would give him the edge he'd begun to lose the minute he'd tasted her. "You'd have to be unconscious not to realize it."

"And I'm not." Still, she backed away, relying on poise to get her out before she lost whatever slim advantage she had. "But it's your kitchen—and it'll be *my* kitchen—that's my main concern right now. With the amount of money you're paying me, you should be grateful I understand the priorities. I'll have a tentative list of changes and new equipment you'll have to order on Monday."

"Fine. We'll go to dinner Saturday."

Summer paused at the door, turned and shook her head. "No."

"I'll pick you up at eight."

It was rare that anyone ignored a statement she'd made. Rather than temper, Summer tried the patient tone she remembered from her governess. It was bound to infuriate. "Blake, I said no."

If he was infuriated, he concealed it well. Blake merely smiled at her—as one might smile at a fussy child. Two, it seemed, could play the same game with equal skill. "Eight," he repeated and sat on the corner of his desk. "We can even have tacos if you like."

"You're very stubborn."

"Yes, I am."

"So am I."

"Yes, you are. I'll see you Saturday."

She had to put a lot of effort into the glare because she wanted to laugh. In the end, Summer found satisfaction by slamming the door, quite loudly.

Chapter 4

"Incredible nerve," Summer mumbled. She took another bite of her hot dog, scowled and swallowed. "The man has incredible nerve."

"You shouldn't let it affect your appetite, *cara*." Carlo patted her shoulder as they strolled along the sidewalk toward the proud, weathered bricks of Independence Hall.

Summer bit into the hot dog again. When she tossed her head, the sun caught at the ends of her hair and flicked them with gold. "Shut up, Carlo. He's so *arrogant*." With her free hand, she gestured wildly while continuing to munch, almost vengefully, on the dog and bun. "Carlo, I don't take orders from anyone, especially some tailored, polished, American executive with dictatorial tendencies and incredible blue eyes."

Carlo lifted a brow at her description, then shot an approving look at a leggy blonde in a short pink skirt who passed them. "Of course not, *mi amore*," he said absently, craning his neck to follow the blonde's progress down the street. "This Philadelphia of yours has the most fascinating tourist attractions, *sì*?"

"I make my own decisions, run my own life," Summer grumbled, jerking his arm when she saw where his attention had wandered. "I take requests, Franconi, not orders."

"It's always been so." Carlo gave a last wistful look over his shoulder. Perhaps he could talk Summer into stopping somewhere, a park bench, an outdoor café, where he could get a more...complete view of Philadelphia's attractions. "You must be tired of walking, love," he began.

"I'm definitely not having dinner with him tonight."

"That should teach him to push Summer Lyndon around." The park, Carlo thought, might have the most interesting of possibilities.

She gave him a dangerous stare. "You're amused because you're a man."

"*You're* amused," Carlo corrected, grinning. "And interested."

"I am not."

"Oh, yes, *cara mia,* you are. Why don't we sit so I can take in the...beauty and attractions of your adopted city? After all—" he tipped the brim of his hat at a strolling brunette in brief shorts "—I'm a tourist, *sì*?"

She caught the gleam in his eyes, and the reason for it. After letting out a huff of breath, Summer turned a sharp right. "I'll show you tourist attractions, *amico*."

"But Summer…" Carlo caught sight of a redhead in snug jeans walking a poodle. "The view from out here is very educational and uplifting."

"I'll lift you up," she promised and ruthlessly dragged him inside. "The Second Continental Congress met here in 1775, when the building was known as the Pennsylvania State House."

There was an echoing of feet, of voices. A group of schoolchildren flocked by led by a prim, stern-faced teacher wearing practical shoes. "Fascinating," Carlo muttered. "Why don't we go to the park, Summer. It's a beautiful day." For female joggers in tiny shorts and tiny shirts.

"I'd consider myself a poor friend if I didn't give you a brief history lesson before you leave this evening, Carlo." She linked her arm more firmly through his. "It was actually July 8, not July 4, 1776, that the Declaration of Independence was read to the crowd in the yard outside this building."

"Incredible." Hadn't that brunette been heading for the park? "I can't tell you how interesting I find this American history, but some fresh air perhaps—"

"You can't leave Philadelphia without seeing the Liberty Bell." Taking him by the hand, Summer dragged him along. "A symbol of freedom is international, Carlo." She didn't even hear his muttered assent as her thoughts began to swing back to Blake again. "Just what was he trying to prove with that gloss and machismo?" she demanded. "Telling me he'd pick me up at eight after I'd refused to go." Gritting her teeth, she put her hands on her hips and glared at Carlo. "Men— you're all basically the same, aren't you?"

"But no, *carissima*." Amused, he gave her a charming smile and ran his fingers down her cheek. "We are all unique, especially Franconi. There are women in every city of the world who can attest to that."

"Pig," she said bluntly, refusing to be swayed with humor. She sidled closer to him, unconcerned that there was a group of three female college students hanging on every word. "Don't throw your women up to me, you Italian lecher."

"Ah, but, Summer…" He brought her palm to his lips, watching the three young women over it. "The word is…connoisseur."

Her comment was an unladylike snort. "You—men," she corrected, jerking her hand from his, "think of women as something to toy with, enjoy for a while, then disregard. No one's ever going to play that game with me."

Grinning from ear to ear, Carlo took both her hands

and kissed them. "Ah, no, no, *cara mia.* A woman, she is like the most exquisite of meals."

Summer's eyes narrowed. As the three girls edged closer she struggled with a grin of her own. "A meal? You dare to compare a woman with a meal?"

"An exquisite one," Carlo reminded her. "One you anticipate with great excitement, one you linger over, savor, even worship."

Her brows arched. "And when your plate's clean, Carlo?"

"It stays in your memory." Touching his thumb and forefinger together, he kissed them dramatically. "Returns in your dreams and keeps you forever searching for an equally sensual experience."

"Very poetic," she said dryly. "But I'm not going to be anyone's entrée."

"No, my Summer, you are the most forbidden of desserts, and therefore, the most desirable." Irrepressible, he winked at the trio of girls. "This Cocharan, do you not think his mouth waters whenever he looks at you?"

Summer gave a short laugh, took two steps away, then stopped. The image had an odd, primitive appeal. Intrigued, she looked back over her shoulder. "Does it?"

Because he knew he'd distracted her, Carlo slipped an arm around her waist and began to lead her from the building. There was still time for fresh air and leggy joggers in the park. Behind them, the three girls muttered in disappointment. "*Cara,* I am a man who has made a study of *amore.* I know what I see in another man's eyes."

Summer fought off a surge of pleasure and shrugged. "You Italians insist on giving a pretty label to basic lust."

With a huge sigh, Carlo led her outside. "Summer, for a woman with French blood, you have no romance."

"Romance belongs in books and movies."

"Romance," Carlo corrected, "belongs everywhere." Though she'd spoken lightly, Carlo understood that she was being perfectly frank. It worried him and, in the way of friend for friend, disappointed him. "You should try candlelight and wine and soft music, Summer. Let yourself experience it. It won't hurt you."

She gave him a strange sidelong smile as they walked. "Won't it?"

"You can trust Carlo like you trust no one else."

"Oh, I do." Laughing again, she swung an arm around his shoulders. "I trust no one else, Franconi."

That too, was the unvarnished truth. Carlo sighed again but spoke with equal lightness. "Then trust yourself, *cara.* Be guided by your own instincts."

"But I do trust myself."

"Do you?" This time it was Carlo who slanted a look at her. "I think you don't trust yourself to be alone with the American."

"With Blake?" He could feel her stiffen with outrage

under the arm he still held around her waist. "That's absurd."

"Then why are you so upset about the idea of having a simple dinner with him?"

"Your English is suffering, Carlo. Upset's the wrong word. I'm annoyed." She made herself relax under his arm again, then tilted her chin. "I'm annoyed because he assumed I'd have dinner with him, then continued to assume I would even after I'd refused. It's a normal reaction."

"I believe your reaction to him is very normal. One might say even—ah—basic." He took out his dark glasses and adjusted them meticulously. Perhaps squint lines added character to a face, but he wanted none on his. "I saw what was in your eyes as well that day in the kitchen."

Summer scowled at him, then lifted her chin a bit higher. "You don't know what you're talking about."

"I'm a gourmet," Carlo corrected with a sweep of his free arm. "Of food, yes, but also of love."

"Just stick to your pasta, Franconi."

He only grinned and patted her flank. "*Carissima,* my pasta never sticks."

She uttered a single French word in the most dulcet tones. It was one most commonly seen scrawled in Parisian alleyways. In tune with each other, they walked on, but both were speculating about what would happen that evening at eight.

* * *

It was quite deliberate, well thought out and very satisfying. Summer put on her shabbiest jeans and a faded T-shirt that was unraveled at the hem on one sleeve. She didn't bother with even a pretense of makeup. After seeing Carlo off at the airport, she'd gone through the drive-in window at a local fast-food restaurant and had picked up a cardboard container of fried chicken, complete with French fries and a tiny plastic bowl of coleslaw.

She opened a can of diet soda and flicked the television on to a syndicated rerun of a situation comedy.

Picking up a drumstick, Summer began to nibble. She'd considered dressing to kill, then breezing by him when he came to the door with the careless comment that she had a date. Very self-satisfying. But this way, Summer decided as she propped up her feet, she could be comfortable and insult him at the same time. After a day spent walking around the city while Carlo ogled and flirted with every female between six and sixty, comfort was every bit as important as the insult.

Satisfied with her strategy, Summer settled back and waited for the knock. It wouldn't be long, she mused. If she was any judge of character, she'd peg Blake as a man who was obsessively prompt. And fastidious, she added, taking a pleased survey of her cluttered, comfortably disorganized apartment.

Let's not forget smug, she reminded herself as she

polished off the drumstick. He'd arrive in a sleek, tailored suit with the shirt crisp and monogrammed on the cuffs. There wouldn't be a smudge on the Italian leather of his shoes. Not a hair out of place. Pleased, she glanced down at the tattered hem on her oldest jeans. A pity they didn't have a few good holes in them.

Grinning gleefully, she reached for her soda. Holes or not, she certainly didn't look like a woman waiting anxiously to impress a man. And that, Summer concluded, was what a man like Blake expected. Surprising him would give her a great deal of pleasure. Infuriating him would give her even more.

When the knock came, Summer glanced around idly before unfolding her legs. Taking her time, she rose, stretched, then moved to the door.

For the second time, Blake wished he'd had a camera to catch the look of blank astonishment on her face. She said nothing, only stared. With a hint of a smile on his lips, Blake tucked his hands into the pockets of his snug, faded jeans. There was no one, he reflected, whom he'd ever gotten more pleasure out of outwitting. So much so, it was tempting to make a career out of it.

"Dinner ready?" He took an appreciative sniff of the air. "Smells good."

Damn his arrogance—and his perception, Summer thought. How did he always manage to stay one step ahead of her? Except for the fact that he wore tennis shoes—tattered ones—he was dressed almost identically to her. It was only more annoying that he looked every bit as natural, and every bit as attractive, in jeans and a T-shirt as he did in an elegant business suit. With an effort, Summer controlled her temper, and twin surges of humor and desire. The rules might have changed, but the game wasn't over.

"*My* dinner's ready," she told him coolly. "I don't recall inviting you."

"I did say eight."

"I did say no."

"Since you objected to going out—" he took both her hands before breezing inside "—I thought we'd just eat in."

With her hands caught in his, Summer stood in the open doorway. She could order him to leave, she considered. Demand it… And he might. Although she didn't mind being rude, she didn't see much satisfaction in winning a battle so directly. She'd have to find another, more devious, more gratifying method to come out on top.

"You're very persistent, Blake. One might even say pigheaded."

"One might. What's for dinner?"

"Very little." Freeing one hand, Summer gestured toward the take-out box.

Blake lifted a brow. "Your penchant for fast food's very intriguing. Ever thought of opening your own chain—Minute Croissants? Drive Through Pastries?"

She wouldn't be amused. "You're the businessman," she reminded him. "I'm an artist."

"With a teenager's appetite." Strolling over, Blake plucked a drumstick from the box. He settled on the couch, then propped his feet on the coffee table. "Not bad," he decided after the first bite. "No wine?"

No, she didn't want to be amused, was determined not to be, but watching him make himself at home with her dinner, Summer fought off a grin. Maybe her plan to insult him hadn't worked, but there was no telling what the evening might bring. She only needed one opening to give him a good, solid jab. "Diet soda." She sat down and lifted the can. "There's more in the kitchen."

"This is fine." Blake took the drink from her and sipped. "Is this how one of the greatest dessert chefs spends her evenings?"

Lifting a brow, Summer took the can back from him. "*The* greatest dessert chef spends her evenings as she pleases."

Blake crossed one ankle over the other and studied her. The flecks in her eyes were more subtle this evening—perhaps because she was relaxed. He liked to think he could make them glow again before the night was over. "Yes, I'm sure you do. Does that extend to other areas?"

"Yes." Summer took another piece of chicken before

handing Blake a paper napkin. "I've decided your company's tolerable—for the moment."

Watching her, he took another bite. "Have you?"

"That's why you're here eating half my meal." She ignored his chuckle and propped her own feet on the table beside his. There was something cozy about the setting that appealed to her—something intimate that made her wary. She was too cautious a woman to allow herself to forget the effect that one kiss had had on her. She was too stubborn a woman to back down.

"I'm curious about why you insisted on seeing me tonight." A commercial on floor wax flicked across the television screen. Summer glanced at it before turning to Blake. "Why don't you explain?"

He took a plastic fork and sampled the coleslaw. "The professional reason or the personal one?"

He answered a question with a question too often, she decided. It was time to pin him down. "Why don't you take it one at a time?"

How did she eat this stuff? he wondered as he dropped the fork back into the box. When you looked at her you could see her in the most elegant of restaurants—flowers, French wine, starchily correct waiters. She'd be wearing silk and toying with some exotic dessert.

Summer rubbed the bottom of one bare foot over the top of the other while she took another bite of chicken.

Blake smiled even as he asked himself why she attracted him.

"Business first then. We'll be working together closely for several months at least. I think it's wise if we get to know each other—find out how the other works so we can make the proper adjustments when necessary."

"Logical." Summer plucked out a couple of French fries before offering the box to Blake. "It's just as well that you find out up front that I don't make adjustments at all. I work only one way—my way. So...personal?"

He enjoyed her confidence and the complete lack of compromise. He planned to explore the first and undo the second. "Personally, I find you a beautiful, interesting woman." Dipping his hand into the box, he watched her. "I want to take you to bed." When she said nothing, he nibbled on a fry. "And I think we should get to know each other first." Her stare was direct and unblinking. He smiled. "Logical?"

"Yes, and egotistical. You seem to have your share of both qualities. But—" she wiped her fingers on the napkin before she picked up the soda again "—you're honest. I admire honesty in other people." Rising, she looked down at him. "Finished?"

His gaze remained as cool as hers while he handed her the box. "Yeah."

"I happen to have a couple of éclairs in the fridge, if you're interested."

"Supermarket special?"

Her lips curved, slowly, slightly. "No. I do have some standards. They're mine."

"Then I could hardly insult you by turning them down."

This time she laughed. "I'm sure diplomacy's your only motive."

"That, and basic gluttony," he added as she walked away. *She's a cool one,* Blake reflected, thinking back to her reaction, or lack of one, to his statement about taking her to bed. The coolness, the control, intrigued him. Or perhaps more accurately, challenged him.

Was it a veneer? If it was, he'd like the opportunity to strip off the layers. Slowly, he decided, even lazily, until he found the passion beneath. It would be there—he imagined it would be like one of her desserts—dark and forbidden beneath a cool white icing. Before too much time had passed, Blake intended to taste it.

Her hands weren't steady. Summer cursed herself as she opened the refrigerator. He'd shaken her—just as he'd meant to. She only hoped he hadn't been able to see through her off-hand response. Yes, he'd intended to shake her, but he'd said precisely what he'd meant. That she understood. At the moment, she didn't have the time to absorb and dissect her feelings. There was only her first reaction—not shock, not outrage, but a kind of nervous excitement she hadn't experienced in years.

Silly, Summer told herself while she arranged éclairs on two Meissen plates. She wasn't a teenager who delighted in fluttery feelings. Nor would she tolerate being informed she was about to become someone's lover. Affairs, she knew, were dangerous, time-consuming and distracting. And there always seemed to be one party who was more involved, therefore, more vulnerable, than the other. She wouldn't allow herself to be in that position.

But the little twinges of nervous excitement remained.

She was going to have to do something about Blake Cocharan, Summer decided as she poured out two cups of coffee. And she was going to have to do it quickly. The problem was—what?

As Summer arranged cups and plates on a tray, she decided to do what she did best under pressure. She'd wing it.

"You're about to have a memorable, sensuous experience."

Blake glanced up at the announcement and watched her come into the room, tray in hand. Desire hit him surprisingly hard, surprisingly fast. It warned him that if he wanted to stay in control, he'd have to play the game with skill.

"My éclairs aren't to be taken lightly," Summer continued. "Nor are they to be eaten with anything less than reverence."

He waited until she sat beside him again before he took a plate. Very skillfully done, he thought again as her scent drifted to him. "I'll do my best."

"Actually—" she brought down the side of her fork and broke off the first bite "—no effort's required. Just taste buds." Unable to resist, Summer brought the fork to his lips.

He watched her, and she him, as she fed him. The light slanted through the window behind them and caught in her eyes. More green now, Blake thought, almost feline. A man, any man, could lose himself trying to define that color, read that expression. The rich cream and flaky pastry melted in his mouth. Exotic, unique, desirable—like its creator. The first taste, like the first kiss, demanded more.

"Incredible," he murmured, and as her lips curved, he wanted them under his.

"Naturally." As she broke off another portion, Blake's hand closed over her wrist. Her pulse scrambled briefly, he could feel it, but her eyes remained cool and level.

"I'll return the favor." He said it quietly, and his fingers stayed lightly on her wrist as he took the fork in his other hand. He moved slowly, deliberately, keeping his eyes on hers, bringing the pastry to her lips, then pausing. He watched them part, saw the tip of her tongue. It would have been so easy to close his mouth over hers just then—from the rapid beat of her pulse under his fingers, he knew there'd be no resistance. Instead, he fed her the éclair, his stomach muscles tightening as he imagined the taste that was even now lying delicately on her tongue.

She'd never felt anything like this. She'd sampled her own cooking countless times, but had never had her senses so heightened. The flavor seemed to fill her mouth. Summer wanted to keep it there, exploring the sensation that had become so unexpectedly, so intensely, sexual. It took a conscious effort to swallow, and another to speak.

"More?" she asked.

His gaze flicked down from her eyes to her mouth then back again. "Always."

A dangerous game. She knew it, but opted to play. And to win. Taking her time, she fed him the next bite. Was the color of his eyes deeper? She didn't think she was imagining it, nor the waves of desire that seemed to pound over her. Did they come from her, or from him?

On the television, someone broke into raucous laughter. Neither of them noticed. It would be wise to step back now, cautiously. Even as the thought passed through her mind, she opened her mouth for the next taste.

Some things exploded on the tongue, others heated it or tantalized. This was a cool, elegant experience, no less sensual than champagne, no less primitive than ripened fruit. Her nerves began to calm, but her awareness intensified. He was wearing some subtle cologne that made her think of the woods in autumn. His eyes were the deep blue of an evening sky. When his knee brushed hers, she felt a warmth that seeped through two layers of material and touched flesh. Moment after moment passed without her being aware that they weren't speaking, only slowly, luxuriously, feeding each other. The intimacy wrapped around her, no less intense, no less exciting than lovemaking. The coffee sat cooling. Shadows spread through the room as the sun went down.

"The last bite," Summer murmured, offering it. "You approve?"

He caught the ends of her hair between his thumb and finger. "Completely."

Her skin tingled, much too pleasantly. Although she didn't shift away, Summer set the fork down with great care. She was feeling soft—too soft. And too vulnerable. "One of my clients has a secret passion for éclairs. Four times a year I go to Brittany and make him two dozen. Last fall he gave me an emerald necklace."

Blake lifted a brow as he twined a strand of her hair around his finger. "Is that a hint?"

"I'm fond of presents," she said easily. "But then, that sort of thing isn't quite ethical between business associates."

As she leaned forward for her coffee, Blake tightened his fingers in her hair and held her still. In the moment her eyes met his, he saw mild surprise and mild annoyance. She didn't like to be held down by anyone.

"Our business association is only one level. We're both acutely aware of that by this time."

"Business is the first level, and the first priority."

"Maybe." It was difficult to admit, even to himself, that he was beginning to have doubts about that. "In any case, I haven't any intention of staying at level one."

If she were ever going to handle him, it would have to be now. Summer draped her arm negligently across the back of the sofa and wished her stomach would unknot. "I'm attracted to you. And I think it should be difficult, and interesting, to work around that for the next few months. You said you wanted to understand me. I rarely explain myself, but I'll make an exception." Leaning forward again, she plucked a cigarette from its holder. "Have you a light?"

It was strange how easily she drew feelings from him without warning. Now it was annoyance. Blake took out his lighter and flicked it on. He watched her pull in smoke, then blow it out quickly in a gesture he realized came more from habit than pleasure. "Go on."

"You said you knew my mother," Summer began. "You'd know of her in any case. She's a beautiful, talented, intelligent woman. I love her very much, both as a mother, and as a person who's full of the joy of life. If she has one weakness, it is men."

Summer folded her legs under her and concentrated on relaxing. "She's had three husbands, and innumerable lovers. She's always certain each relationship is forever. When she's involved with a man, she's blissfully happy. His interests are her interests, his dislikes her dislikes. Naturally, when it ends, she's crushed."

Again, Summer drew on her cigarette. She'd expected him to make some passing comment. When instead, he only listened, only watched, she went further than she'd intended. "My father is a more practical man, and yet he's been through two wives and quite a few discreet affairs. Unlike my mother, who accepts flaws—even enjoys them for a short time—he looks for perfection. Since there is no perfection in people, only in what people create, he's continually disappointed. My mother looks for elation and romance, my father looks for the perfect companion. I don't look for either of those."

"Why don't you tell me what you look for then?"

"Success," she said simply. "Romance has a beginning, so it follows it has an end. A companion demands compromise and patience. I give all my patience to my work, and I have no talent for compromise."

It should have satisfied him, even relieved him. After all, he wanted nothing more than a casual affair, no strings, no commitments. He didn't understand why he wanted to shake the words back down her throat, only knew that he did. "No romance," he said with a nod. "No companionship. That doesn't rule out the fact that you want me, and I want you."

"No." The smoke was leaving a bitter taste in her

mouth. As Summer crushed out her cigarette she thought how much their discussion sounded like a negotiation. Yet wasn't that how she preferred things? "I said it would be difficult to work around, but it's also necessary. You want a service from me, Blake, and I agreed to give you that, because I want the experience and the publicity I'll get out of it. But changing the tone and face of your restaurant is going to be a long, complicated process. Combining that with my other commitments, I won't have time for any personal distractions."

"Distractions?" Why should that one word have infuriated him? It did, just as her businesslike dismissal of desire infuriated him. Perhaps she hadn't meant it as a challenge, but he couldn't take it as anything less. "Does this distract you?" He ran his finger down the side of her throat before he cupped the back of her neck.

She could feel the firm pressure of each of his fingers against her skin. And in his eyes, she could see the temper, the need. Both pulled at her. "You're paying me a great deal of money, to do a job, Blake." Her voice was steady. Good. Her heartbeat wasn't. "As a businessman, you should want the complications left to a minimum."

"Complications," he repeated. He drew his other hand through her hair so that her face was tilted back. Summer felt a jolt of excitement shoot down her spine.

"Is this—" he brushed his lips over her cheek "—a complication?"

"Yes." Her brain sent out the signal to pull away, but her body refused the command.

"And a distraction?"

He took his mouth on a slow journey to hers, but only nibbled. There was no pressure but the slight grip he kept on the base of her neck with fingers moving slowly, rhythmically over her skin. Summer didn't move away, though she told herself she still could. She'd never permitted herself to be seduced, and tonight was no different.

Just a sample, she thought. She knew how to taste and judge, then step away from even the most tempting of flavors. Just as she knew how to absorb every drop of pleasure from that one tiny test.

"Yes," she murmured and let her eyes flutter closed. She needed no visual image now, but only the sensations. Warm, soft, moist—his mouth against hers. Firm, strong, persuasive—the fingers against her skin. Subtle, male, intriguing—the scent that clung to him. When he spoke her name, his voice flowed over her like a breeze, one that carried a trace of heat and the hint of a storm.

"How simple do you want it to be, Summer?" It was happening again, he realized. That total involvement he neither looked for nor wanted—the total involvement he couldn't resist. "There's only you and me."

"There's nothing simple about that." Even as she disagreed, her arms were going around him, her mouth was seeking his again.

It was only a kiss. She told herself that as his lips slanted lightly over hers. She could still end it, she was still in control. But first, she wanted just one more taste. Without thinking, she touched the tip of his tongue with hers, to fully explore the flavor. Her own moan sounded softly in her ears as she drew him closer. Body against body, firm and somehow right. This new thought drifted to her even as the sensation concentrated on the play of mouth to mouth.

Why had kisses seemed so basic, so simplistic before this? There were hundreds of pulse points in her body she'd remained unaware of until this moment. There were pleasures deeper, richer than she'd ever imagined that could be drawn out and exploited by the most elemental gesture between a man and a woman. She'd thought she'd known the limits of her own needs, the depth of her own passions…until now. Barely touching her, Blake was tearing something from her that wasn't calm, ordered and disciplined. And when it was totally free, what then?

She found herself at the verge of something she'd never come to before—where emotions commanded her mind completely. A step further and he would have all of her. Not just her body, not just her thoughts, but that most private, most well guarded possession, her heart.

She felt a greed for him and pulled away from it. If

she were greedy, if she took, then he would too. He still held her, lightly enough for her to draw back, firmly enough to keep her close. She was breathless, moved. As she struggled to think clearly, Summer decided it would be foolish to try to deny either.

"I think I proved my point," she managed.

"Yours?" Blake countered as he ran a hand up her back. "Or mine?"

She took a deep breath, expelling it slowly. That one small show of emotion had desire clawing at him again. "I've mixed enough ingredients to know that business affairs and personal affairs aren't palatable. On Monday, I go to work for Cocharan. I intend to give you your money's worth. There can't be anything else."

"There's quite a bit else already." He cupped her chin in his hand so that their eyes held steady. Inside he was a mass of aching needs and confusion. With that kiss, that long, slow kiss, he'd all but forgotten his strictest rule. *Keep the emotions harnessed, both in business and in pleasure. Otherwise, you make mistakes that aren't easily rectified.* He needed time, and he realized he needed distance. "We know each other better now," he said after a moment. "When we make love, we'll understand each other."

Summer remained seated when he rose. She wasn't completely sure she could stand. "On Monday," she said in a firmer voice, "we'll be working together. That's all there is between us from this point on."

"When you deal with as many contracts as I do, Summer, you learn that paper is just that: paper. It's not going to make any difference."

He walked to the door thinking he needed some fresh air to clear his head, a drink to settle his nerves. And distance, a great deal of distance, before he forgot everything except the raging need to have her.

With his hand on the knob, Blake turned around for one last look at her. There was something in the way she frowned at him, with her eyes focused and serious, her lips soft in a half pout that made him smile.

"Monday," he told her, and was gone.

Chapter 5

Why in hell couldn't he stop thinking of her? Blake sat at his desk examining the details of a twenty-page contract in preparation for what promised to be a long, tense meeting in the boardroom. He wasn't taking in a single word. Uncharacteristic. He knew it, resented it and could do nothing about it.

For days Summer had been slipping into his mind and crowding out everything else. For a man who took order and self-control for granted, it was nerve-racking.

Logically, there was no reason for his obsession with her. Blake called it obsession, for lack of a better term, but it didn't please him. She was beautiful, he mused as his thoughts drifted further away from clauses and terms. He'd known hundreds of beautiful women. She was intelligent, but intelligent women had been in his life before. Desirable—even now in his neat, quiet office he could feel the first stirrings of need. But he was no stranger to desire.

He enjoyed women, as friends and as lovers. Enjoyment, Blake reflected, was perhaps the key word—he'd never looked for anything deeper in a relationship with a woman. But he wasn't certain it was the proper word to describe what was already between himself and Summer. She moved him—too strongly, too quickly—to the point where his innate control was shaken. No, he didn't enjoy that, but it didn't stop him from wanting more. Why?

Utilizing his customary method of working through a problem, Blake leaned back and, picking up a pen, began to list the possibilities.

Perhaps part of the consistent attraction was the fact that he liked outmaneuvering her. It wasn't easily done, and took quick thinking and careful planning. Up till this point, he'd countered her at every turn. Blake was realistic enough to know that that wouldn't last, but he was human enough to want to try. Just where would they clash next? he wondered. Over business…or over something more personal? In either case he wanted to go head to head with her just as much—well, almost as much—as he wanted to make love with her.

And perhaps another reason was that he knew the attraction was just as strong on her part—yet she continued to refuse it. He admired that strength of will in her. She mistrusted intimacy, he mused. Because of her parents' track record? Yes, partially, he decided. But he didn't think that was all of it. He'd just have to dig a bit deeper to get the whole picture.

He wanted to dig, he realized. For the first time in his life Blake wanted to know a woman completely. Her thought process, her eccentricities, what made her laugh, what annoyed, what she really wanted for and in her life. Once he knew all there was to know... He couldn't see past that. But he wanted to know her, understand her. And he wanted her as a lover as he'd never wanted anything else.

When the buzzer on his desk sounded, Blake answered it automatically with his thoughts still centering on Summer Lyndon.

"Your father's on his way back, Mr. Cocharan."

Blake glanced down at the contract on his desk and mentally filed it. He still needed an hour with it before the board meeting. "Thanks." Even as he released the intercom button, the door swung open. Blake Cocharan II strolled into the room and took it over.

In build and coloring, he was similar to his son. Exercise and athletics had kept him trim and hard over the years. There were threads of gray in the dark hair that was covered by a white sea captain's hat. But his eyes were young and vibrant. He walked with the easy rolling gait of a man more accustomed to decks than floors. He wore canvas on his sockless feet, and a Swiss watch on his wrist. When he grinned, the lines etched by time and squinting at the sun fanned out from his eyes and mouth. As he stood to greet him, Blake caught the salty, sea-breezy scent he always associated with his father.

"B.C." Their hands clasped, one older and rougher than the other, both firm. "Just passing through?"

"On my way to Tahiti, going to do some sailing." B.C. grinned again, appealingly, as he ran a finger along the brim of his cap. "Want to play hookey and crew for me?"

"Can't. I'm booked solid for the next two weeks."

"You work too hard, boy." In an old habit, B.C. walked over to the bar at the west side of the room and poured himself bourbon, neat.

Blake grinned at his father's back as B.C. tossed down three fingers of liquor. It was still shy of noon. "I came by it honestly."

With a chuckle, B.C. poured a second drink. When it had been his office, he'd stocked only the best bourbon. He was glad his son carried on the tradition. "Maybe— but I learned to play just as hard."

"You paid your dues, B.C."

"Yeah." Twenty-five years of ten-hour days, he reflected. Of hotel rooms, airports and board meetings. "So did the old man—so've you." He turned back to his son. Like looking into a mirror that's twenty years past, he thought, and smiled rather than sighed. "I've told you before, you can't wrap your life up in hotels."

He sipped appreciatively at the bourbon this time, then swirled it. "Gives you ulcers."

"Not so far." Sitting again, Blake steepled his fingers, watching his father over them. He knew him too well, had apprenticed under him, watched him wheel and deal. Tahiti might be his destination, but he hadn't stopped off in Philadelphia without a reason. "You came in for the board meeting."

B.C. nodded before he found some salted almonds under the bar. "Have to put in my two cents worth now and again." He popped two nuts in his mouth and bit down with relish. He was always grateful that the teeth were still his and his eyesight was keen. If a man had those, and a forty-foot sloop, he needed little else. "If we buy the Hamilton chain, it's going to mean twenty more hotels, over two thousand more employees. A big step."

Blake lifted a brow. "Too big?"

With a laugh, B.C. dropped down into a chair across from the desk. "I didn't say that, don't think that—and apparently you don't think so either."

"No, I don't." Blake waved away his father's offering of almonds. "Hamilton's an excellent chain, simply mismanaged at this point. The buildings themselves are worth the outlay." He gave his father a mild, knowledgeable look. "You might check out the Hamilton Tahiti while you're there."

Grinning, B.C. leaned back. The boy was sharp, he thought, pleased. But then he came by that honestly, too.

"Thought crossed my mind. By the way, your mother sends her love."

"How is she?"

"Up to her neck in a campaign to save another crumbling ruin." The grin widened. "Keeps her off the streets. Going to meet me on the island next week. Hell of a first mate, your mother." He nibbled on another almond, pleased to think of having some time alone with his wife in the tropics. "So, Blake, how's your sex life?"

Too used to his father to be anything but amused, Blake inclined his head. "Adequate, thanks."

With a short laugh, B.C. downed the rest of his drink. "Adequate's a disgrace to the Cocharan name. We do everything in superlatives."

Blake drew out a cigarette. "I've heard stories."

"All true," his father told him, gesturing with the empty glass. "One day I'll have to tell you about this dancer in Bangkok in '39. In the meantime, I've heard you plan to do some face-lifting right here."

"The restaurant." Blake nodded and thought of Summer. "It promises to be…fascinating work."

B.C. caught the tone and began to gently probe. "I can't disagree that the place needs a little glitzing up. So you hired on a French chef to oversee the operation."

"Half French."

"A woman?"

"That's right." Blake blew out smoke, aware which path his father was trying to lead him down.

B.C. stretched out his legs. "Knows her business, does she?"

"I wouldn't have hired her otherwise."

"Young?"

Blake drew on his cigarette and suppressed a smile. "Moderately, I suppose."

"Attractive?"

"That depends on your definition—I wouldn't call her attractive." Too tame a word, Blake thought, much, much too tame. Exotic, alluring—those suited her more. "I can tell you that she's dedicated to her profession, an ambitious perfectionist and that her éclairs..." His thoughts drifted back to that intoxicating interlude. "Her éclairs are an experience not to be missed."

"Her éclairs," B.C. repeated.

"Fantastic." Blake leaned back in his chair. "Absolutely fantastic." He kept the grin under control as his buzzer sounded again.

"Ms. Lyndon is here, Mr. Cocharan."

Monday morning, he thought. Business as usual. "Send her in."

"Lyndon." B.C. set down his glass. "That's the cook, isn't it?"

"Chef," Blake corrected. "I'm not sure if she answers to the term 'cook.'"

The knock was brief before Summer walked in. She

carried a slim leather folder in one hand. Her hair was braided and rolled at the nape of her neck so that the hints of gold threaded through the brown. Her suit in a deep plum color was Chanel, simple and exquisite over a high-necked lace blouse that rose to frame her face. The strict professionalism of her attire made Blake instantly speculate on what she wore beneath—something brief, silky and sexy, the same color as her skin.

"Blake." Following her own self-lecture on priorities, Summer held out her hand. Impersonal, businesslike and formal. She wasn't going to think about what happened when his mouth touched hers. "I've brought you the list of changes of equipment and suggestions we spoke about."

"Fine." He saw her turn her head as B.C. rose from his chair. And he saw the gleam light his father's eyes as it always did when he was in the company of a beautiful woman. "Summer Lyndon, Blake Cocharan II. B.C., Ms. Lyndon will be managing the kitchen here at the Philadelphia Cocharan House."

"Mr. Cocharan." Summer found her hand enveloped in a large, calloused one. He looks, she realized with a jolt, exactly as Blake will in thirty years. Distinguished, weathered, with that perennial touch of polish. Then B.C. grinned, and she understood that Blake would still be dangerous in three decades.

"B.C.," he corrected, lifting her fingers to his lips. "Welcome to the family."

Summer shot Blake a quick look. "Family?"

"We consider anyone associated with Cocharan House part of the family." B.C. gestured to the chair he'd vacated. "Please, sit down. Let me get you a drink."

"Thank you. Perhaps some Perrier." She watched B.C. cross the room before she sat and laid the folder on her lap. "I believe you're acquainted with my mother, Monique Dubois."

That stopped him. B.C. turned, the bottle of Perrier still in his hand, the glass in the other still empty. "Monique? You're Monique's girl? I'll be damned."

And so he might be, B.C. thought. Years before— was it nearly twenty now?—during a period of marital upheaval on both sides, he'd had a brief, searing affair with the French actress. They'd parted on amicable terms and he'd reconciled with his wife. But the two weeks with Monique had been...memorable. Now he was in his son's office pouring Perrier for her daughter. Fate, he thought wryly, was a tricky sonofabitch.

If Summer had suspected before that her mother and Blake's father had once been lovers, she was now certain of it. Her thoughts on fate directly mirrored his as she crossed her legs. Like mother, like daughter? she wondered. Oh, no, not in this case. B.C. was still staring at her. For a reason she didn't completely understand, she decided to make it easy for him.

"Mother is a loyal client of Cocharan Houses; she'll stay nowhere else. I've already mentioned to Blake that we once had dinner with your father. He was very gracious."

"When it suits him," B.C. returned, relieved. *She knows,* he concluded before his gaze strayed to Blake's. There he saw a frown of concentration that was all too familiar. *And so will he if I don't watch my step,* B.C. decided. *Hot water,* he mused. *After twenty years I could still be in hot water.* His wife was the love of his life, his best friend, but twenty years wasn't long enough to be safe from a transgression.

"So—" he finished pouring the Perrier, then brought it to her "—you decided against following in your mother's footsteps and became a chef instead."

"I'm sure Blake would agree that following in a parent's footsteps is often treacherous."

Instinct told Blake that it wasn't business she spoke of now. A look passed between his father and Summer that he couldn't comprehend. "It depends where the path leads," Blake countered. "In my case I preferred to look at it as a challenge."

"Blake takes after his grandfather," B.C. put in. "He has that cagey kind of logic."

"Yes," Summer murmured. "I've seen it in action."

"Apparently you made the right choice," B.C. went on. "Blake told me about your éclairs."

Slowly, Summer turned her head until she was facing Blake again. The muscles in her stomach, in her thighs, tightened with the memory. Her voice remained calm and cool. "Did he? Actually, my specialty is the bombe."

Blake met her gaze directly. "A pity you didn't have one available the other night."

There were vibrations there, B.C. thought, that didn't need to bounce off a third party. "Well, I'll let you two get on with your business. I've some people to see before the board meeting. A pleasure meeting you, Summer." He took her hand again and held it as his eyes held hers. "Please, give my best to your mother."

She saw his eyes were like Blake's, in color, in shape, in appeal. Her lips curved. "I will."

"Blake, I'll see you this afternoon."

He only murmured an assent, watching Summer rather than his father. The door closed before he spoke. "Why do I feel as though there were messages being passed in front of me?"

"I have no idea," Summer said coolly as she lifted the folder. "I'd like you to glance over these papers while I'm here, if you have time." Zipping open the folder, she pulled them out. "That way, if there are any questions or any disagreements, we can get through them now before I begin downstairs."

"All right." Blake picked up the first sheet but studied her over it. "Is that suit supposed to keep me at a distance?"

She sent him a haughty look. "I have no idea what you're talking about."

"Yes, you do. And another time I'd like to peel it off you, layer by layer. But at the moment, we'll play it your way." Without another word, he lowered his gaze to the paper and started to read.

"Arrogant swine," Summer said distinctly. When he didn't even bother to look up she folded her arms over her chest. She wanted a cigarette to give her something to do with her hands, but refused herself the luxury. She would sit like a stone, and when the time came, she would argue for every one of the changes she'd listed. And win every one of them. On that level *she* was in complete control.

She wanted to hate him for realizing she'd worn the elegant, career-oriented suit to set a certain tone. Instead, she had to respect him for being perceptive enough to pick up on small details. She wanted to hate him for making her want so badly with only a look and a few words. It wasn't possible when she'd spent the remainder of the weekend alternately wishing she'd never met him and wishing he'd come back and bring her that excitement again. He was a problem; there was no denying it. She understood that you solved problems one step at a time. Step one, her kitchen—accent on the personal pronoun.

"Two new gas ovens," he murmured as he scanned the sheet. "One electric oven and two more ranges of each kind." Without lowering it, he glanced at her over the top of the page.

"I believe I explained to you before the need for both gas and electric ovens. First, yours are antiquated. Second, in a restaurant of this size the need for two gas ovens is imperative."

"You specify brands."

"Of course, I know what I like to work with."

He only lifted a brow, thinking that procurement was going to grumble. "All new pots and pans?"

"Definitely."

"Perhaps we should have a yard sale," Blake mumbled as he went back to the sheet. He hadn't the vaguest idea what a *sautoir* was or why she required three of them. "And this particular heavy-duty mixer?"

"Essential. The one you have is adequate. I don't accept adequate."

He smothered a laugh as he recalled his father's view on adequate in relation to love lives. "Did you list so much of this in French to confuse me?"

"I listed in French," Summer countered, "because French is correct."

He made an indefinable sound as he passed over the next sheet. "In any case, I've no intention of quibbling over equipment in French or English."

"Good. Because I've no intention of working with any less than the best." She smiled at him and settled back. First point taken.

Blake flipped over the second sheet and went on to the third. "You intend to rip out the existing counters, have the new ranges built in, add an island and an additional six feet of counter space."

"More efficient," Summer said easily.

"And time-consuming."

"In a hurry? You hired me, Blake, not Minute Chef." His quick grin made her eyes narrow. "My function is to organize your kitchen, which means making it as efficient and creative as I know how. Once the nuts and bolts of that are done, I'll beef up your menu."

"And this—" he flipped through the five typed sheets "—is all necessary for that?"

"I don't bother with anything that isn't necessary when it comes to business. If you don't agree," she said as she rose, "we can terminate the agreement. Hire LaPointe," she suggested, firing up. "You'll have an ostentatious, overpriced, second-rate kitchen that produces equally ostentatious, overpriced and second-rate meals."

"I have to meet this LaPointe," Blake murmured as he stood. "You'll get what you want, Summer." As a satisfied smile formed on her lips, he narrowed his eyes. "And you damn well better deliver what you promised."

The fire leapt back, accenting the gold in her irises. And as he saw it, he wanted.

"I've given you my word. Your middle-class restaurant with its mediocre prime rib and soggy pastries will be serving the finest in haute cuisine within six months."

"Or?"

So he wanted collateral, Summer thought, and heaved a breath. "Or my services for the term of the contract are gratis. Does that satisfy you?"

"Completely." Blake held out a hand. "As I said, you'll have precisely what you've asked for, down to the last egg beater."

"A pleasure doing business with you." Summer tried to draw her hand away and found it caught firm. "Perhaps you don't," she began, "but I have work to do. You'll excuse me?"

"I want to see you."

She let her hand remain passively in his rather than risk a struggle she might lose. "You have seen me."

"Tonight."

"Sorry." She smiled again, though her teeth were beginning to clench. "I have a date."

She felt the quick increase in pressure of his fingers over hers and was perversely pleased. "All right, when?"

"I'll be in the kitchen every day, and some evenings, to oversee the remodeling. You need only ride the elevator down."

He drew her closer, and though the desk remained between them, Summer felt that the ground beneath was a bit less firm. "I want to see you alone," he said quietly. Lifting her hand to his lips, he kissed her fingers slowly, one by one. "Away from here, outside of business hours."

If Blake Cocharan II had been anything like Blake Cocharan III in his youth, Summer could understand how her mother had become so quickly, so heatedly involved. The yearning was there, and the temptation—but she wasn't Monique. In this case, she was determined history would not repeat itself. "I've explained to you why that's not possible. I don't enjoy covering the same ground twice."

"Your pulse is racing," Blake pointed out as he ran a finger across her wrist.

"It generally does when I become annoyed."

"Or aroused."

Tilting her head, she sent him a killing look. "Would you amuse yourself with LaPointe in this way?"

Temper stirred and he suppressed it, knowing she wanted him to be angry. "At the moment, I don't care whether you're a chef or a plumber or a brain surgeon. At the moment," he repeated, "I only care that you're a woman, and one who I desire very much."

She wanted to swallow because her throat had gone dry but fought off the need. "At the moment I *am* a chef with a specific job to do. I'll ask you again to excuse me so I can begin to do it."

This time, Blake thought as he released her hand. But, by God, this time was the last time. "Sooner or later, Summer."

"Perhaps," she agreed as she picked up her leather folder. "Perhaps not." In one quick gesture, she zipped it closed. "Enjoy your day, Blake." As if her legs weren't weak and watery, she strolled to the door and out.

Summer continued to walk calmly through the outer office, over the plush carpet, past the busy secretaries and through the reception area. Once in the elevator, she leaned back against the wall and let out the long, tense breath she'd been holding. Nerves jumping, she began the ride down.

That was over, she told herself. She'd faced him in his office and won every point.

Sooner or later, Summer.

She let out another breath. Almost every point, she corrected. The important thing now was to concentrate on her kitchen, and to keep busy. It wasn't going to help matters if she allowed herself to think of him as she had over the weekend.

As her nerves began to calm, Summer straightened away from the wall. She'd handled herself well, she'd made herself clear and *she'd* walked out on him. All in all, a successful morning. She pressed a hand against her stomach, where a few muscles were still jumping. Damn it, things would be simpler if she didn't want him so badly.

When the doors slid open she stepped out, then wound her way around to the kitchen. In the prelunch bustle, she went unnoticed. She approved of the noise.

A quiet kitchen to Summer meant there was no communication. Without that, there was no cooperation. For a moment, she stood just inside the doorway to watch.

She approved of the smells. It was a mixture of lunchtime aromas over the still-lingering odors of breakfast. Bacon, sausage and coffee. She caught the scent of baking chicken, of grilled meat, of cakes fresh from the oven. Narrowing her eyes, she envisioned the room as it would be in a short time. Made to her order. Better, Summer decided with a nod.

"Ms. Lyndon."

Distracted, she frowned up at a big man in white apron and cap. "Yes?"

"I'm Max." His chest expanded, his voice stiffened. "Head chef."

Ego in danger, she thought as she extended a hand. "How do you do, Max. I missed you when I was in last week."

"Mr. Cocharan has instructed me to give you full cooperation during this—transition period."

Marvelous, she thought with an inward moan. Resentment in a kitchen was as difficult to deal with as a deflated soufflé. Left to herself, she might have been able to keep injured feelings to a minimum, but the damage had already been done. She made a mental note to give Blake her opinion of his tact and diplomacy.

"Well, Max, I'd like to go over the proposed structural changes with you, since you know the routine here better than anyone else."

"Structural changes?" he repeated. His full, round face flushed. The moustache over his mouth quivered. She caught the gleam of a single gold tooth. "In *my* kitchen?"

My kitchen, Summer mentally corrected, but smiled. "I'm sure you'll be pleased with the improvements—and the new equipment. You must have found it frustrating trying to create something special with outdated appliances."

"This oven," he said and gestured dramatically toward it, "this range—both have been here since I began at Cocharan. We are none of us outdated."

So much for cooperation, Summer thought wryly. If it was too late for a friendly transition of authority, she'd have to go with the *coup*. "We'll be receiving three new ovens," she began briskly. "Two gas, one electric. The electric will be used exclusively for desserts and pastries. This counter," she continued, walking toward it without looking back to see if Max was following, "will be removed and the ranges I specified built into a new counter—butcher block. The grill remains. There'll be an island here to provide more working area and to make use of what is now essentially wasted space."

"There is no wasted space in my kitchen."

Summer turned and aimed her haughtiest stare. "That isn't a matter for debate. Creativity will be the first priority of this kitchen, efficiency the second. We'll be expected to produce quality meals during the remodeling—difficult but not impossible if everyone makes the necessary adjustments. In the meantime, you and I will go over the current menu with an eye toward adding excitement and flair to what is now pedestrian."

She heard him suck in his breath but continued before he could rage. "Mr. Cocharan contracted me to turn this restaurant into the finest establishment in the city. I fully intend to do just that. Now, I'd like to observe the staff in lunch preparations." Unzipping her leather folder, Summer pulled out a note pad and pen. Without another word she began walking through the busy kitchen.

The staff, she decided after a few moments, was well trained and more orderly than many. Credit Max. Cleanliness was obviously a first priority. Another point for Max. She watched a cook expertly bone a chicken. Not bad, Summer decided. The grill was sizzling, pots steaming. Lifting a lid, she ladeled out a small portion of the soup du jour. She sampled it, holding the taste on her tongue a moment.

"Basil," she said simply, then walked away. Another cook drew apple pies from an oven. The scent was strong and wholesome. Good, she mused, but any experienced grandmother could do the same. What was needed was some pizzazz. People would come to this

restaurant for what they wouldn't get at home. Char-
lottes, Clafouti, flambées.

The structural changes came from her practical side,
but the menu—the menu stemmed from her creativity,
which was always paramount.

As she surveyed the kitchen, the staff, drew in the
smells, absorbed the sounds, Summer felt the first real
stirrings of excitement. She would do it, and she would
do it for her own satisfaction just as much as in answer to Blake's challenge. When she was finished, this
kitchen would bear her mark. It would be different entirely from jetting from one place to the next to create
a single memorable dish. This would have continuity,
stability. A year from now, five years from now, this
kitchen would still retain her touch, her influence.

The thought pleased her more than she'd expected.
She'd never looked for continuity, only the flash of an
individual triumph. And wouldn't she be behind the
scenes here? She might be in the kitchen in Milan or
Athens, but the guests in the dining room knew who
was preparing the Charlotte Royal. Clients wouldn't
come into the restaurant anticipating a Summer Lyndon dessert, but a Cocharan Hotel meal.

Even as she mulled the thought over in her mind, she
found it didn't matter. Why, she was still unsure. For
now, she only knew the pleasurable excitement of planning. *Think about it later,* she advised herself as she
made a final note. There were months to worry about

consequences, reasons, pitfalls. She wanted to begin, get elbow deep in a project she now, for whatever reason, considered peculiarly her own.

Slipping her folder under her arm, she walked out. She couldn't wait to start working on menus.

Chapter 6

Russian Beluga Malasol Caviar—that should be available from lunch to late-night dining. All night through room service.

Summer made another scrawled note. During the past two weeks, she'd changed the projected menu a dozen times. After one abortive session with Max, she'd opted to go solo on the task. She knew the ambience she wanted to create, and how to do so through food.

To save herself time, she'd set up a small office in a storage room off the kitchen. There, she could oversee the staff and the beginnings of the remodeling while having enough privacy to work on what was now her pet project.

Avoiding Blake had been easy because she'd kept herself so thoroughly busy. And it appeared he was just as involved in some complicated corporate deal. Buying out another hotel chain, if rumor were fact. Summer had little interest in that, for her concentration focused on items like medallions of veal in champagne sauce.

As long as the remodeling was going on, the staff remained in a constant state of panic or near panic. She'd come to accept that. Most of the kitchens she'd worked in were full of the tension and terror only a cook would understand. Perhaps it was that creative tension, and the terror of failure, that helped form the best meals.

For the most part, she left the staff supervision to Max. She interfered with the routine he'd established as little as possible, incorporating the changes she'd initiated unobtrusively. She'd learned the qualities of diplomacy and power from her father. If it placated Max at all, it wasn't apparent in his attitude toward Summer. That remained icily polite. Summer shrugged this off and concentrated on perfecting the entrées her kitchen would offer.

Calf's Liver Berlinoise. An excellent entrée, not as popular certainly as a broiled filet or prime rib, but excellent. As long as she didn't have to eat it, Summer thought with a smirk as she noted it down.

Once she'd organized the meat and poultry, she'd put her mind to the seafood. And naturally there had to be a cold buffet available twenty-four hours a day through room service. That was something else to work out. Soups, appetizers, salads—all of those had to be considered, decided on and confirmed before she began on the desserts. And at the moment, she'd have traded any of the elegant offerings jotted down in front of her for a cheeseburger on a sesame seed bun and a bag of chips.

"So this is where you've been hiding." Blake leaned against the doorway. He'd just completed a grueling four-hour meeting and had fully intended to go up to his suite for a long shower and a quiet, solitary meal. Instead, he'd found himself heading for the kitchen, and Summer.

She looked as she had the first time he'd seen her— her hair down, her feet bare. On the table in front of her were reams of scrawled-on paper and a half-empty glass of diluted soda. Behind her, boxes were stacked, sacks piled. The room smelled faintly of pine cleaner and cardboard. In her own way, she looked competent and completely in charge.

"Not hiding," she corrected. "Working." Tired, she thought. He looked tired. It showed around the eyes. "Been busy? We haven't seen you down here for the past couple of weeks."

"Busy enough." Stepping inside, he began to poke through her notes.

"Wheeling and dealing from what I hear." She leaned back, realizing all at once that her back ached. "Taking over the Hamilton chain."

He glanced up, then shrugged and looked back at her notes again. "It's a possibility."

"Discreet." She smiled, wishing she weren't quite so glad to see him again. "Well, while you've been playing Monopoly, I've been dealing with more intimate matters." When he glanced at her again, with his brow raised exactly as she'd expected it to be, she laughed. "Food, Blake, is the most basic and personal of desires, no matter what anyone might say to the contrary. For many, eating is a ritual experienced three times a day. It's a chef's job to make each experience memorable."

"For you, eating's a jaunt through adolescence."

"As I said," Summer continued mildly, "food is very personal."

"Agreed." After another glance around the room, he looked back at her. "Summer, it's not necessary for you to work in a storage room. It's a simple matter to set you up in a suite."

She pushed through the papers, looking for her list on poultry. "This is convenient to the kitchen."

"There's not even a window. The place is packed with boxes."

"No distractions." She shrugged. "If I'd wanted a suite, I'd have asked for one. For the moment, this suits me." And it's several hundred feet away from you, she added silently. "Since you're here, you might want to see what I've been doing."

He lifted a sheet of paper that listed appetizers. "*Coquilles St. Jacques, Escargots Bourguignonne, Pâté de Campagne.* Is it too personal a question to ask if you ever eat what you recommend?"

"From time to time, if I trust the chef. You'll see, if you go more thoroughly through my notes, that I want to offer a more sophisticated menu, because the American palate is becoming more sophisticated."

Blake smiled at the term *American,* and the way she said it, before he sat across from her. "Is it?"

"It's been a slow process," she said dryly. "Today, you can find a good food processor in almost every kitchen. With one, and a competent cookbook, even you could make an acceptable mousse."

"Amazing."

"Therefore," she continued, ignoring him, "to lure people into a restaurant where they'll pay, and pay well to be fed, you have to offer them the superb. A few blocks down the street, they can get a wholesome, filling meal for a fraction of what they'll pay in the Cocharan House." Summer folded her hands and rested her chin on them. "So you have to give them a very special ambience, incomparable service and exquisite food." She picked up her soda and sipped. "Personally, I'd rather pick up a take-out pizza and eat it at home, but…" She shrugged.

Blake scanned the next sheet. "Because you like pizza, or you like being alone?"

"Both. Now—"

"Do you stay out of restaurants because you spend

so much time in a kitchen behind them or because you simply don't like being in a group?"

She opened her mouth to answer and found she didn't know. Uncomfortable, she toyed with her soda. "You're getting more personal, and off the point."

"I don't think so. You're telling me we have to appeal to people who're becoming sophisticated enough to make dishes that were once almost exclusively professionally prepared, as well as draw in clientele who might prefer a quick, less expensive meal around the corner. You, due to your profession and your taste, fall into both categories. What would a restaurant have to offer not only to bring you in, but to make you want to come back?"

A logical question. Summer frowned at it. She hated logical questions because they left you no choice but to answer. "Privacy," she answered at length. "It isn't an easy thing to accomplish in a restaurant, and of course, not everyone looks for it. Many go out to eat to see and be seen. Some, like myself, prefer at least the illusion of solitude. To accomplish both, you have to have a certain number of tables situated in such a way that they seem removed from the rest."

"Easily enough done with the right lighting, a clever arrangement of foliage."

"The key words are right and clever."

"And privacy is your prerequisite in choosing a restaurant."

"I don't generally eat in them," Summer said with a restless movement of her shoulders. "But if I do, privacy ranks equally with atmosphere, food and service."

"Why?"

She began to push the papers together on her desk and stack them. "That's definitely a personal question."

"Yes." He covered her hands with one of his to still them. "Why?"

She stared at him a moment, certain she wouldn't answer. Then she found herself drawn by the quiet look and the gentle touch. "I suppose it stems back to eating in so many restaurants as a child. And I suppose one of the reasons I first became interested in cooking was as a defense against the interminable ritual of eating out. My mother was—is—of the type who goes out to see and be seen. My father often considered eating out a business. So much of my parents' lives, and therefore mine, was public. I simply prefer my own way."

Now that he was touching her, he wanted more. Now that he was learning of her, he wanted all. He should have known better than to believe it would be otherwise. He'd nearly convinced himself that he had his feelings for her under control. But now, sitting in the cramped storage room with kitchen sounds just outside the door, he wanted her as much—more—than ever.

"I wouldn't consider you an introvert, or a recluse."

"No." She didn't even notice that she'd laced her fingers with his. There was something so comfortable, so right about the gesture. "I simply like to keep my private life just that. Mine and private."

"Yet, in your field, you're quite a celebrity." He shifted and under the table his leg brushed against hers. He felt the warmth glow through him and the need double.

Without thinking, she moved her leg so that it brushed his again. The muscles in her thighs loosened. "Perhaps. Or you might say my desserts are celebrities."

Blake lifted their joined hands and studied them. Hers was shades lighter than his, inches smaller and more narrow. She wore a sapphire, oval, deeply blue in an ornate antique setting that made her fingers look that much more elegant. "Is that what you want?"

She moistened her lips, because when his eyes came back to hers they were intense and as darkly blue as the stone on her hand. "I want to be successful. I want to be considered the very best at what I do."

"Nothing more?"

"No, nothing." Why was she breathless? she asked herself frantically. Young girls got breathless—or romantics. She was neither.

"When you have that?" Blake rose, drawing her to her feet without effort. "What else?"

Because they were standing, she had to angle her head to keep her eyes level with his. "It's enough." As she said it, Summer had her first doubts of the truth of that statement. "What about you?" she countered.

"Aren't you looking for success—more success? The finest hotels, the finest restaurants."

"I'm a businessman." Slowly, he walked around the table until nothing separated them. Their hands were still joined. "I have a standard to maintain or improve. I'm also a man." He reached for her hair, then let it flow through his fingers. "And there're things other than account books I think about."

They were close now. Her body brushed his and caused her skin to hum. She forgot all the rules she'd set out for both of them and reached up to touch his cheek. "What else do you think about?"

"You." His hand was at her waist, then sliding gently up her back as he drew her closer. "I think very much about you, and this."

Lips touched—softly. Eyes remained open and aware. Pulses throbbed. Desire tugged.

Lips parted—slowly. A look said everything there was to say. Pulses hammered. Desire tore free.

She was in his arms, clinging, greedy, burning. Every hour of the past two weeks, all the work, the planning, the rules, melted away under a blaze of passion. If she sensed impatience in him, it only matched her own. The kiss was hard, long, desperate. Body strained against body in exquisite torment.

Tighter. Whether she said the word aloud or merely thought it, he seemed to understand. His arms curved around her, crushing her to him as she wanted to be.

She felt the lines and planes of his body mold to hers even as his mouth molded to hers, and somehow she seemed softer than she'd ever imagined herself to be.

Feminine, sultry, delicate, passionate. Was it possible to be all at once? The need grew and expanded—for him—for a taste and touch she'd found nowhere else. The sound she made against his lips came as much from confusion as from pleasure.

Good God, how could a woman take him so far with only a kiss? He was already more than half-mad for her. Control was losing its meaning in a need that was much more imperative. Her skin would slide like silk under his hands—he knew it. He had to feel it.

He slipped a hand under her sweater and found her. Beneath his palm, her heartbeat pounded. Not enough. The thought raced through his mind that it would never be enough. But questions, reason, were for later. Burying his face against her throat he tasted her skin. The scent he remembered lingered there, enticing him further, drawing him closer to the edge where there could be no turning back. The fatigue he'd felt when he'd entered the room vanished. The tension he felt whenever she was near evaporated. At that moment, he considered her completely his without realizing he'd wanted exclusive possession.

Her hair brushed over his face, cloud soft, fragrant. It made him think of Paris, right before the heat of summer took over from spring. But her skin was hot and vibrating, making him envision long humid nights when lovemaking would be slow, endlessly slow. He wanted her there, in the cramped little room where the floor was littered with boxes.

She couldn't think. Summer could feel her bones dissolve and her mind empty. Sensation after sensation poured over her. She could have drowned in them. Yet she wanted more—she could feel her body craving more, wanting all. Storm, thunder, heat. Just once...the longing seeped into her with whispering promises and dark pleasure. She could let herself be his, take him as hers. Just once. And then...

With a moan, she tore her mouth from his and buried her face against his shoulder. Once with Blake would haunt her for the rest of her life.

"Come upstairs," Blake murmured. Tilting her head back, he ran kisses over her face. "Come up with me where I can make love with you properly. I want you in my bed, Summer. Soft, naked, mine."

"Blake..." She turned her face away and tried to steady her breathing. What had happened to her—when—how? "This is a mistake—for both of us."

"No." Taking her by the shoulders, he kept her facing him. "This is right—for both of us."

"I can't get involved—"

"You already are."

She let out a deep breath. "No further than this. It's already more than I intended."

When she started to back away, he held her firmly in front of him. "I need a reason, Summer, a damn good one."

"You confuse me." Summer blurted it out before she realized it, then swore at the admission. "Damn it, I don't like to be confused."

"And I ache for you." His voice was as impatient as hers, his body as tense. "I don't like to ache."

"We've got a problem," she managed, dragging a hand through her hair.

"I want you." Something in the way he said it made her hand pause in midair and her gaze lift to his. There was nothing casual in those three words. "I want you more than I've ever wanted anyone. I'm not comfortable with that."

"A big problem," she whispered and sat unsteadily on the edge of the table.

"There's one way to solve it."

She managed a smile. "Two ways," she corrected. "And I think mine's the safest."

"Safest." Reaching down, he ran a fingertip over the curve of her cheek. "You want safety, Summer?"

"Yes." It was easily said because she'd discovered it was true. Safety was something she'd never thought about until Blake, because she'd never felt endangered until then. "I've made myself a lot of promises, Blake, set a lot of goals. Instinct tells me you could interfere. I always go with my instincts."

"I've no intention of interfering with your goals."

"Nevertheless, I have a few very strict rules. One of them is never to become intimate with a business associate or a client. In one point of view, you fall into both categories."

"How do you intend to prevent it from happening? Intimacies come in a lot of degrees, Summer. You and I have already reached some of them."

How could she deny it? She wanted to run from it. "We managed to keep out of each other's way for two weeks," she pointed out. "It's simply a matter of continuing to do so. Both of us are very busy at the moment, so it shouldn't be too difficult."

"Eventually one of us is going to break the rules."

And it could be me just as easily as it could be him, she thought. "I can't think about eventually, only about now. I'll stay downstairs and do my job. You stay upstairs and do yours."

"Like hell," Blake muttered and took a step forward. Summer was halfway to her feet when a knock sounded on her door.

"Mr. Cocharan, there's a phone call for you. Your secretary says it's urgent."

Blake controlled his fury. "I'll be there." He gave Summer a long, hard look. "We're not finished."

She waited until he'd reached the door. "I can turn this place into a palace or a greasy spoon," she said quietly. "It's your choice."

Turning around, he measured her. "Blackmail?"

"Insurance," she corrected and smiled. "Play it my way, Blake and everybody's happy."

"Your point, Summer," he acknowledged with a nod. "This time."

When the door closed behind him, she sat again. She may have outmaneuvered him this time, she mused, but the game was far from over.

Summer gave herself another hour before she left her temporary office to go back to the kitchen. Busboys wheeled in and out with trays of dirty dishes. The dishwasher hummed busily. Pots simmered. Someone sang as she basted a chicken. Two hours to the dinner rush. In another hour, the panic and confusion would set in.

It was then, when the scent of food hit her, that Summer realized she hadn't eaten. Deciding to kill two birds with one stone, she began to root through the cupboards. She'd find something for a late lunch, and see just how provisions were organized.

She couldn't complain about the latter. The cupboards were not only well stocked, they were systematically stocked. Max had a number of excellent qualities, she thought. A pity an open mind wasn't among them. She continued to scan shelf after shelf, but the item she was looking for was nowhere to be found.

"Ms. Lyndon?"

Hearing Max's voice behind her, Summer slowly

closed the cabinet door. She didn't have to turn around to see the cold politeness in his eyes or the tight disapproval of his mouth. She was going to have to do something about this situation before long, she decided. But at the moment she was a bit tired, quite a bit hungry and not in the mood to deal with it.

"Yes, Max." She opened the next door and surveyed the stock.

"Perhaps I can help you find what you're looking for."

"Perhaps. Actually, I'm checking to see how well stocked we are while searching out a jar of peanut butter. Apparently—" she closed that door and went on to the next "—we're very well stocked indeed, and very well organized."

"My kitchen is completely organized," Max began stiffly. "Even in the midst of all this—this carpentry."

"The carpentry's almost finished," she said easily. "I think the new ovens are working out well."

"To some, new is always better."

"To some," she countered, "progress is always a death knell. Where do I find the peanut butter, Max? I really want a sandwich."

This time she did turn, in time to see his eyebrows rise and his mouth purse. "Below," he said with a hint of a smirk as he pointed. "We keep such things on hand for the children's menu."

"Good." Unoffended, Summer crouched down and found it. "Would you like to join me?"

"Thank you, no. I have work to do."

"Fine." Summer took two slices of bread and began to spread the peanut butter. "Tomorrow, nine o'clock, you and I will go over the proposed menus in my office."

"I'm very busy at nine."

"No," she corrected mildly. "We're very busy from seven to nine, then things tend to ease off, particularly midweek, until the lunch rush. Nine o'clock," she repeated over his huff of breath. "Excuse me, I have to get some jelly for this."

Leaving Max gritting his teeth, Summer went to one of the large refrigerators. Pompous, narrow-minded ass, she thought as she found a restaurant-sized jar of grape jelly. As long as he continued to be uncooperative and stiff, things were going to be difficult. More than once, she'd expected Max to turn in his resignation—and there were times, though she hated to be so hard line, that she wished he would.

The changes in the kitchen were already making a difference, she thought as she closed the second slice of bread over the jelly and peanut butter. Any fool could see that the extra range, the more efficient equipment, tightened the flow of preparation and improved the quality of food. Annoyed, she bit into her sandwich just as excited chatter broke out behind her.

"Max'll be furious. *Fur-i-ous.*"

"Nothing he can do about it now."

"Except yell and throw things."

Perhaps it was the underlying glee in the last statement that made Summer turn. She saw two cooks huddled over the stove. "What'll Max be furious about?" she asked over another mouthful of sandwich.

The two faces turned to her. Both were flushed either from the heat of the stove or excitement. "Maybe you ought to tell him, Ms. Lyndon," one of the cooks said after a moment of indecision. The glee was still there, she noticed, barely suppressed.

"Tell him what?"

"Julio and Georgia eloped—we just got word from Julio's brother. They took off for Hawaii."

Julio and Georgia? After a quick flip through her mental file, Summer placed them as two cooks who worked the four-to-eleven shift. A glance at her watch told her they were already fifteen minutes late.

"I take it they won't be coming in today."

"They quit." One of the cooks snapped his fingers. "Just like that." He glanced across the room where Max was babying a rack of lamb. "Max'll hit the roof."

"He won't solve anything up there," she murmured. "So we're two short for the dinner shift."

"Three," the second cook corrected. "Charlie called in sick an hour ago."

"Wonderful." Summer finished off her sandwich,

then rolled up her sleeves. "Then the rest of us better get to work."

With an apron covering her jeans and sweater, Summer took over one section of the new counter. Perhaps it wasn't her usual style, she mused as she began mixing the first oversized bowl of cake batter, but circumstances called for immediate action. And, she thought as she licked some batter from her knuckle, they damn well better get the stereo speakers in before the end of the week. Summer might bake without Chopin in an emergency once, but she wouldn't do it twice.

She was arranging several layers of Black Forest cake in the oven when Max spoke over her shoulder.

"You're making yourself some dessert now?" he began.

"No." Summer set the timer, then moved back to the counter to start preparations on chocolate mousse. "It seems there's been a wedding and an illness—though I don't think the first has anything to do with the second. We're shorthanded tonight. I'm taking over the desserts, Max, and I don't exchange small talk when I'm working."

"Wedding? What wedding?"

"Julio and Georgia eloped to Hawaii, and Charlie's sick. I have this mousse to deal with at the moment."

"Eloped!" he exploded. "Eloped without my permission?"

She took the time to look over her shoulder. "I suppose Charlie should have checked with you before he got sick as well. Save the hysterics, Max, and have someone peel me some apples. I want to do a *Charlotte de Pommes* after this."

"Now you're changing my menu!" he exploded.

She whirled, fire in her eyes. "I have a dozen different desserts to make in a very short time. I'd advise you to stay out of my way while I do it. I'm not known for graciousness when I'm cooking."

He sucked in his stomach and pulled back his shoulders. "We'll see what Mr. Cocharan has to say about this."

"Terrific. Keep him out of my way, too, for the next three hours or someone's going to end up with a face full of my best whipped cream." Spinning back around, she went to work.

There wasn't time, she couldn't take the time, to study and approve each dessert as it was completed. Later, Summer would think of the hours as assembly line work. At the moment, she was too pressed to think. Julio and Georgia had been the dessert chefs. It was now up to her to do the work of two people in the same amount of time.

She ignored the menu and went with what she knew she could make from memory. The diners that evening were in for a surprise, but as she finished topping the second Black Forest cake, Summer decided it would be a pleasant one. She arranged the cherries quickly, cursing the need to rush. Impossible to create when one was on such a ridiculous timetable, she thought, and muttered bad temperedly under her breath.

By six, the bulk of the baking was done and she concentrated on the finishing touches of a line of desserts designed to satisfy an army. Chocolate icing there, a dab of cream here, a garnish, a spoon of jam or jelly. She was hot, her arms aching. Her once-white apron was streaked and splashed. No one spoke to her, because she wouldn't answer. No one approached her, because she tended to snarl.

Occasionally she would indicate with a wave of her arm a section of dishes that were to be taken away. This was done instantly, and without a sound. If there was talk, it was done in undertones and out of her hearing. None of them had ever seen anything quite like Summer Lyndon on a roll.

"Problems?"

Summer heard Blake speak quietly over her shoulder but didn't turn. "Cars are made this way," she mumbled, "not desserts."

"Early reports from the dining room are more than favorable."

She grunted and rolled out pastry dough for tarts. "The next time I'm in Hawaii, I'm going to look up Julio and Georgia and knock their heads together."

"A bit testy, aren't you?" he murmured and earned

a lethal glare. "And hot." He touched her cheek with a fingertip. "How long have you been at it?"

"Since a bit after four." After shrugging his hand away she began to rapidly cut out pastry shells. Blake watched, surprised. He'd never seen her work quickly before. "Move."

He stepped back but continued to watch her. By his calculations, she'd worked on the menus in the window-less storage room for more than six hours, and had now been on her feet for nearly three. Too small, he thought as a protective urge moved through him. Too delicate.

"Summer, can't someone else take over now? You should rest."

"No one touches my desserts." This was said in such a strong, authoritative voice that the image of a delicate flower vanished. He grinned despite himself.

"Anything I can do?"

"I'll want some champagne in an hour. Dom Peri-gnon, '73."

He nodded as an idea began to form in his mind. She smelled like the desserts lined on the counter in front of her. Tempting, delicious. Since he'd met her, Blake had discovered he possessed a very demanding sweet tooth. "Have you eaten?"

"A sandwich a few hours ago," she said testily. "Do you think I could eat at a time like this?"

He glanced at the sumptuous array of cakes and pas-tries. He could smell delicately roasted meats, spicy sauces. Blake shook his head. "No, of course not. I'll be back."

Summer muttered something, then fluted the edges of her pastry shells.

Chapter 7

By eight o'clock, Summer was finished, and not in the best of humors. For nearly four hours, she'd whipped, rolled, fluted and baked. Often, she'd spent twice that time, and twice that effort, perfecting one single dish. That was art. This, on the other hand, had been labor, plain and simple.

She felt no flash of triumph, no glow of self-satisfaction, but simply fatigue. An army cook, she thought disdainfully; it was hardly different from producing the quickest and easiest for the masses. At the moment, if she never saw the inside of another egg again, it would be too soon.

"There should be enough made up to get us through the dinner hour, and room service tonight," she told Max briskly as she pulled off her soiled apron. Critically she frowned at a line of fruit tarts. More than one of them were less than perfect in shape. If there'd been time, she'd have discarded them and made others. "I want someone in touch with personnel first thing in the morning to see about hiring two more dessert chefs."

"Mr. Cocharan has already contacted personnel." Max stood stiffly, not wanting to give an inch, though he'd been impressed with how quickly and efficiently she'd avoided what could easily have been a catastrophe. He clung tightly to his resentment, even though he had to admit—to himself—that she baked the best apricot tart he'd ever tasted.

"Fine." Summer ran a hand over the back of her neck. The skin there was damp, the muscles drawn taut. "Nine o'clock tomorrow, Max, in my office. Let's see if we can get organized. I'm going home to soak in a hot tub until morning."

Blake had been leaning against the wall, watching her work. It had been fascinating to see just how quickly the temperamental artist had put her nose to the grindstone and produced.

She'd shown him two things he hadn't expected—a speed and lack of histrionics when she'd been forced to deal with a less than ideal situation, and a calm acceptance of what was obviously a touchy area with Max. However much she played the role of prima donna, when her back was against the wall, she handled herself very well.

When she removed her apron, he stepped forward. "Give you a lift?"

Summer glanced over at him as she pulled the pins from her hair. It fell to her shoulders, tousled, and a bit damp at the ends from the heat. "I have my car."

"And I have mine." The arrogance, with that trace of aloofness, was still there, even when he smiled.

"And a bottle of Dom Perignon, '73. My driver can pick you up in the morning."

She told herself she was only interested in the wine. The cool smile had nothing to do with her decision. "Properly chilled?" she asked, arching her brow. "The champagne, that is."

"Of course."

"You're on, Mr. Cocharan. I never turn down champagne."

"The car's out in the back." He took her hand rather than her arm as she'd expected. Before she could make any counter move, he was leading her from the kitchen. "Would it embarrass you if I said I was very impressed with what you did this evening?"

She was used to accolades, even expected them. Somehow, she couldn't remember ever getting so much pleasure from one before. She moved her shoulders, hoping to lighten her own response. "I make it my business to be impressive. It doesn't embarrass me."

Perhaps if she hadn't been tired, he wouldn't have seen through the glib answer so easily. When they reached his car, Blake turned and took her by the shoulders. "You worked very hard in there."

"Just part of the service."

"No," he corrected, soothing the muscles. "That's not what you were hired for."

"When I signed the contract, that became my kitchen. What goes out of it has to satisfy my standards, my pride."

"Not an easy job."

"You wanted the best."

"Apparently I got it."

She smiled, though she wanted badly just to sit down. "You definitely got it. Now, you did say something about champagne?"

"Yes, I did." He opened the door for her. "You smell of vanilla."

"I earned it." When she sat, she let out a long, pleasurable sigh. Champagne, she thought, a hot bath with mountains of bubbles, and smooth, cool sheets. In that order. "Chances are," she murmured, "even as we speak, someone in there is taking the first bite of my Black Forest cake."

Blake shut the driver's door, then glanced at her as he started the ignition. "Does it feel odd?" he asked. "Having strangers eat something you spent so much time and care creating?"

"Odd?" Summer stretched back, enjoying the plush luxury of the seat and the view of the dusky sky through the sun roof. "A painter creates on canvas for whoever will look, a composer creates a symphony for whoever will listen."

"True enough." Blake maneuvered his way onto the street and into the traffic. The sun was red and low. The night promised to be clear. "But wouldn't it be more gratifying to be there when your desserts are served?"

She closed her eyes, completely relaxed for the first time in hours. "When one cooks in one's own kitchen for friends, relatives, it can be a pleasure or a duty. Then there might be the satisfaction of watching something you've cooked being appreciated. But again, it's a pleasure or a duty, not a profession."

"You rarely eat what you cook."

"I rarely cook for myself," she countered. "Except the simpler things."

"Why?"

"When you cook for yourself, there's no one there to clean up the mess."

He laughed and turned into a parking lot. "In your own odd way you're a very practical woman."

"In every way I'm a practical woman." Lazily, she opened her eyes. "Why did we stop?"

"Hungry?"

"I'm always hungry after I work." Turning her head, she saw the blue neon sign of a pizza parlor.

"Knowing your tastes by now, I thought you'd find this the perfect accompaniment to the champagne."

She grinned as the fatigue was replaced with the first real stirrings of hunger. "Absolutely perfect."

"Wait here," he told her as he opened the door. "I had someone call ahead and order it when I saw you were nearly finished."

Grateful, and touched, Summer leaned back and closed her eyes again. When was the last time she'd allowed anyone to take care of her? she wondered. If memory served her, the last time she'd been pampered she'd been eight, and cranky with a case of chicken pox. Independence had always been expected of her, by her parents, and by herself. But tonight, this one time, it was a rather sweet feeling to let someone else make the arrangements with her comfort in mind.

And she had to admit, she hadn't expected simple consideration from Blake. Style, yes, credit where credit was due, yes—but not consideration. He'd put in a hard day himself, she thought, remembering how tired he'd looked that afternoon. Still, he'd waited long past the time when he could have had his own dinner in comfort, relaxed in his own way. He'd waited until she was finished.

Surprises, she mused. Blake Cocharan III definitely had some surprises up his sleeve. She'd always been a sucker for them.

When Blake opened the car door, the scent of pizza rolled pleasurably inside. Summer took the box from him, then leaned over and kissed his cheek. "Thanks."

"I should've tried pizza before," he murmured.

She settled back again, letting her eyes close and her lips curve. "Don't forget the champagne. Those are two of my biggest weaknesses."

"I've made a note of it." Blake pulled out of the parking lot and joined the traffic again. Her simple gratitude shouldn't have surprised him. It certainly shouldn't have moved him. He had the feeling she would have had the same low-key, pleased reaction if he'd presented her with a full-length sable or a bracelet of blue-white diamonds. With Summer, it wouldn't be the gift, but the nature of the giving. He found he liked that idea very much. She wasn't a woman who was easily impressed, he mused, yet she was a woman who could be easily pleased.

Summer did something she rarely did unless she was completely alone. She relaxed, fully. Though her eyes were closed, she was no longer sleepy, but aware. She could feel the smooth motion of the car beneath her, hear the rumble of traffic outside the windows. She had only to draw in a breath to smell the tangy scent of sauce and spice. The car was spacious, but she could sense the warmth of Blake's body across the seat.

Pleasant. That was the word that drifted through her mind. So pleasant, there seemed to be no need for caution, for defenses. It was a pity, she reflected, that they weren't driving aimlessly...

Strange, she'd never chosen to do anything aimlessly. And yet, tonight, to drive…along a long, deserted beach—with the moon full, shining off the water, and the sand white. You'd be able to hear the surf ebb and flow, and see the hundreds of stars you so rarely noticed in the city. You'd smell the salt and feel the spray. The moist, warm air would flow over your skin.

She felt the car swing off the road, then purr to a stop. For an extra moment, Summer held on to the fantasy.

"What're you thinking?"

"About the beach," she answered. "Stars." She caught herself, surprised that she'd indulged in what could only be termed romanticism. "I'll take the pizza," she said, straightening. "You can bring the champagne."

He put a hand on her arm, lightly but it stopped her. Slowly he ran a finger down it. "You like the beach?"

"I never really thought about it." At the moment, she found she'd like nothing better than to rest her head against his shoulder and watch waves surge against the shore. Star counting. Why should she want to indulge in something so foolish now when she never had before? "For some reason, it just seemed like the night for it." And she wondered if she were answering his question or her own.

"Since there's no beach, we'll just have to come up with something else. How's your imagination?"

"Good enough." Quite good enough, Summer thought, to see where she'd end up if she didn't change the mood—hers as well as his. "And at the moment, I imagine the pizza's getting cold, and the champagne warm." Opening the door, she climbed out with the box in hand. Once inside the building, Summer started up the stairs.

"Does the elevator ever work?" Blake shifted the bag in his arm and joined her.

"Off and on—mostly it's off. Personally, I don't trust it."

"In that case, why'd you pick the fourth floor?"

She smiled as they rounded the second landing. "I like the view—and the fact that salesmen are usually discouraged when they're faced with more than two flights of steps."

"You could've chosen a more modern building, with a view, a security system and a working elevator."

"I look at modern tools as essential, a new car, well tuned, as imperative." Drawing out her keys, Summer jiggled them lightly as they approached her door. "As to living arrangements, I'm a bit more open-minded. My flat in Paris has temperamental plumbing and the most exquisite cornices I've ever seen."

When she opened the door, the scent of roses was overwhelming. There were a dozen white in a straw basket, a dozen red in a Sevres vase, a dozen yellow in a pottery jug and a dozen pink in Venetian glass.

"Run into a special at the florist's?"

Summer raised her brows as she set the pizza on

the dinette. "I never buy flowers for myself. These are from Enrico."

Blake set the bag next to the box and drew out the champagne. "All?"

"He's a bit flamboyant—Enrico Gravanti—you might've heard of him. Italian shoes and bags."

Two hundred million dollars worth of shoes and bags, as Blake recalled. He flicked a finger down a rose petal. "I hadn't heard Gravanti was in town. He normally stays at the Cocharan House."

"No, he's in Rome." As she spoke, Summer went into the kitchen for plates and glasses. "He wired these when I agreed to make the cake for his birthday next month."

"Four dozen roses for a cake?"

"Five," Summer corrected as she came back in. "There's another dozen in the bedroom. They're rather lovely, a kind of peach color." In anticipation, she held out both glasses. "And, after all, it is one of my cakes."

With a nod of acknowledgment, Blake loosened the cork. Air fizzed out while the champagne bubbled toward the lip of the bottle. "So, I take it you'll be going to Italy to bake it."

"I don't intend to ship it air freight." She watched the pale gold liquid rise in the glass as Blake poured. "I should only be in Rome two days, three at most." Raising the glass to her lips, she sipped, eyes closed, senses keen. "Excellent." She sipped again before she opened her eyes and smiled. "I'm starving." After lifting the lid on the box, she breathed deep. "Pepperoni."

"Somehow I thought it suited you."

With a laugh, an easy one, she sat down. "Very perceptive. Shall I serve?"

"Please." And as she began to, Blake flicked on his lighter and set the three staggered-length tapers she had on the table burning. "Champagne and pizza," he said as he turned off the lights. "That demands candlelight, don't you think?"

"If you like." When he sat, Summer lifted her first piece. The cheese was hot enough to make her catch her breath, the sauce tangy. "Mmmm. Wonderful."

"Has it occurred to you that we spend a great deal of our time together eating?"

"Hmm—well, it's something I thoroughly enjoy. I always try to look at eating as a pleasure rather than a physical necessity. It adds something."

"Pounds, usually."

She shrugged and reached for the champagne. "Of course, if one isn't wise enough to take one's pleasure in small doses. Greed is what adds pounds, ruins the complexion and makes one miserable."

"You don't succumb to greed?"

She remembered abruptly that it had been just that, exactly that, that she'd felt for him. But she'd controlled it, Summer reminded herself. She hadn't succumbed.

"No." She ate slowly, savoring. "I don't. In my profession, it would be disastrous."

"How do you keep your pleasure in small doses?"

She wasn't sure she trusted the way the question came out. Taking her time, she set a second piece on each plate. "I'd rather have one spoonful of a superb chocolate soufflé than an entire plateful of food that doesn't have flair."

Blake took another bite of pizza. "And this has flair?"

She smiled because it was so obviously not the sort of meal he was used to. "An excellent balance of spices—perhaps just a tad heavy on the oregano—a good marriage of sauce and crust, the proper handling of cheese and the bite of pepperoni. With the proper use of the senses, almost any meal can be memorable."

"With the proper use of the senses," Blake countered, "other things can be memorable."

She reached for her glass again, her eyes laughing over the rim. "We're speaking of food. Taste, of course, is paramount, but appearance…" He linked his hand with hers and she found herself watching him. "Your eyes tell you first of the desire to taste." His face was lean, the eyes a deep blue she found continuously compelling.…

"Then a scent teases you, entices you." His was dark, woodsy, tempting.…

"You hear the way champagne bubbles into a glass

and you want to experience it." Or the way he said her name, quietly.

"After all this," she continued in a voice that was beginning to take on a faint huskiness, a faint trace of feeling, "you have the taste, the texture to explore." And his mouth held a flavor she couldn't forget.

"So—" he lifted her hand and pressed his mouth to the palm "—your advice is to savor every aspect of the experience in order to absorb all the pleasure. Then…" Turning her hand over, he brushed his lips, then the tip of his tongue, over her knuckles. "The most basic of desires becomes unique."

In an arrow-straight line, the heat shot up her arm. "No experience is acceptable otherwise."

"And atmosphere?" Lightly, with just a fingertip, he traced the shape of her ear. "Wouldn't you agree that the proper setting can enhance the same experience? Candlelight, for instance."

Their faces were closer now. She could see the soft shifting light casting shadows, mysteries. "Outside devices can often add more intensity to a mood."

"You could call it romance." He took his fingertip down the length of her jawline.

"You could." Champagne never went to her head, yet her head was light. Slowly, luxuriously, her body was softening. She made an effort to remember why she should allow neither to happen, but no answer came.

"And romance, for some, is another very elemental need."

"For some," he murmured when his lips followed the trail of his fingertip.

"But not for you." He nipped at her lips and found them soft, and warm.

"No, not for me." But her sigh was as soft and warm as her lips.

"A practical woman." He was raising her to her feet so that their bodies could touch.

"Yes." She tilted her head back, inviting the exploration of his lips.

"Candlelight doesn't move you?"

"It's only an attractive device." She curved her arms up his back to bring him closer. "As chefs, we're taught that such things can lend the right mood to our meals."

"And it wouldn't matter if I told you that you were beautiful? In the full sun where your skin's flawless—in candlelight, which turns it to porcelain. It wouldn't matter," he continued as he ran a line of moist heat down her throat, "if I told you you excite me as no other woman ever has? Just looking at you makes me want, touching you drives me mad."

"Words," she managed, though her head was spinning. "I don't need—"

Then his mouth covered hers. The one long, deep kiss made lies of all her practical claims. Tonight, though she'd never wanted such things before, she wanted the romance of soft words, soft lights. She wanted the slow, savoring loving that emptied the mind and made a furnace of the body. Tonight she wanted, and there was only one man. If tomorrow there were consequences, tomorrow was hours away. He was here.

She didn't resist as he lifted her. Tonight, if only for a short while, she'd be fragile, soft. She heard him blow out the candles and the light scent of melted wax followed them toward the bedroom.

Moonlight. The silvery sorcery of moonlight slipped through the windows. Roses. The fragile fragrance of roses floated on the air. Music. The muted magic of Beethoven drifted in from the apartment below.

There was a breeze. Summer felt it whisper over her face as he placed her on the bed. Atmosphere, she thought hazily. If she had planned on a night of lovemaking, she could have set the stage no better. Perhaps... She drew him down to join her.... Perhaps it was fate.

She could see his eyes. Deep blue, direct, involving. He watched her while doing no more than tracing the shape of her face, of her lips, with his finger. Had anyone ever shown her that kind of tenderness? Had she ever wanted it?

No. And if the answer was no, the answer had abruptly changed. She wanted this new experience, the sweetness she'd always disregarded, and she wanted the man who would bring her both.

Taking his face in her hands, she studied him. This was the man she would share this one completely private moment with, the one who would soon know her body as well as her vulnerabilities. She might have wavered over the trust, reminded herself of the pitfalls— if she'd been able to resist the need, and the strength, she saw in his eyes.

"Kiss me again," she murmured. "No one's ever made me feel the way you do when you kiss me."

He felt a surge of pleasure, intense, stunning. Lowering his head, he touched his lips to hers, toying with them, watching her as she watched him while their emotions heightened and their need sharpened. Should he have known she'd be even more beautiful in the moonlight, with her hair spread over a pillow? Could he have known that desire for her would be an ache unlike any desire he'd known? Was it still as simple as desire, or had he crossed some line he'd been unaware of? There were no answers now. Answers were for the daylight.

With a moan, he deepened the kiss and felt her body yield beneath his even as her mouth grew avid. Little tongues of passion flickered, still subdued beneath a gentleness they both seemed to need. Odd, because neither of them had needed it before, or often thought to show it.

Her hands were light on his face, over his neck, then

slowly combing through his hair. Though his body was hard on hers, there was no demand yet.

Savor me. The thought ran silkily through her mind even as Blake's lips journeyed over her face. Slowly. She'd never known a man with such patience or an arousal so heady. Mouth against mouth, then mouth against skin—each drew her deeper and still deeper into a languor that encompassed both body and mind.

Touch me. And he seemed to understand this fresh need. His hands moved, but still without hurry, over her shoulders, down her sides, then up again to whisper over her breasts—until it was no longer enough for either of them. Then wordlessly they began to undress each other.

Fingers of moonlight fell across exposed flesh—a shoulder, the length of an arm, a lean torso. Luxuriously, Summer ran her hands over Blake's chest and learned the muscle and form. Lazily, he explored the length of her and learned the subtle curves and silk. Even when the last barrier of clothing was drawn away, they didn't rush. So much to touch, taste—and time had no meaning.

The breeze flitted in, but they grew warmer. Wherever her fingers wandered, his flesh would burn, then cool only to burn again. As he took his lips over her, finding pleasure, learning secrets, she began to heat. And demand crept into both of them.

More urgently now, with quick moans, trembling

breaths, they took each other further. He hadn't known he could be led, and she'd always refused to be, yet now, one guided the other to the same destination.

Summer felt reality slipping away from her, but had no will to stop it. The music penetrated only faintly into her consciousness, but his murmurs were easily heard. It was his scent, no longer the roses, that titillated. She would feel whatever she was meant to feel, go wherever she was meant to go, as long as he was with her. Along with the strongest physical desire she'd ever known was an emotional need that exploded inside her. She couldn't question it, couldn't refuse it. Her body, mind, heart, ached for him.

With his name trembling on her lips, she took him into her. Then, for both of them, the pleasure was so acute that sanity was forgotten. Sensation—waves, floods, storms—whipped through her. The calm had become a hurricane to revel in. Together, they were swept away.

Had hours passed or minutes? Summer lay in the filtered moonlight and tried to orient herself. She'd never felt quite like this. Sated, exhilarated, exhausted. Once she'd have said it was impossible to be all at once.

She could feel the brush of Blake's hair against her shoulder, the whisper of his breath against her cheek. His scent and hers were mixed now, so that the roses were only an accent. The music had stopped, but she thought she could still hear the echo. His body was pressed into hers, but his weight was a pleasure. She knew, without effort, she could wrap her arms around him and stay just so for the rest of her life. So through the hazy pleasure came the first stirrings of fear.

Oh, God, how far had she gone in such a short time? She'd always been so certain her emotions were perfectly safe. It wasn't the first time she'd been with a man, but she was too aware that it was the first time she'd made love in the true sense of the word.

Mistake. She forced the word into her head even as her heart tried to block it. She had to think, had to be practical. Hadn't she seen what uncontrolled emotions and dreams had done to two intelligent people? Both her parents had spent years moving from relationship to relationship looking for…what?

This, her heart told her, but again she blocked it out. She knew better than to look for something she didn't believe existed. Permanency, commitment—they were illusions. And illusions had no place in her life.

Closing her eyes a moment, she waited for herself to settle. She was a grown woman, sophisticated enough to understand and accept mutual desire that held no strings. *Treat it lightly,* she warned herself. *Don't pretend it's more than it is.*

But she couldn't resist smoothing his hair as she spoke. "Odd how pizza and champagne affect me."

Raising his head, Blake grinned at her. At the moment, he felt he could've taken on the world. "I think it should be your staple diet." He kissed the curve of her shoulder. "It's going to be mine. Want some more?"

"Pizza and champagne?"

Laughing, he nuzzled her neck. "That, too." He shifted, drawing her against his side. It was one more gesture of intimacy that had something inside her trembling.

Set out the rules, Summer told herself. *Do it now, before...before it would be much too easy to forget.*

"I like being with you," she said quietly.

"And I you." He could see the shadows play on the ceiling, hear the muted sound of traffic outside, but he was still saturated with her.

"Now that we've been together like this, it's going to affect our relationship one of two ways."

Puzzled, he turned his head to look at her. "One of two ways?"

"It's either going to increase the tension while we're working, or alleviate it. I'm hoping it alleviates it."

In the darkness he frowned at her. "What happened just now had absolutely nothing to do with business."

"Whatever you and I do together is bound to affect our working relationship." Moistening her lips, she tried to continue in the same light way. "Making love with you was...personal, but tomorrow morning we're back to being associates. This can't change that—I think it'd be a mistake to let it change the tone of our business dealings." Was she rambling? Was she making sense? She wished desperately that he would say something, anything at all. "I think we both knew this was bound to happen. Now that it has, it's cleared the air."

"Cleared the air?" Infuriated, and to his surprise, hurt, he rose on his elbow. "It did a damn sight more than that, Summer. We both know that, too."

"Let's keep it in perspective." How had she begun this so badly? And how could she keep rambling on when she only wanted to curl up next to him and hold on? "We're both unattached adults who're attracted to each other. On that level, we shouldn't expect any more from each other than's reasonable. On a business level, we both have to expect total involvement."

He wanted to push the business level down her throat. Violently. The emotion didn't please him, nor did the sudden realization that he wanted total involvement on a very personal level. With an effort, he controlled the fury. He needed to ask, and answer, some questions for himself—soon. In the meantime, he needed to keep a cool head.

"Summer, I intend to make love with you often, and when I do, business can go to hell." He ran a hand down her side and felt her body respond. If she wanted rules, he thought furiously, he'd give her rules. His. "When we're here, there isn't any hotel or any restaurant. There's just you and me. Back at Cocharan House, we'll be as professional as you want."

She wasn't certain if she wanted to calmly agree with him or scream in protest. She remained silent.

"And now," he continued, drawing her still closer, "I want to make love with you again, then I want to sleep with you. At nine o'clock tomorrow, we'll get back to business."

She might have spoken then, but his mouth touched hers. Tomorrow was hours away.

Chapter 8

Damn, it was frustrating. Blake had heard men complain about women, calling them incomprehensible, contradictory, baffling. Because he'd always found it possible to deal with women on a sensible level, he'd never put much credence in any of it, until Summer. Now, he found himself searching for more adjectives. Rising from his desk, Blake paced to the window and frowned out at his view of the city.

When they'd made love the first time, he realized that he'd never known that a woman could be that soft, that giving. Strong—still strong, yes, but with a fragility that had a man lying in velvet. Had it been his imagination, or had she been totally his in every way one person could belong to another? He'd have sworn that for that space of time she'd thought of nothing but him, wanted nothing but him. And yet, before their bodies had cooled, she'd been so practical, so...unemotional.

Damn, wasn't a man supposed to be grateful for that—a man who wanted the pleasure and companionship of a woman without all the complications? He could remember other relationships where a neat set of rules had proven invaluable, but now...

Below, a couple walked along the sidewalk, their arms slung around each other's shoulders. As he watched he imagined them laughing at something no one else would understand. And as he watched, Blake thought of his own statement of the degrees of intimacy. Instinct told him that he and Summer had shared an intimacy as deep as any two people could experience. Not just a merging of bodies, but a touching, a twining, of thoughts and needs and wants that was absolute. But if his instincts had told him one thing, she had told him another. Which was he to believe?

Frustrating, he thought again and turned away from the window. He couldn't deny that he'd gone to her apartment the night before with the idea of seducing her, and putting an end to the tension between them. But he couldn't deny that he'd been seduced after five minutes alone with her. He couldn't see her and not want to touch her. He couldn't hear her laugh without wanting to taste the curve of her lips. Now that he'd made love with her, he wasn't certain a night would pass without his wanting her again.

There must be a term for what he was experiencing. Blake was always more comfortable when he could label something and therefore file it properly. The most efficient heading, the most logical category. What was it called when you thought of a woman when you should be thinking about something else? What name did you give to this constant edgy feeling?

Love… The word crept up on him, not entirely pleasantly. Good God. Uneasy, Blake sat again and stared at the far wall. He was in love with her. It was just as simple—and just as terrifying—as that. He wanted to be with her, to make her laugh, to make her tremble with desire. He wanted to see her eyes glow with temper, and with passion. He wanted to spend quiet evenings, and wild nights, with her. And he was deadly sure he'd want the same thing twenty years down the road.

Since the first time he'd walked down those four flights of stairs from her apartment, he hadn't thought of another woman. Love, if it could ever be considered logical, was the logical conclusion. And he was stuck with it. Taking out a cigarette, Blake ran his fingers down the length of it. He didn't light it, but continued to stare at the wall.

Now what? he asked himself. He was in love with a woman who'd made herself crystal clear on her feelings about commitments and relationships. She wanted no part of either. He, on the other hand, believed in the permanency, and even the romance, of marriage—

though he'd never considered it specifically applying to himself.

Things were different now. He was a man too well ordered, both outwardly and mentally, not to see marriage as the direct result of love. With love, you wanted stability, vows, endurance. He wanted Summer. Blake leaned back in his chair. And he firmly believed there was always a way to get what you wanted.

If he even mentioned the word love, she'd be gone in a flash. Even he wasn't completely comfortable with it as yet. Strategy, he told himself. It was all a matter of strategy—or so he hoped. He simply had to convince her that he was essential to her life, that theirs was the relationship designed to break her set of rules.

Apparently the game was still on—and he still intended to win. Frowning at the wall, he began to work his way through the problem.

Summer was having problems of her own. Four cups of strong black coffee hadn't quite brought her up to maximum working level. Ten hours' sleep suited her well, eight could be tolerated. With less than that, and she'd had a good deal less than that the night before, she edged perilously close to nastiness. Add to that a state of emotional turmoil, and Max's frigid resentment, and it didn't promise to be the most pleasant or productive morning.

"By using one of the traditional French garnitures for the roast of lamb, we'll add something European and attractive to the entrée." Summer folded her hands on some of the scattered papers on her desk. She'd brought a few of Enrico's flowers in and set them in a water glass. They helped cover some of the dusty smell.

"My roast of lamb is perfect as it is."

"For some tastes," Summer said evenly. "For mine it's only adequate. I don't accept adequate." Their eyes warred, violently. As neither gave way, she continued. "I prefer to go with *clamart,* artichoke hearts filled with buttered peas, and potatoes sautéed in butter."

"We've always used watercress and mushrooms."

Meticulously, she changed the angle of a rosebud. The small distraction helped her keep her temper. "Now, we use *clamart.*" Summer noted it down, underlined it, then went on. "As to the prime rib—"

"You will not touch my prime rib."

She started to snap back but managed to grit her teeth instead. It was common knowledge in the kitchen that the prime rib was Max's specialty, one might say his baby. The wisest course was to give in graciously on this point, and hold a hard line on others. Her British heritage of fair play came through.

"The prime rib remains precisely as it is," she told him. "My function here is to improve what needs improving while incorporating the Cocharan House standard." Well said, Summer congratulated herself while Max huffed and subsided. "In addition, we'll keep the New York strip and the filet." Sensing he was mollified, Summer hit him with the poultry entrée. "We'll continue to serve the very simple roast chicken, with the choice of potatoes or rice and the vegetables of the day, but we add pressed duck."

"Pressed duck?" Max blustered. "We have no one on staff who's capable of preparing that dish properly, nor do we have a duck press."

"No, which is why I've ordered one, and why I'm hiring someone who can use it."

"You're bringing someone into my kitchen just for this!"

"I'm bringing someone into *my* kitchen," she corrected, "to prepare the pressed duck and the lamb dish among other things. He's leaving his current job in Chicago to come here because he trusts my judgment. You might begin to do the same." With this, she began to tidy papers. "That's all for today, Max. I'd like you to take along these notes." While the headache began to drum inside her head, she handed him a stack of papers. "If you have any suggestions on what I've listed, please jot them down." She bent back over her work as he rose and strode silently out of the room.

Perhaps she shouldn't have been so abrupt. Summer understood injured feelings and fragile egos. She might have handled it better. Yes, she might have—with a weary sigh, she rubbed her temple—if she wasn't feeling a bit injured and fragile herself. Your own fault, she reminded herself; then propping her elbows on the table, she dropped her head into the cupped hands.

Now that it was tomorrow, she had to face the consequences. She'd broken one of her own primary rules. Never become intimate with a business associate. She should have been able to shrug and say rules were made to be broken, but... It worried her more that it wasn't that particular rule that was causing the turmoil, but another she'd broken. Never let anyone who could really matter get too close. Blake, if she didn't draw in the lines now and hold them, could really matter.

Drinking more coffee and wishing for an aspirin, she began to go over everything again. She was certain she'd been casual enough, and clear enough, the night before over the lack of ties and obligations. But when they'd made love again, nothing she'd said had made sense. She shook her head, trying to block that out. That morning they'd been perfectly at ease with each other—two adults preparing for a workday without any morning-after awkwardness. That's what she wanted.

Too many times, she'd seen her mother glowing and bubbling at the beginning of an affair. This man was *the* man—this man was the most exciting, the most considerate, the most poetic. Until the bloom faded. Summer's belief was that if you didn't glow, you didn't fade, and life was a lot simpler.

Yet she still wanted him.

After a brief knock, one of the kitchen staff stuck

his head around her door. "Ms. Lyndon, Mr. Cocharan would like to see you in his office."

Summer finished off her rapidly cooling coffee. "Yes? When?"

"Immediately."

She lifted a brow. No one summoned her immediately. People requested her, at her leisure. "I see." Her smile was icy enough to make the messenger shrink back. "Thank you."

When the door closed again she sat perfectly still. These were working hours, she reflected, and she was under contract. It was reasonable and right that he should ask her to come to his office. That was acceptable. But she was still Summer Lyndon—she went to no one immediately.

She spent the next fifteen minutes deliberately dawdling over her papers before she rose. After strolling through the kitchen, and taking the time to check on the contents of a pot or skillet on the way, she went to an elevator. On the ride up, she glanced at her watch, pleased to note that she'd arrive nearly twenty-five minutes after the call. As the doors opened she flicked a speck of lint from the sleeve of her blouse, then sauntered out.

"Mr. Cocharan would like to speak to me?" She gave the words the intonation of a question as she smiled down at the receptionist.

"Yes, Ms. Lyndon, you're to go right through. He's been waiting."

Unsure if the last statement had been censure or warning, Summer continued down the hall to Blake's door. She gave a peremptory knock before going in. "Good morning, Blake."

When she entered, he set aside the file in front of him and leaned back in his chair. "Have trouble finding an elevator?"

"No." Crossing the room, she chose a chair and settled down. He looked, she thought, as he had the first time she'd come into his office—aloof, aristocratic. This then was the perfect level for them to deal on. "This is one of the few hotels that has elevators one doesn't grow old waiting for."

"You're aware what the term immediately means."

"I'm aware of it. I was busy."

"Perhaps I should make it clear that I don't tolerate being kept waiting by an employee."

"And I'll make two things clear," she tossed back. "I'm not merely an employee, but an artist. Secondly, I don't come at the snap of anyone's fingers."

"It's eleven-twenty," Blake began with a mildness Summer instantly suspected. "On a workday. My signature is at the base of your checks. Therefore, you do answer to me."

The faint, telltale flush crept along her cheekbones.

"You'd turn my work into something to be measured in dollars and cents and minute by minute—"

"Business is business," he countered, spreading his hands. "I think you were quite clear on that subject."

She'd maneuvered herself successfully toward that particular corner, and he'd given her a helpful shove into it. As a result, her attitude only became more haughty. "You'll notice I *am* here at present. You're wasting time."

As an ice queen, she was magnificent, Blake thought. He wondered if she realized how a change of expression, a tone of voice, could alter her image. She could be half a dozen women in the course of a day. Whether she knew it or not, Summer had her mother's talent. "I received another dissatisfied call from Max," he told her flatly.

She arched a brow and looked like royalty about to dispense a beheading. "Yes?"

"He objects—strongly—to some of the proposed changes in the menu. Ah—" Blake glanced down at the pad on his desk "—pressed duck seems to be the current problem, though several others were tossed in around it."

Summer sat straighter in her chair, tilting up her chin. "I believe you contracted me to improve the quality of Cocharan House dining."

"I did."

"That is precisely what I'm doing."

The French was beginning to seep into the intonation of her voice, her eyes were beginning to glow. Despite the fact it annoyed him, she was undeniably at her most attractive this way. "I also contracted you to manage the kitchen—which means you should be able to control your staff."

"Control?" She was up, and the ice queeen was now the enraged artist. Her gestures were broad, her movements dramatic. "I would need a whip and chain to control such a narrow-minded, ill-tempered old woman who worries only about his own egocentricities. *His* way is the only way. *His* menu is carved in stone, sacrosanct. Pah!" It was a peculiarly French expletive that would have been ridiculous coming from anyone else. From Summer, it was perfect.

Blake tapped his pen against the edge of his desk while he watched the performance. He was nearly tempted to applaud. "Is this what's known as artistic temperament?"

She drew in a breath. Mockery? Would he dare? "You've yet to see true temperament, *mon ami.*"

He only nodded. It was tempting to push her into full gear—but business was business. "Max has worked for Cocharan for over twenty-five years." Blake set down the pen and folded his hands—calm, in direct contrast to Summer's temper. "He's loyal and efficient, and obviously sensitive."

"Sensitive." She nearly spat the word. "I give him his

prime rib and his precious chicken, but still, he's not satisfied. I will have my pressed duck and my *clamart*. *My* menu won't read like something from the corner diner."

He wondered if he recorded the conversation and played it back to her, she'd see the absurdity of it. At the moment, though he had to clear his throat to disguise a chuckle, he doubted it. "Exactly," Blake said and kept his face expressionless. "I've no desire to interfere with the menu. The point is, I've no desire to interfere at all."

Far from mollified, Summer tossed her hair behind her shoulders and glared at him. "Then why do you bother me with these trivialities?"

"These trivialities," he countered, "are your problem, not mine. As manager, part of your function is to do simply that. Manage. If your supervisory chef is consistently dissatisfied, you're not doing your job. You're free to make whatever compromises you think necessary."

"Compromises?" Her whole body stiffened. Again, he thought she looked magnificent. "I don't make compromises."

"Being hardheaded won't bring peace to your kitchen."

She let out her breath in a hiss. "Hardheaded!"

"Exactly. Now, the problem of Max is back in your court. I don't want any more phone calls."

In a low, dangerous voice, she let out a stream of

French, and though he was certain it was colloquial, he caught the drift. With a toss of her head, she started toward the door.

"Summer."

She turned, and the stance reminded him of one of the mythical female archers whose aim was killingly true. She wouldn't even wince as her arrow went straight through the heart. Ice queen or warrior, he wanted her. "I want to see you tonight."

Her eyes went to slits. "You dare."

"Now that we've tabled the first issue, it's time to go onto the second. We might have dinner."

"You tabled the first issue," she retorted. "I don't table things so easily. Dinner? Have dinner with your account book. That's what you understand."

He rose and approached her without hurry. "We agreed that when we're away from here, we're not business associates."

"We're not away from here." Her chin was still angled. "I'm standing in your office, where I was summoned."

"You won't be standing in my office tonight."

"I stand wherever I choose tonight."

"So tonight," he continued easily, "we won't be business associates. Weren't those your rules?"

Personal and professional, and that tangible line of demarcation. Yes, that's the way she'd wanted it, but it wasn't as easy for her to make the separation as she'd thought it would be. "Tonight," she said with a shrug, "I may be busy."

Blake glanced at his watch. "It's nearly noon. We might consider this lunch hour." He looked back at her, half smiling. Lifting a hand, he tangled it in her hair. "During lunch hour, there's no business between us, Summer. And tonight, I want to be with you." He touched his lips to one corner of her mouth, then the other. "I want to spend long—" his lips slanted over hers softly "—private hours with you."

She wanted it too, why pretend otherwise? She'd never believed in pretenses, only in defenses. In any event, she'd already decided to handle Max and the kitchen in her own way. Linking her hands around his neck, she smiled back at him. "Then tonight, we'll be together. You'll bring the champagne?"

She was softening, but not yielding. Blake found it infinitely more exciting than submission. "For a price."

Her laugh was wicked and warm. "A price?"

"I want you to do something for me you haven't done before."

She tilted her head, then touched the tip of her tongue to her lip. "Such as?"

"Cook for me."

Surprise lit her eyes before the laughter sprang out again. "Cook for you? Well, that's a much different request from what I expected."

"After dinner I might come up with a few others."

"So you want Summer Lyndon to prepare your dinner." She considered it as she drew away. "Perhaps I will, though such a thing usually costs much more than a bottle of champagne. Once in Houston I prepared a meal for an oil man and his new bride. I was paid in stock certificates. Blue chip."

Blake took her hand and brought it to his lips. "I bought you a pizza. Pepperoni."

"That's true. Eight o'clock then. And I'd advise you to eat a very light lunch today." She reached for the door handle, then glanced over her shoulder with a grin. "You do like *Cervelles Braisées*?"

"I might, if I knew what it was."

Still smiling, she opened the door. "Braised calf's brains. *Au revoir.*"

Blake stared at the door. She'd certainly had the last word that time.

The kitchen smelled of cooking and sounded like a drawing room. Strains of Chopin were muted as Summer rolled the boneless breasts of chicken in flour. On the range, the clarified butter was just beginning to deepen in color. Perfect. Stuffed tomatoes were already prepared and waiting in the refrigerator. Buttered peas were just beginning to simmer. She would sauté the potato balls while she sautéed the *suprêmes*.

Timing, of course, was critical. *Suprêmes de Volaille à Brun* had to be done to the instant, even a minute of overcooking and she would, like any temperamental cook, throw them out in disgust. Hot butter sizzled as she slipped the floured chicken into it.

She heard the knock but remained where she was. "It's open," she called out. Meticulously, she adjusted the heat under the skillet. "I'll take the champagne in here."

"*Chérie,* if I'd only thought to bring some."

Stunned, Summer turned and saw Monique, glorious in midnight black and silver, framed by her kitchen doorway. "Mother!" With the kitchen fork still in her hand, Summer closed the distance and enveloped her mother.

With that part bubbling, part sultry laugh she was famous for, Monique kissed both of Summer's cheeks, then drew her daughter back. "You are surprised, *oui*? I adore surprises."

"I'm astonished," Summer countered. "What're you doing in town?"

Monique glanced toward the range. "At the moment, apparently interrupting the preparations for an intimate *tête à tête.*"

"Oh!" Whipping around, Summer dashed back to the skillet and turned the chicken breasts, not a second too soon. "What I meant was, what are you doing in Philadelphia?" She checked the flame again, and was satisfied. "Didn't you once say you'd never set foot in the town of the hardware king again?"

"Time mellows one," Monique claimed with a characteristic flick of the wrist. "And I wanted to see my daughter. You are not so often in Paris these days."

"No, it doesn't seem so, does it?" Summer split her attention between her mother and her range, something she would have done for no one else. "You look wonderful."

Monique's smooth cheeks dimpled. "I feel wonderful, *mignonne*. In six weeks, I start a new picture."

"A new picture." Carefully Summer pressed a finger to the top of the chicken. When they sprang back, she removed them to a hot platter. "Where?"

"In Hollywood. They have pestered me, and at last I give in." Monique's infectious laugh bubbled out again. "The script is superb. The director himself came to Paris to woo me. Keil Morrison."

Tall, somewhat gangly, intelligent face, fiftyish. Summer had a clear enough picture from the glossies, and from a party for a reigning box office queen where she'd prepared *île Flottante*. From her mother's tone of voice, Summer knew the answer before she asked the question. "And the director?"

"He, too, is superb. How would you feel about a new step poppa, *chérie*?"

"Resigned," Summer said, then smiled. That was too hard a word. "Pleased, of course, if you're happy, Mother." She began to prepare the brown butter sauce while Monique expounded.

"Oh, but he is brilliant and so sensitive! I've never met a man who so understands a woman. At last, I've found my perfect match. The man who finally brings everything I need and want into my life. The man who makes me feel like a woman."

Nodding, Summer removed the skillet from the heat and stirred in the parsley and lemon juice. "When's the wedding?"

"Last week." Monique smiled brilliantly as Summer glanced up. "We were married quietly in a little churchyard outside Paris. There were doves—a good sign. I tore myself away from Keil because I wanted to tell you in person." Stepping forward, she flashed a thin diamond-crusted band. "Elegant, *oui*? Keil doesn't believe in the—how do you say?—ostentatious."

So, for the moment, neither would Monique DuBois Lyndon Smith Clarion Morrison. She supposed, when the news broke, the glossies and trades would have a field day. Monique would eat up every line of publicity. Summer kissed her mother's cheek. "Be happy, *ma mère*."

"I'm ecstatic. You must come to California and meet my Keil, and then—" She broke off as the knock interrupted her. "Ah, this must be your dinner guest. Shall I answer for you?"

"Please." With the tongue caught between her teeth, Summer poured the sauce over the *suprêmes*. She'd serve them within five minutes or dump them down the sink.

When the door opened, Blake was treated to a slightly more voluptuous, slightly more glossy, version of Summer. The candlelight disguised the years and enhanced the classic features. Her lips curved slowly, in the way her daughter's did, as she offered her hand.

"Hello, Summer is busy in the kitchen. I'm her mother, Monique." She paused a moment as their hands met. "But you are familiar to me, yes. But yes!" she continued before Blake could speak. "The Cocharan House. You are the son—B.C.'s son. We've met before."

"A pleasure to see you again, Mademoiselle Dubois."

"This is odd, *oui*? And amusing. I stay in your hotel while in Philadelphia. Already my bags are checked in and my bed turned down."

"You'll let me know personally if there's anything I can do for you while you stay with us."

"Of course." She studied him in the brief but thorough way a woman of experience has. Like mother, like daughter, she mused. Each had excellent taste. "Please, come in. Summer is putting the finishing touches on your meal. I've always admired her skill in the kitchen. Myself, I'm helpless."

"Diabolically helpless," Summer put in as she entered with the hot platter. "She always made sure she burned things beyond recognition, and therefore, no one asked her to cook."

"An intelligent move, to my thinking," Monique said easily. "And now, I'll leave you to your dinner."

"You're welcome to join us, Mother."

"Sweet." Monique framed Summer's face in her hands and kissed both cheeks again. "But I need my beauty rest after the long flight. Tomorrow, we catch up, *non*? Monsieur Cocharan, we will all have dinner at your wonderful hotel before I go?" In her sweeping way, she was at the door. *"Bon appétit."*

"A spectacular woman," Blake commented.

"Yes." Summer went back to the kitchen for the rest of the meal. "She continually amazes me." After placing the vegetables on the table, she picked up her glass. "She's just taken her fourth husband. Shall we drink to them?"

He began to remove the foil from the bottle, but her tone had him pausing. "A bit cynical?"

"Realistic. In any case, I do wish her happiness." When he removed the cork, she took it and absently waved it under her nose. "And I envy her perennial optimism." After both glasses were filled, Summer touched hers to his. "To the new Mrs. Morrison."

"To optimism," Blake countered before he drank.

"If you like," Summer said with a shrug as she sat. She transferred one of the *suprêmes* from the platter to his plate. "Unfortunately the calf's brains looked poor today, so we have to settle for chicken."

"A pity." The first bite was tender and perfect.

"Would you like some time off to spend with your mother while she's in town?"

"No, it's not necessary. Mother'll divide her time between shopping and the health spa during the day. She tells me she's about to begin a new film."

"Really." It only took him a minute to put things together. "Morrison—the director?"

"You're very quick," Summer acknowledged, toasting him.

"Summer." He laid a hand over hers. "Do you object?"

She opened her mouth to answer quickly, then thought it over. "No. No, object isn't the word. Her life's her own. I simply can't understand how or why she continually plunges into relationships, tying herself up into marriages which on the average have lasted 5.2 years apiece. Is the word optimism, I wonder, or gullibility?"

"Monique doesn't strike me as a gullible woman."

"Perhaps it's a synonym for romantic."

"No, but romantic might be synonymous with hope. Her way isn't yours."

Yet we both chose lovers from the same bloodline, Summer reminded herself. Just what would Blake's reaction be to that little gem? Keep the past in the past, Summer advised herself. And concentrate on the moment. She smiled at him. "No, it's not. And how do you find my cooking?"

Perhaps it was best to let the subject die, for a time. He needed to ease her over that block gently. "As I find everything about you," Blake told her. "Magnificent."

She laughed as she began to eat again. "It wouldn't be advisable for you to become too used to it. I rarely prepare meals for only compliments."

"That had occured to me. So I brought what I thought was the proper token."

Summer tasted the wine again. "Yes, the champagne is excellent."

"But an inadequate token for a Summer Lyndon meal."

When she shot him a puzzled look, he reached in his inside pocket and drew out a small thin box.

"Ah, presents." Amused, she accepted the box.

"You mentioned a fondness for them." Blake saw the amusement fade as she opened the box.

Inside were diamonds—elegant, even delicate in the form of a slender bracelet. They lay white and regal against the dark velvet of the box.

She wasn't often overwhelmed. Now, she found herself struggling through waves of astonishment. "The meal's too simple for a token like this," she managed. "If I'd known, I'd've prepared something spectacular."

"I wouldn't have thought art ever simple."

"Perhaps not, but..." She looked up, telling herself she wasn't supposed to be moved by such things. They were only pretty stones after all. But her heart was full.

"Blake, it's lovely, exquisite. I think you've taken me too seriously when I talk of payments and gifts. I didn't do this tonight for any reason more than I wanted to do it."

"This made me think of you," he said as if she hadn't spoken. "See how cool and haughty the stones are? But..." He slipped the bracelet out of the box. "If you look closely, if you hold it to light, there's warmth, even fire." As he spoke, he let the bracelet dangle from his fingers so that it caught and glittered with the flames from the candles. At that moment, it might have been alive.

"So many dimensions, from every angle you can see something different. A strong stone, and more elegant than any other." Laying the bracelet over her wrist, he clasped it. His gaze lifted and locked on hers. "I didn't do this tonight for any reason other than I wanted to do it."

She was breathless, vulnerable. Would it be like this every time he looked at her? "You begin to worry me," Summer whispered.

The one quiet statement had the need whipping through him almost out of control. He rose, then, drawing her to her feet, crushed her against him before she could agree or protest. "Good."

His mouth wasn't patient this time. There seemed to be a desperate need to hurry, take all, take everything. Hunger that had nothing to do with the meal still unfinished on the table sped through him. She was every desire, and every answer. Biting off an oath, he pulled her to the floor.

This was the whirlwind. She'd never been here before, trapped, exhilarated. Elated by the speed, trembling from the power, Summer moved with him. There was no patience with clothes this time. They were tugged and pulled and tossed aside until flesh could meet flesh. Hot and eager, her body arched against his. She wanted the wind and the fury that only he could bring her.

As his hands sped over her, she delighted in their firmness, in the strength of each individual finger. Her own demands raged equally. Her mouth raced down his throat, teeth nipping, tongue darting. Each unsteady breath told her that she drove him just as he drove her. There was pleasure in that, she discovered. To give passion, and to have it returned to you. Even though her mind clouded, she knew the instant his control snapped.

He was rough, but she delighted in it. She had taken him beyond the civilized only by being. His mouth was everywhere, tasting, on a crazed journey from her lips to her breasts—lingering—then lower, still lower, until she caught her breath in astonished excitement.

The world peeled away, the floor, the walls, ceiling, then the sky and the ground itself. She was beyond all that, in some spiraling tunnel where only the senses ruled. Her body had no bounds, and she had no control.

She moaned, struggling for a moment to pull it back, but the first peak swept her up, tossing her blindly. Even the illusion of reason shattered.

He wanted her like this. Some dark, primitive part of him needed to know he could bring her to this throbbing, mindless world of sensations. She shuddered beneath him, gasping, yet he continued to drive her up again and again with hands and mouth only. He could see her face in the candlelight—those flickers of passion, of pleasure, of need. She was moist and heated. And he was greedy.

Her skin pulsed under him everywhere he touched. When he touched his mouth to the sensitive curve where thigh meets hip, she arched and moaned his name. The sound of it tore through him, pounding in his blood long after there was silence.

"Tell me you want me," he demanded as he raced up her shuddering body again. "And only me."

"I want you." She could think of nothing. She would have given him anything. "Only you."

They joined in a violence that went on and on, then shattered into a crystal contentment.

She lay beneath him knowing she'd never gather the strength to move. There was barely the strength to breathe. It didn't seem to matter. For the first time, she noticed the floor was hard beneath her, but it didn't inspire her to shift to a more comfortable position. Sighing, she closed her eyes. Without too much effort, she could sleep exactly where she was.

Blake moved, only to draw himself up and take his weight on his own arms. She seemed so fragile suddenly, so completely without defense. He hadn't been gentle with her, yet during the loving, she'd seemed so strong, so full of fire.

He gave himself the enjoyment of looking at her while she half dozed, wearing nothing more than diamonds at her wrist. As he watched, her eyes fluttered open and she watched him, catlike from half-lowered lids. Her lips curved. He grinned at her, then kissed them.

"What's for dessert?"

Chapter 9

Unfortunately, Summer was going to need a phone in her office. She preferred to work undisturbed, and phones had a habit of disturbing, but the final menu was almost completed. She was approaching the practical stage of selective marketing. With so many new things—and difficult-to-come-by items—on the bill of fare, she would have to begin the process of finding the best suppliers. It was a job she would have loved to have delegated, but she trusted her own negotiating skills, and her own intuition, more than anyone else's. When choosing a supplier of the best oysters or okra, you needed both.

After tidying her morning's work, Summer gave the stack of papers a satisifed nod. Her instincts about taking this very different sort of job had been valid. She was doing it, and doing it well. The kitchen remodeling was exactly what she'd envisioned, the staff was well trained—and with her carefully screened and selected additions would be only more so. The two new pastry chefs were better than she'd expected them to be. Julio and Georgia had sent a postcard from Hawaii, and it had been taped, with some honor, to the front of a refrigerator. Summer had only had a moment's temptation to throw darts at it.

She'd interfered very little with the setup in the dining room. The lighting there was excellent, the linen impeccable. The food—her food—alone would be all the refreshing the restaurant required.

Soon, she thought, she'd be able to have the new menus printed. She had only to pin down a few prices first and haggle over terms and delivery hours. The next step was the installation of a phone. Choosing to deal with it immediately, she headed for the door. She entered the kitchen from one end as Monique entered from the other. All work ceased.

It amused Summer, and rather pleased her, that her mother had that stunning effect on people. She could see Max standing, staring, with a kitchen spoon in one hand that dripped sauce unheeded onto the floor. And, of course, Monique knew how to make an entrance. It might be said she was a woman made for entrances.

She smiled slowly—it almost appeared hesitantly—as she stepped in, bringing the scent of Paris and spring with her. Her eyes were more gray than her daughter's and, despite the difference in years and experience, held more innocence. Summer had yet to decide if it was calculated or innate.

"Perhaps someone could help me?"

Six men stepped forward. Max came perilously close to allowing the stock from the spoon to drip on Monique's shoulder. Summer decided it was time to restore order. "Mother." She brushed her way through the circle of bodies surrounding Monique.

"Ah, Summer, just who I was looking for." Even as she took her daughter's hands, she gave the group of male faces a sweeping smile. "How fascinating. I don't believe I've ever been in a hotel kitchen before. It's so—ah—large, *oui*?"

"Please, Ms. Dubois—madame." Unable to contain himself, Max took Monique's hand. "I'd be honored to show you whatever you'd like to see. Perhaps you'd care to sample some of the soup?"

"How kind." Her smile would have melted chocolate at fifty yards. "Of course, I must see everything where my daughter works."

"Daughter?"

Obviously, Summer mused, Max had heard nothing but violins since Monique walked into the room. "My mother," Summer said clearly, "Monique Dubois. This is Max, who's in charge of the kitchen staff."

Mother? Max thought dumbly. But of course the resemblance was so strong he felt like a fool for not see-ing it before. There wasn't a Dubois film he hadn't seen at least three times. "A pleasure." Rather gallantly, he kissed the offered hand. "An honor."

"How comforting to know my daughter works with such a gentleman." Though Summer's lip curled, she said nothing. "And I would love to see everything, just everything—perhaps later today?" she added before Max could begin again. "Now, I must steal Summer away for just a short time. Tell me, would it be pos-sible to have some champagne and caviar delivered to my suite?"

"Caviar isn't on the menu," Summer put in with an arch look at Max. "As yet."

"Oh." Prettily, Monique pouted. "I suppose some pâté, or some cheese would do."

"I'll see to it personally. Right away, madame."

"So kind." With a flutter of lashes, Monique slipped her arm through Summer's and swept from the room.

"Laying it on a bit thick," Summer muttered.

Monique threw back her head and gave a bubbling laugh. "Don't be so British, *chérie*. I just did you an enormous service. I learned from the delightful young Cocharan this morning that not only is my daughter an employee at this very hotel—which you didn't bother to tell me—but that you had a few internal problems in the kitchen."

"I didn't tell you because it's only a temporary arrangement, and because it's been keeping me quite busy. As to the internal problems…"

"In the form of one very large Max." Monique glided into the elevator.

"I can handle them just fine by myself," Summer finished.

"But it doesn't hurt to have him impressed by your parentage." After pressing the button for her floor, Monique turned to study her daughter. "So, I look at you in the light and see that you've grown more lovely. That pleases me. If one must have a grown daughter, one should have a beautiful grown daughter."

Laughing, Summer shook her head. "You're as vain as ever."

"I'll always be vain," Monique said simply. "God willing I'll always have a reason to be. Now—" she motioned Summer out of the elevator "—I've had my morning coffee and croissants, and my massage. I'm ready to hear about this new job of yours and your new lover. From the look of you, both agree with you."

"I believe it's customary for mothers and daughters to discuss new jobs, but not new lovers."

"Pooh." Monique tossed open the door to her suite. "We were never just mother and daughter, but friends, *n'est-ce pas?* And *chère amies* always discuss new lovers."

"The job," Summer said distinctly as she dropped into a butter-soft daybed and brought up her legs, "is working out quite well. I took it originally because it intrigued me and—well because Blake threw LaPointe up in my face."

"LaPointe? The beady-eyed little man you detest so much? The one who told the Paris papers you were his…"

"Mistress," Summer said violently.

"Ah, yes, such a foolish word, mistress, so antiquated, don't you agree? Unless one considers that mistress is the feminine term for master." Monique smiled serenely as she draped herself on the sofa. "And were you?"

"Certainly not. I wouldn't have let him put his pudgy little hands on me if he'd been half the chef he claims to be."

"You might have sued."

"Then more people would've snickered and said where there's smoke there's fire. The little French swine would've loved that." She was gritting her teeth, so she deliberately relaxed her jaw. "Don't get me started on LaPointe. It was enough that Blake maneuvered me into this job with him as an edge."

"A very clever man—your Blake, that is."

"He's not my Blake," Summer said pointedly. "He's his own man, just as I'm my own woman. You know I don't believe in that sort of thing." The discreet knock had Monique waving negligently and Summer rising to answer. She thought, as the tray of cheeses and fresh fruit and the bucket of iced champagne was wheeled in, that Max must have dashed around like a madman to have it served so promptly. Summer signed the check with a flourish and dismissed the waiter.

Idly Monique inspected the tray before choosing a single cube of cheese. "But you're in love with him."

Busy with the champagne cork, Summer glanced over. "What?"

"You're in love with the young Cocharan."

The cork exploded out, champagne fizzed and geysered from the bottle. Monique merely lifted her glass to be filled. "I'm not in love with him," Summer said with an underlying desperation her mother recognized.

"One is always in love with one's lover."

"No, one is not." With a bit more control, Summer poured the wine. "Affairs don't have to be romantic and flowery. I'm fond of Blake, I respect him. I consider him an attractive, intelligent man and enjoy his company."

"It's possible to say the same of a brother, or an uncle. Even perhaps an ex-husband," Monique commented. "This is not what I think you feel for Blake."

"I feel passion for him," Summer said impatiently. "Passion is not to be equated with love."

"Ah, Summer." Amused, Monique chose a grape. "You can think with your British mind, but you feel with your French heart. This young Cocharan isn't a man any woman would lightly dismiss."

"Like father like son?" The moment it was said, Summer regretted it.

But Monique only smiled, softly, reminiscently. "It occurred to me. I haven't forgotten B.C."

"Nor he you."

Interested, Monique flipped back from the past. "You've met Blake's father?"

"Briefly. When your name was mentioned he looked as though he'd been struck by lightning."

The soft smile became brilliant. "How flattering. A woman likes to believe she remains in a man's memory long after they part."

"You may be flattered. I can tell you I was damned uncomfortable."

"But why?"

"Mother." Restless, Summer rose again and began to pace. "I was attracted to Blake—very much attracted—and he to me. How do you think I felt when I was talking to his father, and both B.C. and I were thinking about the fact that you'd been lovers? I don't think Blake has any idea. If he did, do you realize how awkward the situation would be?"

"Why?"

On a long breath, Summer turned to her mother again. "B.C. was and is married to Blake's mother. I get the impression Blake's rather fond of his mother, and of his father."

"What does that have to do with it?" Monique's gesture was typically French—a slight shrug, a slight lifting of the hand, palm out. "I was fond of his father too. Listen to me," she continued before Summer could retort. "B.C. was always in love with his wife. I knew that then. We consoled each other, made each other laugh in what was a miserable time for both of us. I'm grateful for it, not ashamed of it. Neither should you be."

"I'm not ashamed." Frustrated, Summer dragged a hand through her hair. "I don't ask you to be, but—damn it, Mother, it's awkward."

"Life often is. You'll remind me there are rules, and so there are." She threw back her head and took on the regal haughtiness her daughter had inherited. "I don't play by the rules, and I don't apologize."

"Mother." Cursing herself, Summer went and knelt beside the couch. "I wasn't criticizing you. It's only that what's right for you, what's good for you, isn't right and good for me."

"You think I don't know that? You think I'd have you live my life?" Monique laid a hand on her daughter's head. "Perhaps I've seen more deep happiness than you've seen. But I've also seen more deep despair. I can't wish you the first without knowing you'd face the second. I want for you only what you wish for yourself."

"Some things you're afraid to wish for."

"No, but some things are more carefully wished for. I will give you some advice." She patted Summer's head, then drew her up to sit on the sofa. "When you were a little girl, I gave you none because small children have always been a mystery to me. When you grew up, you wouldn't have listened to any. Perhaps now we've come to the point between mother and daughter when each understands the other is intelligent."

With a laugh, Summer picked a strawberry from the tray. "All right, I'll listen."

"It does not make you less of a woman to need a man." When Summer frowned, she continued. "To need one to exist, yes, this is nonsense. To need one to give one scope and importance, this is dishonest. But to need a man, one man, to bring joy and passion? This is life."

"There can be joy and passion in a woman's life without a man."

"Some joy, some passion," Monique agreed. "Why settle for some? What is it that you prove by cutting off what is a natural need? Perhaps it's a foolish woman who takes a different man as a husband, four times. Again, I don't apologize, but only remind you that Summer Lyndon is not Monique Dubois. We look for different things in different ways. But we are both women. I don't regret my choices."

With a sigh, Summer laid her head on her mother's shoulder. "I want to be able to say that for myself. I've always thought I could."

"You're an intelligent woman. What choice you make will be right for you."

"My greatest fear has always been to make a mistake."

"Perhaps your greatest fear is your greatest mistake." She touched Summer's cheek again. "Come, pour me some more champagne. I'll tell you of my Keil."

When Summer returned to the kitchen, her mind was still playing back her conversation with Monique. It was rare that Monique pressed her for details about her personal life, and rarer still for her to offer advice. It was true that most of the hour they'd spent together had been devoted to a listing of Keil Morrison's virtues, but in those first few moments, Monique had said things designed to make Summer think—designed to make her begin to doubt her own list of priorities.

But when she approached the swinging doors leading into the kitchen, and the sounds of the argument met her, she knew her thinking would have to wait.

"My casserole's perfect."

"Too much milk, too little cheese."

"You've never been able to admit that my casseroles are better than yours."

Perhaps the scene was laughable—huge Max and little Charlie, the undersized Korean cook who came no higher than his superior's breastbone. They stood, glaring at each other, while both of them held a solid grip on a spinach casserole. It might have been laughable, Summer thought wearily, if the rest of the kitchen staff hadn't already been choosing up sides while the luncheon orders were ignored.

"Inferior work," Max retorted. He'd yet to forgive Charlie for being out sick three days running.

"Your casseroles are always inferior work. Mine are perfect."

"Too much milk," Max said solidly. "Not enough cheese."

"Problem?" Summer stepped up, lining herself between them.

"This scrawny little man who masquerades as a cook is trying to pass this mass of soggy leaves off as a spinach casserole." Max tried to tug the glass dish away and found that the scrawny little man was surprisingly strong.

"This big lump of dough who calls himself a chef is jealous because I know more about vegetables than he does."

Summer bit down hard on her bottom lip. Damn it, it was funny, but the timing was all wrong. "Perhaps the rest of you might get back to work," she began coolly, "before what clientele we have left in the dining room evacuates to the nearest golden arches for decent service. Now…" She turned back to the two opponents. Any moment, she decided, there'd be bared teeth and snarls. "This, I take it, is the casserole in question."

"The dish is a casserole," Max tossed back. "What's in it is garbage." He tugged again.

"Garbage!" The little cook squealed in outrage, then curled his lip. "Garbage is what you pass off as prime rib. The only thing edible on the plate is the tiny spring of parsley you part with." He tugged back.

"Gentlemen, might I ask a question?" Without waiting for an answer, she touched a finger to the dish. It was still warm, but cooling fast. "Has anyone tasted the casserole?"

"I don't taste poison." Max gave the dish another yank. "I pour poison down the sink."

"I wouldn't have this—this ox taste one spoonful of my spinach." Charlie yanked right back. "He'd contaminate it."

"All right, children," Summer said in sweet tones that had both men's annoyance turning on her. "Why don't I do the testing?"

Both men eyed each other warily. "Tell him to let go of my spinach," Charlie insisted.

"Max—"

"He lets go first. I'm his superior."

"Charlie—"

"The only thing superior is his weight." And the tug-of-war began again.

Out of patience, Summer tossed up her hands. "All right, *enough!*"

It might have been the shock of having her raise her voice, something she'd never done in the kitchen—or it might have been that the dish itself was becoming slippery from so much handling. Either way, at her word, the dish fell out of both men's hands with force. It struck the edge of the counter, shattering, so that glass flew even before the casserole and its contents hit the floor. In unison, Max and Charlie erupted with abuse and accusations.

Summer, distracted by the pain in her right arm, glanced down and saw the blood begin to seep from a four-inch gash. Amazed, she stared at it for a full three seconds while her mind completely rejected the idea that blood, her blood, could pour out so quickly.

"Excuse me," she managed at length. "Do you think the two of you could finish this round after I stop bleeding to death?"

Charlie looked over, a torrent of abuse trembling on his tongue. Instead, he stared wide-eyed at the wound, then broke into an excited ramble of Korean.

"If you'd stop interfering," Max began, even as he caught sight of the blood running down Summer's arm. He blanched, then to everyone's surprise, moved like lightning. Grabbing a clean cloth, he pressed it against the gash in Summer's arm. "Sit," he ordered and nudged her onto a kitchen stool. "You," he bellowed at no one in particular, "clean up this mess." Already he was fashioning a tourniquet. "Relax," he said to Summer with unaccustomed gentleness. "I want to see how deep it is."

Giddy, she nodded and kept her eyes trained on the

steam from a pot across the room. It didn't really hurt so very much, she thought as her vision blurred then refocused. She'd probably imagined all that blood.

"What the hell's going on in here?" She heard Blake's voice vaguely behind her. "You can hear the commotion in here clear out to the dining room." He strode over, intending to give both Summer and Max the choice of unemployment or peaceful coexistence. The red-stained cloth stopped him cold. "Summer?"

"An accident," Max said hurriedly while Summer shook her head to clear it. "The cut's deep—she'll need stitches."

Blake was already grabbing the cloth from Max and pushing him aside. "Summer. How the hell did this happen?"

She focused on his face and registered concern and perhaps temper in his eyes before everything started to swim again. Then she made the mistake of looking down at her arm. "Spinach casserole," she said foolishly before she slid from the stool in a dead faint.

The next thing she heard was an argument. *Isn't this where I came in?* she thought vaguely. It only took her a moment to recognize Blake's voice, but the other, female and dry, was a stranger.

"I'm staying."

"Mr. Cocharan, you aren't a relative. It's against hospital policy for you to remain while we treat Ms. Lyndon. Believe me, it's only a matter of a few stitches."

A few stitches? Summer's stomach rolled. She didn't like to admit it, but when it came to needles—the kind the medical profession liked to poke into flesh—she was a complete coward. And if her sense of smell wasn't playing tricks on her, she knew where she was. The odor of antiseptics was much too recognizable. Perhaps if she just sat up and quietly walked away, no one would notice.

When she did sit up, she found herself in a small, curtained examining room. Her gaze lit on a tray that held all the shiny, terrifying tools of the trade.

Blake caught the movement out of the corner of his eye, and was beside her. "Summer, just relax."

Moistening her lips, she studied the room again. "Hospital?"

"Emergency Room. They're going to fix your arm."

She managed a smile, but kept her gaze locked on the tray. "I'd just as soon not." When she started to swing her legs over the side of the examining table, the doctor was there to stop her.

"Lie still, Ms. Lyndon."

Summer stared back at the tough, lined female face. She had frizzy hair the color of a peach, and wire-rim glasses. Summer gauged her own strength against the doctor's and decided she could win. "I'm going home now," she said simply.

"You're going to lie right there and get that arm sewed up. Now be quiet."

Well, perhaps if she recruited an ally. "Blake?"

"You need stitches, love."

"I don't want them."

"Need," the doctor corrected, briskly. "Nurse!" While she scrubbed her hands in a tiny sink, she looked back over her shoulder. "Mr. Cocharan, you'll have to wait outside."

"No." Summer managed to struggle back into a sitting position. "I don't know you," she told the white-coated woman at the sink. "And I don't know her," she added when the nurse pushed passed the curtains. "If I'm going to have to sit here while you sew up my arm with cat gut or whatever it is you use, I'm going to have someone here that I know." She tightened her grip on Blake's hand. "I know him." She lay back down but kept the death hold on Blake's hand.

"Very well." Recognizing both a strong will and basic fear, the doctor gave in. "Just turn your head away," she advised. "This won't take long. I've already used yards of cat gut today."

"Blake." Summer took a deep breath and looked straight into his eyes. She wouldn't think about what the two women on the other side of the table were doing to her arm. "I have a confession to make. I don't deal very well with this sort of thing." She swallowed again when she felt the pressure on her skin. "I have to be tranquilized to get through a dental appointment."

Out of the corner of his eye, he saw the doctor take

the first stitch. "We almost had to do the same thing for Max." He ran his thumb soothingly over his knuckles. "After this, you could tell him you're going to put in a wood-burning stove and a hearth and he wouldn't give you any trouble."

"A hell of a way to get cooperation." She winced, felt her stomach roll and swallowed desperately. "Talk to me—about anything."

"We should take a weekend, soon, and go to the beach. Some place quiet, right on the ocean."

It was a good image, she struggled to focus on it. "Which ocean?"

"Any one you want. We'll do nothing for three days but lie in the sun, make love."

The young nurse glanced over, and a sigh escaped before the doctor caught her eye.

"As soon as I'm back from Rome. All you have to do is find some little island in the Pacific while I'm gone. I'd like a few palm trees and friendly natives."

"I'll look into it."

"In the meantime," the doctor put in as she snipped off a length of bandage, "keep this dressing dry, have it changed every third day and come back in two weeks to have the stitches removed. A nasty slice," she added, giving the bandage a last professional adjustment. "But you'll live."

Cautiously Summer turned her head. The wound was now covered in the sterile white gauze. It looked neat, trim and somehow competent. The nausea faded instantly. "I thought they made the stitches so they dissolved."

"It's a nice arm." The doctor rinsed off her hands in the sink. "We wouldn't want a scar on it. I'll give you a prescription for some pain pills."

Summer set her jaw. "I won't take them."

With a shrug, the doctor dried her hands. "Suit yourself. Oh, and you might try the Solomon Islands off New Guinea." Whipping back the curtain, she strode out.

"Quite a lady," Summer muttered as Blake helped her off the table. "Terrific bedside manner. I can't think why I don't hire her as my personal physician."

The spunk was back, Blake thought with a grin, but kept a supportive arm around her waist. "She was exactly what you needed. You didn't need any more sympathy, or worry, than you were getting from me."

She frowned up at him as he led her into the parking lot. "When I bleed," she corrected, "I need a great deal of sympathy and worry."

"What you need—" he kissed her forehead before opening the car door "—is a bed, a dark room and a few hours' rest."

"I'm going back to work," she corrected. "The kitchen's probably chaos, and I have a long list of phone calls to make—as soon as you arrange to have a phone hooked up for me."

"You're going home, to bed."

"I've stopped bleeding," Summer reminded him. "And though I admit I'm a complete baby when it comes to blood and needles and doctors in white coats, that's done now. I'm fine."

"You're pale." He stopped at a light and turned to her. It wasn't entirely clear to him how he'd gotten through the last hour himself. "You arm's certainly throbbing now, or soon will be. I make it a policy—whenever one of my staff faints on the job, they have the rest of the day off."

"Very liberal and humanitarian of you. I wouldn't have fainted if I hadn't looked."

"Home, Summer."

She sat up, folded her hands and took a deep breath. Her arm *was* throbbing, but she wouldn't have admitted it now for anything. With the new ache, and annoyance, it was easy to forget that she'd clung to his hand a short time before. "Blake, I realize I've mentioned this before, but sometimes it doesn't hurt to reiterate. I don't take orders."

Silence reigned in the car for almost a full minute. Blake turned west, away from Cocharan House and toward Summer's apartment building.

"I'll just take a cab," she said lightly.

"What you'll take is a couple of aspirin, right before I draw the shades and tuck you into bed."

God, that sounded like heaven. Ignoring the image,

she set her chin. "Just because I depended on you—a little—while that woman was plying her needle, doesn't mean I need a keeper."

There was a way to convince her to do as he wanted. Blake considered it. Perhaps the direct way was the best way. "I don't suppose you noticed how many stitches she put in your arm."

"No." Summer looked out the window.

"I did. I counted them as she sewed. Fifteen. You didn't notice the size of the needle, either?"

"No." Pressing a hand to her stomach she glared at him. "Dirty pool, Blake."

"If it works…" Then he slipped a hand over hers. "A nap, Summer. I'll stay with you if you like."

How was she supposed to deal with him when he went from being kind, to filthy, to gentle? How was she supposed to deal with herself when all she really wanted was to curl up beside him where she knew it would be safe and warm? "I'll rest." All at once, she felt she needed to, badly, but it no longer had anything to do with her arm. If he continually stirred her emotions like this, the next few months were going to be impossible. "Alone," she finished firmly. "You have enough to do back at the hotel."

When he pulled up in front of her building, she put out a hand to stop him from turning off the engine. "No, you needn't bother to come up. I'll go to bed, I promise." Because she could feel him tense with an objection, she smiled and squeezed his hand. I have to go up alone, she realized. If he came with her now, everything could change. "I'm going to take those aspirin, turn on the stereo and lie down. I'd feel better if you'd go by the kitchen and make certain everything's all right there."

He studied her face. Her skin was pale, her eyes weary. He wanted to stay with her, have her hold onto him for support again. Even as he sat beside her, he could feel the distance she was putting between them. No, he wouldn't allow that—but for now, she needed rest more than she needed him.

"If that's what you want. I'll call you tonight."

Leaning over, she kissed his cheek, then climbed from the car quickly. "Thanks for holding my hand."

Chapter 10

It was beginning to grate on her nerves. It wasn't as
though Summer didn't enjoy attention. More than enjoying it, she'd come to expect it as a matter of course
in her career. It wasn't as if she didn't enjoy being ca-
tered to. That was something she'd developed a taste
for early on, growing up in households with servants.
But as any good cook knows, sugar has to be dispensed
with a careful hand.

Monique had extended her stay a full week, claim-
ing that she couldn't possibly leave Philadelphia while
Summer was still recovering from an injury. The more
Summer tried to play down the entire incident of her
arm and the stitches, the more Monique looked at her
with admiration and concern. The more admiration and

concern she received, the more Summer worried about that next visit to the doctor.

Though it wasn't in character, Monique had gotten into the habit of coming by Summer's office every day with healing cups of tea and bowls of healthy soup—then standing over her daughter until everything was consumed.

For the first few days, Summer had found it rather sweet—though tea and soup weren't regulars on her diet. As far as she could remember, Monique had always been loving and certainly kind, but never maternal. For this reason alone, Summer drank the tea, ate the soup and swallowed complaints along with them. But as it continued, and as Monique consistently interrupted the final stages of her planning, Summer began to lose patience. She might have been able to tolerate Monique's overreaction and mothering, if it hadn't been for the same treatment by the kitchen staff, headed by Max.

She was permitted to do nothing for herself. If she started to brew a pot of coffee, someone was there, taking over, insisting that she sit and rest. Every day at precisely noon, Max himself brought her in a tray with the luncheon speciality of the day. Poached salmon, lobster soufflé, stuffed eggplant. Summer ate—because like her mother, he hovered over her—while she had visions of a bacon double cheeseburger with a generous side order of onion rings.

Doors were opened for her, concerned looks thrown her way, conciliatory phrases heaped on her until she wanted to scream. Once when she'd been unnerved enough to snap that she had some stitches in her arm, not a terminal illness, she'd been brought yet another soothing cup of tea—with a saucer of plain vanilla cookies.

They were killing her with kindness.

Every time she thought she'd reached her limit, Blake managed to level things for her again. He wasn't callous of her injury or even unkind, but he certainly wasn't treating her as though she were the star attraction at a deathbed.

He had an uncanny instinct for choosing the right time to phone or drop in on the kitchen. He was there, calm when she needed calm, ordered when she yearned for order. He demanded things of her when everyone else insisted she couldn't lift a finger for herself. When he annoyed her, it was in an entirely different way, a way that tested and stretched her abilities rather than smothered them.

And with Blake, Summer didn't have that hampering guilt about letting loose with her temper. She could shout at him knowing she wouldn't see the bottomless patience in his eyes that she saw in Max's. She could be unreasonable and not be worried that his feelings would be hurt like her mother's.

Without realizing it, she began to see him as a pillar

of solidity and sense in a world of nonsense. And, for perhaps the first time in her life, she felt an intrinsic need for that pillar.

Along with Blake, Summer had her work to keep her temper and her nerve ends under some kind of control. She poured herself into it. There were long sessions with the printer to design the perfect menu—an elegant slate gray with the words COCHARAN HOUSE embossed on the front—thick creamy parchment paper inside listing her final choices in delicate script. Then there were the room service menus that would go into each unit—not quite so luxurious, perhaps, but Summer saw to it that they were distinguished in their own right. She talked for hours with suppliers, haggling, demanding and enjoying herself more than she would ever have guessed, until she got precisely the terms she wanted.

It gave her a glow of success—perhaps not the flash she felt on completing some spectacular dish—but a definite glow. She found that in a different way, it was equally satisfying.

And it was unpardonably annoying to be told, after the completion of a particularly long and successful negotiation, that she should take a little nap.

"Chérie." Monique glided into the storage room, just as Summer hung up the phone with the butcher, bearing the inevitable cup of herbal tea. "It's time you had a break. You mustn't push yourself so."

"I'm fine, Mother." Glancing at the tea, Summer sincerely hoped she wouldn't gag. She wanted something carbonated and cold, preferably loaded with caffeine. "I'm just going over the contracts with the suppliers. It's a bit complicated and I've still got one or two calls to make."

If she'd hoped that would be a gentle hint that she needed privacy to work, she was disappointed. "Too complicated when you've already worked so many hours today," Monique insisted and took a seat on the other side of the desk. "You forget, you've had a shock."

"I cut my arm," Summer said with strained patience.

"Fifteen stitches," Monique reminded her, then frowned with disapproval as Summer reached for a cigarette. "Those are so bad for your health, Summer."

"So's nervous tension," she muttered, then doggedly cleared her throat. "Mother, I'm sure Keil's missing you desperately just as you must be missing him. You shouldn't be away from your new husband for so long."

"Ah, yes." Monique sighed and looked dreamily at the ceiling. "For a new bride, a day away from her husband is like a week, a week can be a year." Abruptly, she pressed her hands together, shaking her head. "But my Keil, he is the most understanding of men. He knows I must stay when my daughter needs me."

Summer opened her mouth, then shut it again. Diplomacy, she reminded herself. Tact. "You've been wonderful," she began, a bit guiltily, because it was true. "I can't tell you how much I appreciate all the time, all the trouble, you've taken over this past week or so. But my arm's nearly healed now. I'm really fine. I feel terribly guilty holding you here when you should be enjoying your honeymoon."

With her light, sexy laugh, Monique waved a hand. "My sweet, you'll learn that a honeymoon isn't a time or a trip, but a state of mind. Don't concern yourself with that. Besides, do you think I could leave before they take those nasty stitches out of your arm?"

"Mother—" Summer felt the hitch in her stomach and reached for the tea in defense.

"No, no. I wasn't there for you when the doctor treated you, but—" here, her eyes filled and her lips trembled "—I will be by your side when she removes them—one at a time."

Summer had an all-too-vivid picture of herself lying once again on the examining table, the tough-faced doctor over her. Monique, frail in black, would be standing by, dabbing at her eyes with a lacy handkerchief. She wasn't sure if she wanted to scream, or just drop her head between her knees.

"Mother, you'll have to excuse me. I've just remembered, I have an appointment with Blake in his office." Without waiting for an answer, Summer dashed from the storage room.

Almost immediately Monique's eyes were dry and her lips curved. Leaning back in her chair, she laughed in delight. Perhaps she hadn't always known just what to do with a daughter when Summer had been a child, but now… Woman to woman, she knew precisely how to nudge her daughter along. And she was nudging her along to Blake, where Monique had no doubt her strong-willed, practical and much-loved daughter belonged.

"À l'amour," she said and lifted the tea in a toast.

It didn't matter to Summer that she didn't have an appointment, only that she see Blake, talk to him and restore her sanity. "I have to see Mr. Cocharan," she said desperately as she pushed right past the receptionist.

"But, Ms. Lyndon—"

Heedless, Summer dashed through the outer office and tossed open his door without knocking. "Blake!"

He lifted a brow, motioned her inside, then continued with his telephone conversation. She looked, he thought, as if she were on the last stages of a manhunt, and on the wrong side of the bloodhounds. His first instinct might have been to comfort, to soothe, but common sense prevailed. It was all too obvious that she was getting enough of that, and detesting it.

Frustrated, she whirled around the room. Nervous energy flowed from her. She stalked to the window, then, restless, turned away from the view. Ultimately she walked to the bar and poured herself a defiant portion of vermouth. The moment she heard the phone click back on the cradle, she turned to him.

"Something has to be done!"

"If you're going to wave that around," he said mildly,

indicating her glass, "you'd better drink some first. It'll be all over you."

Scowling, Summer took a long sip. "Blake, my mother has to go back to California."

"Oh?" He finished scrawling a memo. "Well, we'll be sorry to see her go."

"*No!* No, she has to go back, but she won't. She insists on staying here and nursing me into catatonia. And Max," she continued before he could comment. "Something has to be done about Max. Today—today it was shrimp salad and avocado. I can't take much more." She sucked in a breath, then continued in a dazed rambling of complaints. "Charlie looks at me as if I were Joan of Arc, and the rest of the kitchen staff is just as bad—if not worse. They're driving me crazy."

"I can see that."

The tone of voice had her pacing coming to a quick halt and her eyes narrowing. "Don't aim that coolly amused smile at me."

"Was I smiling?"

"Or that innocent look, either," she snapped back. "You were smiling inside, and nervous breakdowns are definitely not funny."

"You're absolutely right." He folded his hands on the desk. "Why don't you sit down and start from the beginning."

"Listen—" She dropped into a chair, sipped the vermouth, then was up and pacing again. "It's not that I don't appreciate kindness, but there's a saying about too much of a good thing."

"I think I've heard that."

Ignoring him, she plunged on. "You can ruin a dessert with too much pampering, too much attention, you know."

He nodded. "The same's sometimes said of a child."

"Just stop trying to be cute, damn it."

"It doesn't seem to take any effort." He smiled. She scowled.

"Are you listening to me?" she demanded.

"Every word."

"I wasn't cut out to be pampered, that's all. My mother—every day it's cup after cup of herbal tea until I have visions of sloshing when I walk. 'You should rest, Summer. You're not strong yet, Summer.' Damn it, I'm strong as an ox!"

He took out a cigarette, enjoying the show. "I'd've said so myself."

"And Max! The man's positively smothering me with good will. Lunch every day, twelve on the dot." With a groan, she pressed a hand against her stomach. "I haven't had a real meal in a week. I keep getting these insane cravings for tacos, but I'm so full of tea and lobster bisque I can't do anything about it. If one more person tells me to put up my feet and rest, I swear, I'm going to punch them right in the mouth."

Blake scrutinized the end of his cigarette. "I'll make sure I don't mention it."

"That's just it, you don't." She spun around the desk, then sat on it directly in front of him. "You're the only one around here who's treated me like a normal person since this ridiculous thing happened. You even shouted at me yesterday. I appreciate that."

"Think nothing of it."

With a half laugh, she took his hand. "I'm serious. I feel foolish enough for being so careless as to let an accident like that happen in my kitchen. You don't constantly remind me of it with pats on the head and concerned looks."

"I understand you." Blake linked his fingers with hers. "I've been making a study of you almost from the first instant we met."

The way he said it had her pulse fluctuating. "I'm not an easy person to understand."

"No?"

"I don't always understand."

"Let me tell you about Summer Lyndon, then." He measured her hand against his before he linked their fingers. "She's a beautiful woman, a bit spoiled from her upbringing and her own success." He smiled when her brows drew together. "She's strong and opinionated and intensely feminine without being calculating. She's ambitious and dedicated with a skill for concentration that reminded me once of a surgeon. And she's romantic, though she'll claim otherwise."

"That's not true," Summer began.

"She listens to Chopin when she works. Even while she chooses to have an office in a storage room, she keeps roses on her desk."

"There're reasons why—"

"Stop interrupting," he told her simply, and with a huff, she subsided. "What fears she has are kept way below the surface because she doesn't like to admit to having any. She's tough enough to hold her own against anyone, and compassionate enough to tolerate an uncomfortable situation rather than hurt someone's feelings. She's controlled, and she's passionate. She has a taste for the best champagne and junk food. There's no one I've known who's annoyed me quite so much, or who I'd trust quite so implicitly."

She let out a long breath. It wasn't the first time he'd put her in a position where words were hard to come by. "Not an entirely admirable woman."

"Not entirely," Blake agreed. "But a fascinating one."

She smiled, then sat on his lap. "I've always wanted to do this," she murmured, snuggling. "Sit on some big corporate executive's lap in an elegant office. I'm suddenly quite sure I'd rather be fascinating than admirable."

"I prefer you that way." He kissed her, but lightly.

"You've chased off my nervous breakdown again."

He brushed at her hair, thinking he was close—very close—to winning her completely. "We aim to please."

"Now if I just didn't have to go back down and face all that sugar." She sighed. "And all those earnestly concerned faces."

"What would you rather do?"

Linking her hands around his neck, she laughed and drew back. "If I could do anything I wanted?"

"Anything."

Thoughtfully she ran her tongue over her teeth then grinned. "I'd like to go to the movies, a perfectly dreadful movie, and eat pounds of buttered popcorn with too much salt."

"Okay." He gave her a friendly slap on the bottom. "Let's go find a dreadful movie."

"You mean now?"

"Right now."

"But it's only four o'clock."

He kissed her, then hauled her to her feet. "It's known as playing hookey. I'll fill you in on the way."

She made him feel young, foolishly young and irresponsible, sitting in a darkened corner of the theater with a huge barrel of popcorn on his lap and her hand in his. When he looked back over his life, Blake could remember no time when he hadn't felt secure—but irresponsible? Never that. Having a multimillion dollar business behind him had ingrained in him a very demanding sense of obligation. However much he'd benefited growing up, having enough and always the best, there'd always been the unspoken pressure to maintain that standard—for himself, and for the family business.

Because he'd always taken that position seriously, he was a cautious man. Impulsiveness had never been part of his style. But perhaps that was changing a bit— with Summer. He'd had the impulse to give her whatever she'd wanted that afternoon. If it had been a trip to Paris to eat supper at Maxim's, he'd have arranged it then and there. Then again, he should have known that a box of popcorn and a movie were more her style.

It was that style—the contrast of elegance and simplicity—that had drawn him in from the first. He knew, without question, that there would never be another woman who would move him in the same way.

Summer knew it had been days since she had fully relaxed. In fact, she hadn't been able to relax at all since the accident with anyone but Blake. He'd given her support, but more important, he'd given her space. They hadn't been together often over the past week, and she knew Blake was closing the deal with the Hamilton chain. They'd both been busy, preoccupied, pressured, yet when they were alone and away from Cocharan House, they didn't talk business. She knew how hard he'd worked on this purchase—the negotiations, the paperwork, the endless meetings. Yet he'd put all that aside—for her.

Summer leaned toward him. "Sweet."

"Hmm?"

"You," she whispered under the dialogue on the screen. "You're sweet."

"Because I found a dreadful movie?"

With a chuckle, she reached for more popcorn. "It is dreadful, isn't it?"

"Terrible, which is why the theater's nearly empty. I like it this way."

"Antisocial?"

"No, it just makes it easier—" leaning closer, he caught the lobe of her ear between his teeth "—to indulge in this sort of thing."

"Oh." Summer felt the thrill of pleasure start at her toes and climb upward.

"And this sort of thing." He nipped at the cord of her neck, enjoying her quick little intake of breath. "You taste better than the popcorn."

"And it's excellent popcorn." Summer turned her head so that her mouth could find his.

So warm, so right. Summer felt it was almost possible to say that her lips were made to fit his. If she'd believed in such things... If she'd believed in such things, she might have said that they'd been meant to find each other at this stage of their lives. To meet, to clash, to attract, to merge. One man to one woman, enduringly. When they were close, when his lips were heated on hers, she could almost believe it. She wanted to believe it.

He ran a hand down her hair. Soft, fresh. Just the touch of that and no more could make him want her unreasonably. He never felt stronger than when he was with her. And he never felt more vulnerable. He didn't hear the explosion of sound and music from the speakers. She didn't see the sudden kaleidoscope of color and movement on the screen. Hampered by the small seats, they shifted in an effort to get that much closer.

"Excuse me." The young usher, who had the job until September when school started up again, shifted his feet in the aisle. Then he cleared his throat. "Excuse me."

Glancing up, Blake noticed that the house lights were on and the screen was blank. After a surprised moment, Summer pressed her mouth against his shoulder to muffle a laugh.

"Movie's over," the boy said uncomfortably. "We have to—ah—clear the theater after every show." Glancing at Summer, he decided any man might lose interest in a movie with someone like her around. Then Blake stood, tall, broad shouldered, with that one aloofly raised eyebrow. The boy swallowed. And a lot of guys didn't like to be interrupted.

"Ah—that's the rule, you know. The manager—"

"And reasonable enough," Blake interrupted when he noticed the boy's Adam's apple working.

"We'll just take the popcorn along," Summer said as she rose. She tucked the barrel under one arm and slid her other through Blake's. "Have a nice evening," she told the usher over her shoulder as they walked out.

When they were outside, she burst out laughing. "Poor child, he thought you were going to manhandle him."

"The thought crossed my mind, but only very briefly."

"Long enough for him to get nervous about it." After climbing into the car, she placed the popcorn in her lap. "You know what he thought, don't you?"

"What?"

"That we were having an illicit affair." Leaning over, she nipped at Blake's ear. "The kind where your wife thinks you're at the office, and my husband thinks I'm shopping."

"Why didn't we go to a motel?"

"That's where we're going now." Nibbling on popcorn again, she sent him a wicked glance. "Though I think in our case we might substitute my apartment."

"I'm willing to be flexible. Summer..." He drew her against his side as they breezed through a light. "Just what was that movie about?"

Laughing, she let her head lay against his shoulder. "I haven't the vaguest idea."

Later, they lay naked in her bed, the curtains open to let in the light, the windows up to let in the breeze. From the apartment below came the repetitive sound of scales being played, a bit unsteadily, on the piano. Perhaps she'd dozed for a short time, because the sunlight seemed softer now, almost rosy. But she wasn't in any hurry for night to fall.

The sheets were warm and wrinkled from their bodies. The air was ripe with supper smells—grilling pork from the piano teacher's apartment, spaghetti sauce from the newlyweds next door. The breeze carried the mix of both, appealingly.

"It's nice," Summer murmured, with her head nestled in the curve of her lover's shoulder. "Just being here like this, knowing that anything there is to do can be done just as well tomorrow. You probably haven't played hookey enough." She was quite sure she hadn't.

"If I did, the business would suffer and the board would begin to grumble. Complaining's one of their favorite things."

Absently, she rubbed the bottom of her foot over the top of one of his. "I haven't asked you about the Hamilton chain because I thought you probably got enough of that at the office, and from the press, but I'd like to know if you got what you wanted."

He thought about reaching for a cigarette then decided it wasn't worth the effort. "I wanted those hotels. As it turned out, the deal satisfied all parties in the end. You can't ask for more than that."

"No." Thoughtfully, she rolled over so that she could look at him directly. Her hair brushed over his chest.

"Why did you want them? Is it the acquisition itself, the property or just a matter of enjoying the wheeling and dealing? The strategy of negotiations?"

"It's all of that. Part of the enjoyment in business is setting up deals, working out the flaws, following through until you've gotten what you were aiming for. In some ways it's not that different from art."

"Business isn't art," Summer corrected archly.

"There are parallels. You set up an idea, work out the flaws, then follow through until you've created what you wanted."

"You're being logical again. In art you use the emotion in equal parts with the mind. You can't do that in business." Her shrug was typically French. Somehow she became more French whenever her craft was under discussion. "This is all facts and figures."

"You left out instinct. Facts and figures aren't enough without that."

She frowned, considering. "Perhaps, but you wouldn't follow instinct over a solid set of facts."

"Even a solid set of facts varies according to the circumstances and the players." He was thinking of her now, and himself. Reaching up, he tucked her hair behind her ear. "Instincts are very often more reliable."

And she was thinking of him now, and herself. "Often more," Summer murmured, "but not always more. That leaves room for failure."

"No amount of planning, no amount of facts, precludes failure."

"No." She laid her head on his shoulder again, trying to ward off the little trickle of panic that was trying to creep in.

He ran a hand down her back. She was still so cautious, he thought. A little more time, a little more room—a change of subject. "I have twenty new hotels to oversee, to reorganize," he began. "That means twenty more kitchens that have to be studied and graded. I'll need an expert."

She smiled a little as she lifted her head again. "Twenty is a very demanding and time-consuming number."

"Not for the best."

Tilting her head, she looked down her straight, elegant nose. "Naturally not, but the best is very difficult to come by."

"The best is currently very soft and very naked in my arms."

Her lips curved slowly, the way he most enjoyed them. "Very true. But this, I think, is not a negotiating table."

"You've a better idea how to spend the evening?"

She ran a fingertip along his jawline. "Much better."

He caught her hand in his and, drawing her finger into his mouth, nipped lightly. "Show me."

The idea appealed, and excited. It seemed that whenever they made love she was quickly dominated by her own emotions and his skill. This time, she would set the pace, and in her own time, in her own way, she would destroy the innate control that brought her both admiration and frustration. Just the thought of it sent a thrill racing up her spine.

She brought her mouth close to his, but used her tongue to taste. Slowly, very slowly, she traced his lips. Already she could feel the heat rising. With a lazy sigh, she shifted so that her body moved over his as she trailed kisses down his jaw.

A strong face, she thought, aristocratic but not soft, intelligent, but not cold. It was a face some women would find haughty—until they looked into the eyes. She did so now and saw the intensity, the heat, even the ruthlessness.

"I want you more than I should," she heard herself say. "I have you less than I want."

Before he could speak, she crushed her mouth to his and started the journey for both of them.

He was still throbbing from her words alone. He'd wanted to hear that kind of admission from her; he'd waited to hear it. Just as he'd waited to feel this strong, pure emotion from her. It was that emotion that stripped away all his defenses even as her seeking hands and mouth exploited the weaknesses.

She touched. His skin heated.

She tasted. His blood sang.

She encompassed. His mind swam.

Vulnerable. Blake discovered the new sensation in himself. She made him so. In the soft, lowering light—near dusk—he was trapped in that midnight world of quietly raging powers. Her fingers were cool and very sure as they stroked, enticed. He could feel them slide leisurely over him, pausing to linger while she sighed. And while she sighed, she exploited. His body was weighed down with layer after layer of pleasures—to be seduced so carefully, to be desired so fully.

With long, lengthy, openmouthed kisses, she explored all of him, reveling in the firm masculinity of his body—knowing she would soon rip apart that impenetrable control. She was obsessed with it, and with him. Could it be that now, after she'd made love with him, after she'd begun to understand the powers and weaknesses in his body, she would find even more delight in learning of them again?

There seemed to be no end to the variations of her feelings, to the changes of sensations she could experience when she was with him like this. Each time, every time, was as vital and unique as the first had been. If this was a contradiction to everything she'd ever believed was true about a man and woman, she didn't question it now. She exalted in it.

He was hers. Body and mind—she felt it. Almost tangibly she could sense the polish, the civilized sheen, that was so much a part of him melt away. It was what she wanted.

There was little sanity left. As she roamed over him the need became more primitive, more primal. He wanted more, endlessly more, but the blood was drumming in his head. She was so agile, so relentless. He experienced a wave of pure helplessness for the first time in his life. Her hands were clever—so clever he couldn't hear the quick unsteadiness of her breathing. He could feel her tormenting him exquisitely, but he couldn't see the flickers of passion or depth of desire in her eyes. He was blind and deaf to everything.

Then her mouth was devouring his and everything savage that civilized men restrain tore from him. He was mad for her. In his mind were dark swirling colors, in his ears was a wild rushing like a sea crazed by a storm. Her name ripped from him like an oath as he gripped her, rolling her to her back, enclosing her, possessing her.

And there was nothing but her, to take, to drown in, to ravage and to worship until passion spun from its peak and emptied him.

Chapter 11

"I'm starving."

It was full dark, with no moon to shed any trickle of light into the room. The darkness itself was comfortable and easy. They were still naked and tangled on Summer's bed, but the piano had been silent for an hour. There were no more supper smells in the air. Blake drew her a bit closer and kept his eyes shut, though it wasn't sleep he sought. Somehow in the silence, in the darkness, he felt closer to her.

"I'm starving," Summer repeated, a bit sulkily this time.

"You're the chef."

"Oh, no, not this time." Rising on her elbow, Summer glared at him. She could see the silhouette of his profile, the long line of chin, the straight nose, the sweep of brow. She wanted to kiss all of them again, but knew it was time to make a stand. "It's definitely your turn to cook."

"My turn?" He opened one eye, cautiously. "I could send out for pizza."

"Takes too long." She rolled on top of him to give him a smacking kiss—and a quick jab in the ribs. "I said I was starving. That's an immediate problem."

He folded his arms behind his head. He, too, could see only a silhouette—the drape of her hair, slope of her shoulder, the curve of her breasts. It was enough. "I don't cook."

"Everyone cooks something," she insisted.

"Scrambled eggs," he said, hoping it would discourage her. "That's about it."

"That'll do." Before he could think of anything to change her mind, she was off the bed and switching on the bedside lamp.

"Summer!" He tossed his arm over his eyes to shield them and tried a halfhearted moan. She grinned at that before she turned to the closet to find a robe.

"I have eggs, and a skillet."

"I make very bad eggs."

"That's okay." She found his slacks, shook them out briefly, then tossed them on top of him. "Real hunger makes allowances."

Resigned, Blake put his feet on the floor. "Then I don't expect a critique afterward."

While she waited, he slipped into a pair of brief jockey shorts. They were dark blue, cut low at the waist, high at the thigh. Very sexy, she mused, and very discreet. Strange how such an incidental thing could reflect a personality.

"Cooks like to be cooked for," she told him as he drew on his slacks.

He shrugged into his shirt, leaving it unbuttoned. "Then don't interfere."

"Wouldn't dream of it." Hooking her arm through his, Summer led him to the kitchen. Again, she switched on lights and made him wince. "Make yourself at home," she invited.

"Aren't you going to assist?"

"No, indeed." Summer took the top off the cookie jar and plucked out the familiar sandwich cookie. "I don't work overtime and I never assist."

"Union rules?"

"My rules."

"You're going to eat cookies?" he asked as he rummaged for a bowl. "And eggs?"

"This is just the appetizer," she said with her mouth full. "Want one?"

"I'll pass." Sticking his head in the refrigerator, he found a carton of eggs and a quart of milk.

"You might want to grate a bit of cheese," Summer began, then shrugged when he sent her an arch look. "Sorry. Carry on." Blake broke four eggs into the bowl then added a dollop of milk. "One should measure, you know."

"One shouldn't talk with one's mouth full," he said mildly and began to beat the eggs.

Overbeating them, she thought but managed to restrain herself. But when it came to cooking, willpower wasn't her strong suit. "You haven't heated up the pan, either." Undaunted by being totally ignored, she took another cookie. "I can see you're going to need lessons."

"If you want something to do, make some toast."

Obligingly she took a loaf of bread from the bin and popped two pieces in the toaster. "It's characteristic of cooks to get a bit testy when they're watched, but a good chef has to overcome that—and distractions." She waited until he'd poured the egg mixture into a skillet before going to him. Wrapping her arms around his waist, she pressed her lips to the back of his neck. "All manner of distraction. And you've got the flame up too high."

"Do you like your eggs singed or burned clear through?"

With a laugh, she ran her hands up his bare chest. "Singed is fine. I have a nice little white Bordeaux you might've put in the eggs, but since you didn't, I'll just pour some into glasses." She left him to cook and, by the time Blake had finished the eggs, she had buttered toast on a plate and chilled wine in glasses. "Impressive," Summer decided as she sat at the dinette. "And aromatic."

But it's the eyes that tell you first, he remembered. "Attractive?" He watched as she spooned eggs on her plate.

"Very, and—" she took a first testing bite "—yes, and quite good, all in all. I might consider putting you on the breakfast shift, on a trial basis."

"I might consider the job, if cold cereal were the basic menu."

"You'll have to expand your horizons." She continued to eat, enjoying the hot, simple food on an empty stomach. "I believe you could be quite good at this with a few rudimentary lessons."

"From you?"

She lifted her wine, and her eyes laughed over the rim. "If you like. You certainly couldn't have a better teacher."

Her hair was still rumpled around her face—his hands had done that. Her cheeks were flushed, her eyes bright and flecked with gold. The robe threatened to slip off one shoulder, and left a teasing hint of skin exposed. As passion had stripped away his control, now emotions stripped away all logic.

"I love you, Summer."

She stared at him while the smile faded slowly. What went through her she didn't recognize. It didn't seem to be any one sensation, but a cornucopia of fears, excitement, disbelief and longings. Oddly, no one of them seemed dominant at first, but were so mixed and muddled she tried to grip any one of them and hold on to it. Not knowing what else to do, she set the glass down precisely, then stared at the wine shimmering inside.

"That wasn't a threat." He took her hand, holding it until she looked up at him again. "I don't see how it could come as that much of a surprise to you."

But it had. She expected affection. That was something she could deal with. She understood respect. But love—that was such a fragile word. Such an easily broken word. And something inside her begged for it to be taken from him, cherished, protected. Summer struggled against it.

"Blake, I don't need to hear that sort of thing the way other women do. Please—"

"Maybe you don't." He hadn't started the way he'd intended to, but now that he had, he'd finish. "But I need to say it. I've needed to for a long time now."

She drew her hand from his and nervously picked up her glass again. "I've always thought that words are the first thing that can damage a relationship."

"When they're not said," Blake countered. "It's a lack of words, a lack of meaning, that damages a relationship. This one isn't a word I use casually."

"No." She could believe that. It might have been the belief that had the fear growing stronger. Love, when it was given demanded some kind of return. She wasn't ready—she was sure she wasn't ready. "I think it's best, if we want things to go on as they are, that we—"

"I don't want things to go on as they are," he interrupted. He'd rather have felt annoyance than this panic that was sneaking in. He took a moment, trying to alleviate both. "I want you to marry me."

"No." Summer's own panic became full-blown. She stood quickly, as if that would erase the words, put back the distance. "No, that's impossible."

"It's very possible." He rose too, unwilling to have her draw away from him. "I want you to share my life, my name. I want to share children with you and all the years it takes to watch them grow."

"Stop." She threw up her hand, desperate to halt the words. They were moving her, and she knew it would be too easy to say yes and make that ultimate mistake.

"Why?" Before she could prevent it, he'd taken her face in his hands. The touch was gentle, though there was steel beneath. "Because you're afraid to admit it's something you want, too?"

"No, it's not something I want—it's not something I believe in. Marriage—it's a license that costs a few dollars. A piece of paper. For a few thousand dollars more, you can get a divorce decree. Another piece of paper."

He could feel her trembling and cursed himself for not knowing how to get through. "You know better than that. Marriage is two people who make promises to each other, and who make the effort to keep them. A divorce is giving up."

"I'm not interested in promises." Desperate, she pushed his hands from her face and stepped back. "I don't want any made to me, and I don't want to make any. I'm happy with my life just as it is. I have my career to think of."

"That's not enough for you, and we both know it. You can't tell me you don't feel for me. I can see it. Every time I'm with you it shows in your eyes, more each time." He was handling it badly, but saw no other course open but straight ahead. The closer he came, the further away she drew. "Damn it, Summer, I've waited long enough. If my timing's not as perfect as I wanted it to be, it can't be helped."

"Timing?" She dragged a hand through her hair. "What are you talking about? You've waited?" Dropping her hands, she began to pace the room. "Has this been one of your long-term plans, all neatly thought out, all meticulously outlined? Oh, I can see it." She let out a trembling breath and whirled back to him. It no longer made any difference to her if she were unreasonable. "Did you sit in your office and go over your strategy point by point? Was this the setting up, the looking for flaws, the following through?"

"Don't be ridiculous—"

"Ridiculous?" she tossed back. "No, I think not. You'd play the game well—disarming, confusing, charming, supportive. Patience, you'd have a lot of that. Did you wait until you thought I was at my most vulnerable?" Her breath was heaving now, and the words were tumbling out on each one. "Let me tell you something, Blake, I'm not a hotel chain you can acquire by waiting until the market's ripe."

In a slanted way she'd been killingly accurate. And the accuracy put him on the defensive. "Damn it, Summer, I want to marry you, not acquire you."

"The words are often one and the same, to my way of thinking. Your plan's a little off the mark this time, Blake. No deal. Now, I want you to leave me alone."

"We have a hell of a lot of talking to do."

"No, we have no talking to do, not about this. I work for you, for the term of the contract. That's all."

"Damn the contract." He took her by the shoulders, shaking her once in frustration. "And damn you for being so stubborn. I love you. That's not something you can brush aside as if it doesn't exist."

To their mutual surprise, her eyes filled abruptly, poignantly. "Leave me alone," she managed as the first tears spilled out. "Leave me completely alone."

The tears undermined him as her temper never would have done. "I can't do that." But he released her when he wanted to hold her. "I'll give you some time, maybe we both need time, but we'll have to come back to this."

"Just go away." She never allowed tears in front of anyone. Though she tried to dash them away, others fell quickly. "Go away." On the repetition she turned from him, holding herself stiff until she heard the click of the door.

She looked around, and though he was gone, he was everywhere. Dropping to the couch, she let herself weep and wished she were anywhere else.

She hadn't come to Rome for the cathedrals or the fountains or the art. Nor had she come for culture or history. As Summer took a wicked cab ride from the airport into the city, she was more grateful for the crowded streets and noise than the antiquity. Perhaps she'd stayed in America too long this time. Europe was fast cars, crumbling ruins and palaces. She needed Europe again, Summer told herself. As she zipped past the Trevi Fountain she thought of Philadelphia.

A few days away, she thought. Just a few days away, doing what she was best at, and everything would fall back into perspective again. She'd made a mistake with Blake—she'd known from the beginning it had been a mistake to get involved. Now it was up to her to break it off, quickly, completely. Before long he'd be grateful to her for preventing him from making an even larger mistake. Marriage—to her. Yes, she imagined he'd be vastly relieved, within even a few weeks.

Summer sat in the back of the cab watching Rome skim by and was more miserable than she'd ever been in her life.

When the cab squealed to a halt at the curb she climbed out. She stood for a moment, a slender woman in white fedora and jacket with a snakeskin bag slung carelessly over one shoulder. She was dressed like a woman of confidence and experience. In her eyes was a child who was lost.

Mechanically she paid off the driver, accepted her bag and his bow, then turned away. It was only just past 10:00 a.m. in Rome, and already hot under a spectacular sky. She remembered she'd left Philadelphia in a thunderstorm. Walking up the steps to an old, distinguished building, she knocked sharply five times. After a reasonable wait, she knocked again, harder.

When the door opened, she looked at the man in the short silk robe. It was embroidered, she noticed, with peacocks. On anyone else it would've looked absurd. His hair was tousled, his eyes half-closed. A night's growth of beard shadowed his chin.

"Hello, Carlo. Wake you up?"

"Summer!" He swallowed the string of Italian abuse that had been on his tongue and grabbed her. "A surprise, *si*?" He kissed her soundly, twice, then drew her away. "But why do you bring me a surprise at dawn?"

"It's after ten."

"Ten is dawn when you don't begin to sleep until five. But come in, come in. I don't forget you come for Gravanti's birthday."

Outside, Carlo's home was distinguished. Inside it

was opulent. Dominated by marble and gold, the entrance hall only demonstrated the beginning of his penchant for the luxurious. They walked through and under arches into a living area crowded with treasures, small and large. Most of them had been given to him by pleased clients—or women. Carlo had a talent for picking lovers who remained amiable even when they were no longer lovers.

There was a brocade at the windows, Oriental carpets on the floor and a Tintoretto on the wall. Two sofas were piled with cushions deep enough to swim in. An alabaster lion, nearly two feet in height, sat beside one. A three-tiered chandelier shot out splinters of refracted light from its crystals.

She ran her finger down a porcelain ewer in delicate Chinese blue and white. "New?"

"*Sì.*"

"Medici?"

"But of course. A gift from a…friend."

"Your friends are always remarkably generous."

He grinned. "But then, so am I."

"Carlo?"

The husky, impatient voice came from up the curving marble stairs. Carlo glanced up, then looked back at Summer and grinned again.

Summer removed her white fedora. "A friend, I take it."

"You'll give me a moment, *cara*." He was heading

for the steps as he spoke. "Perhaps you could go into the kitchen, make coffee."

"And stay out of the way," Summer finished as Carlo disappeared upstairs. She started toward the kitchen, then went back to take her suitcase with her. There wasn't any use leaving Carlo with something like luggage to explain to his friend.

The kitchen was as spectacular as the rest of the house and as large as the average hotel room. Summer knew it as well as she knew her own. It was all in ebonies and ivories with what appeared to be acres of counter space. It boasted two ovens, a restaurant-sized refrigerator, two sinks and a dishwasher that could handle the aftermath of an embassy dinner. Carlo Franconi had never been one to do anything in a small way.

Summer opened a cabinet for the coffee beans and grinder. On impulse, she decided to make crêpes. Carlo, she mused, might be just a little while.

When he did come, she was just finishing up at the stove. "Ah, *bella,* you cook for me. I'm honored."

"I had a twinge of guilt about disrupting your morning. Besides—" She slipped crêpes, pregnant with warm apples and cinnamon, onto plates. "I'm hungry." Summer set them on a scrubbed worktable while Carlo pulled up chairs. "I should apologize for coming like this without warning. Was your friend annoyed?"

He flashed a grin as he sat. "You don't give me enough credit."

"Scusi." She passed the small pitcher of cream. "So, we'll be working together for Enrico's birthday."

"My veal, with spaghetti. Enrico has a weakness for my spaghetti. Every Friday, he is in my restaurant eating." Carlo started immediately on the crêpe. "And you make the dessert."

"A birthday cake." Summer drank coffee while her crêpe cooled untouched. Suddenly, she had no appetite for it. "Enrico requested something special, created just for him. Knowing his vanity, and his fondness for chocolate and whipped cream, it was easy to come up with it."

"But the dinner isn't for two more days. You come early?"

She shrugged and toyed with her coffee. "I wanted to spend some time in Europe."

"I see." And he thought he did. She was looking a bit hollow around the eyes. A sign of romantic trouble. "Everything goes well in Philadelphia?"

"The remodeling's done, the new menus printed. I think the kitchen staff is going to do very well. I hired Maurice from Chicago. You remember?"

"Oh, yes, pressed duck."

"It's an exciting menu," she went on. "Just the sort I'd have if I ever decided to have a place of my own. I suppose I developed a bit of respect for you, Carlo, when I started to deal with the paperwork."

"Paperwork." He finished off his crêpes and eyed hers. "Ugly but necessary. You aren't eating, Summer."

"Hmm? No, I guess it's a touch of jet lag." She waved at her plate. "Go ahead."

Taking her at her word, he switched plates. "You solved the problem of Max?"

Absently she touched her arm. The stitches, thank God, were a thing of the past. "We're managing. Mother came to visit for a while. She always makes an impression."

"Monique! So, how is she?"

"Married again," Summer said simply and lifted her coffee. "A director this time, another American."

"She's happy?"

"Naturally." The coffee was strong—stronger than she'd grown used to in America. She thought in frustration that nothing was as it once was for her. "They're starting a film together in another few weeks."

"Perhaps her wisest choice. Someone who would understand her artistic temperament, her needs." He lingered over the perfect melding of spices and fruit. "And how is your American?"

Summer set down her coffee and stared at Carlo. "He wants to marry me."

Carlo choked on a bite of crêpe and grabbed for his cup. "So—congratulations."

"Don't be silly." Unable to sit, she rose, sticking her

hands in the pockets of her long, loose jacket. "I'm not going to."

"No?" Going to the stove, Carlo poured them both more coffee. "Why not? You find him unattractive, maybe? Bad tempered, stupid?"

"Of course not." Impatient, she curled and uncurled her fingers inside the jacket pockets. "That has nothing to do with it."

"What has?"

"I've no intention of getting married to anyone. That's one merry-go-round I can do without."

"You don't choose to grab for the brass ring, maybe because you're afraid you'd miss."

She lifted her chin. "Be careful, Carlo."

He shrugged at the icy tone. "You know I say what I think. If you'd wanted to hear something else, you wouldn't have come here."

"I came here because I wanted a few days with a friend, not to discuss marriage."

"You're losing sleep over it."

She'd picked up her cup and now slammed it down again. Coffee spilled over the sides. "It was a long flight and I've been working hard. And, yes, maybe I'm upset over the whole thing," she continued before Carlo could speak. "I hadn't expected this from him, hadn't wanted it. He's an honest man, and I know when he says he loves me and wants to marry me, he means it. For the moment. That doesn't make it any easier to say no."

Her fury didn't unnerve him. Carlo was well used to passionate emotions from women—he preferred them. "And you—how do you feel about him?"

She hesitated, then walked to the window. She could look out on Carlo's garden from there—a quiet, isolated spot that served as a border between the house and the busy streets of Rome. "I have feelings for him," Summer murmured. "Stronger feelings than are wise. If anything, they only make it more important that I break things off now. I don't want to hurt him, Carlo, any more than I want to be hurt myself."

"You're so sure love and marriage would hurt?" He put his hands on her shoulders and kneaded them lightly. "When you look so hard at the what-ifs in life, *cara mia,* you miss much living. You have someone who loves you, and though you won't say the words, I think you love him back. Why do you deny yourself?"

"Marriage, Carlo." She turned, her eyes earnest. "It's not for people like us, is it?"

"People like us?"

"We're so wrapped up in what it is we do. We're used to coming and going as we please, when we please. We have no one to answer to, no one to consider but ourselves. Isn't that why you've never married?"

"I could say I'm a generous man, and feel it would be too selfish to limit my gifts to only one woman." She smiled, fully, the way he'd wanted to see her smile.

Gently, he brushed the hair away from her face. "But to you, the truth is I've never found anyone who could make my heart tremble. I've looked. If I found her, I'd run for a license and a priest quickly."

With a sigh, she turned back to the window. The flowers were a tapestry of color in the strong sun. "Marriage is a fairy tale, Carlo, full of princes and peasants and toads. I've seen too many of those fairy tales fade."

"We write our own stories, Summer. A woman like you knows that because you've always done so."

"Maybe. But this time I just don't know if I have the courage to turn the next page."

"Take your time. There's no better place to think about life and love than *Roma*. No better man to think about them with than Franconi. Tonight, I cook for you. Linguini——" he kissed the tips of his fingers "——to die for. You can make me one of your babas— just like when we were students, *sì*?"

Turning back to him, Summer wrapped her arms around his neck. "You know, Carlo, if I were the marrying kind, I'd take you, for your pasta alone."

He grinned. "*Carissima,* even my pasta is nothing compared to my—"

"I'm sure," she interrupted dryly. "Why don't you get dressed and take me shopping? I need to buy something fantastic while I'm in Rome. I haven't given my mother a wedding present yet."

* * *

How could he have been so stupid? Blake flicked on his lighter and watched the flame cut through the darkness. It wouldn't be dawn for an hour yet, but he'd given up on sleep. He'd given up on trying to imagine what Summer was doing in Rome while he sat wakeful in an empty suite of rooms and thought of her. If he went to Rome...

No, he'd promised himself he'd give her some room, especially since he'd handled everything so badly. He'd given them both some room.

More strategy, he thought derisively and drew hard on the cigarette. Was that what the whole thing was about? He'd always enjoyed challenges, problems. Summer was certainly both. Was that the reason he wanted her? If she'd agreed to marry him, he could have congratulated himself on a plan well thought out and perfectly executed. Another Cocharan acquisition. Damn it.

He rose. He paced. Smoke curled from the cigarette between his fingers, then disappeared into the half-light. He knew better than that, even if she didn't. If it were true that he'd treated the whole affair like a problem to be carefully solved, it was only because that was his make-up. But he loved her, and if he were sure of anything, it was that she loved him too. How was he going to get over that wall she'd erected?

Go back to the way things were? Impossible. He

looked out at the city as the darkness began to soften. In the east, the sky was just beginning to lighten with the first hints of pink. Suddenly he realized he'd watched too many sunrises alone. Too much had changed between them now, Blake mused. Too much had been said. You couldn't take love back and lock it away for convenience's sake.

He'd stayed away from her for a full week before she'd gone to Rome. It had been much harder than he'd imagined it would be, but her tears that night had pushed him to it. Now he wondered if that had been yet another mistake. Perhaps if he'd gone to her the next day…

Shaking his head, he moved away from the window again. All along, his mistake had been trying to treat the situation with logic. There wasn't any logic in loving someone, only feelings. Without logic, he lost all advantage.

Madly in love. Yes, he thought the term very apt. It was all madness, an incurable madness. If she'd been with him, he could have shown her. Somehow, when she came back, he thought violently, he'd take that damn wall down piece by piece until she was forced to face the madness, too.

When the phone rang he stared at it. Summer? "Hello."

"Blake?" The voice was a little too sulky, a little too French.

"Yes. Monique?"

"I'm sorry to disturb you, but I always forget how much time is different between west and east. I was just going to bed. You were up?"

"Yes." The sun was slowly rising, the room was pale with light. Most of the city wasn't yet awake, but he was. "Did you have a good trip back to California?"

"I slept almost the whole way. Thank God, because there have been so many parties. So little changes in Hollywood—some of the names, some of the faces. Now, to be chic, one must wear sunglasses on a string. My mother did this, but only to keep from losing them."

He smiled because Monique demanded smiles. "You don't need trends to be chic."

"How flattering." Her voice was very young and very pleased.

"What can I do for you, Monique?"

"Oh, so sweet. First I must tell you how lovely it was to stay in your hotel again. Always the service is impeccable. And Summer's arm, it's better, no?"

"Apparently. She's in Rome."

"Oh, yes, my memory. Well, she was never one to sit too long in one space, my Summer. I saw her only briefly before I left. She seemed...preoccupied."

He felt his stomach muscles knotting, his jaw tightening. Deliberately he relaxed both. "She's been working very hard on the kitchen."

Monique's lips curved. He gives away nothing, this

one, she thought with approval. "Yes, well I may see her again for a short time. I must ask you a favor, Blake. You were so kind during my visit."

"Whatever I can do."

"The suite where I stayed, I found it so restful, so *agréable*. I wonder if you could reserve it for me again, in two days' time."

"Two days?" His brow creased, but he automatically reached for a pen to jot it down. "You're coming back east?"

"I'm so foolish, so—what is it?—absent-minded, *oui*? I have business to take care of there, and with Summer's accident, it all went out of my head. I must come back and tie up the ends that are loose. And the suite?"

"Of course, I'll see to it."

"*Merci*. And perhaps, I could ask one more thing of you. I will have a small party on Saturday evening— just a few old friends and some wine. I'd be very grateful if you could stop by for a few minutes. Around eight?"

There was nothing he wanted less at the moment than a party. But manners, upbringing and business left him only one answer. Again, he automatically noted down the date and time. "I'd be happy to."

"Marvelous. Till Saturday then, *au revoir*."

After hanging up the phone, Monique gave a tinkle of laughter. True, she was an actress, not a screenwriter, but she thought her little scenario was brilliant. Yes, absolutely brilliant.

Picking up the phone, she prepared to send a cablegram. To Rome.

Chapter 12

Chérie. Must return to Philadelphia for some unfinished business before filming begins. Will be at Cocharan House in my suite over the weekend. Having a little soirée Saturday evening. Do come. 8:30. A bientôt. Mother.

And just what was she up to? Summer glanced over the cable again as she cruised above the Atlantic. Unfinished business? Summer could think of no business Monique would have in Philadelphia, unless it involved husband number two. But that was ancient history, and Monique always had someone else handle her business dealings. She'd always claimed a good actress was a child at heart and had no head for business. It was another one of her diabolically helpless ways that made it possible for her to do only exactly as she wanted. What

Summer couldn't figure out was why Monique would want to come back east.

With a shrug, Summer slipped the cable back into her bag.

She didn't feel like hassling with people and cocktail talk in just over five hours. The day before, she'd outdone herself with the creation of a birthday cake shaped like Enrico's palatial home outside Rome, and filled with a wickedly wonderful combination of chocolate and cream. It had taken her twelve hours. And for once, at the host's insistence, she'd remained and joined the party for champagne and dessert.

She'd thought it would be good for her. The people, the elegance, the celebratory atmosphere. It had done no more than show her that she didn't want to be in Rome exchanging small talk and drinking wine. She wanted to be home. Home, though it surprised her, was Philadelphia.

She didn't long for Paris and her odd little flat on the Left Bank. She wanted her fourth-floor apartment in Philadelphia, where there were memories of Blake in every corner. However foolish it made her, however unwise or impractical it was, she wanted Blake.

Now, flying home, she found that hadn't changed. It was Blake she wanted to go to when she was on the ground again. It was to Blake she wanted to tell all the foolish stories she'd heard in Enrico's dining room. It was Blake she wanted to hear laugh. It was Blake she wanted to curl up next to now that the nervous energy of the past few days was draining.

Sighing, she tilted her seat back and closed her eyes. But she would do her duty and go to her mother's suite. Perhaps Monique's little party was the perfect diversion. It would give Summer just a bit more time before she faced Blake again. Blake, and the decision she had thought was already made.

B.C. ran a finger around the inside of the snug collar of his shirt and hoped he didn't look as nervous as he felt. Seeing Monique again after all these years— having to introduce Lillian to her. *Monique, my wife, Lillian. Lillian, Monique Dubois, a former lover. Small world, isn't it?*

Though he was a man who appreciated a good joke, this one eluded him.

It seemed there was no statute of limitations on marital transgressions. It was true that he'd only strayed once, and then during an unofficial separation from his wife that had left him angry, bitter and frightened. A crime committed once, was still a crime committed.

He loved Lillian, had always loved her, but he'd never be able to deny that the brief affair with Monique had happened. And he couldn't deny that it had been exciting, passionate and memorable.

They'd never contacted each other again, though once or twice he'd seen her when he was still actively working in the business. Even that had been so long ago.

So, why had she called him now, twenty years later, insisting that he come—with his wife—to her suite at the Philadelphia Cocharan House? He ran his finger around his collar once again. Something was choking him. Monique's only explanation had been that it concerned the happiness of his son and her daughter.

That had left him with the problem of fabricating a reason for coming into town and insisting that Lillian accompany him. That hadn't been a piece of cake, because he'd married a sharp-minded, independent woman, but it was nothing compared with the next ordeal.

"Are you going to fuss with that tie all day?" B.C. jumped as his wife came up behind him. "Easy." With a laugh, she brushed the back of his jacket, smoothing it over his shoulders in a habit that took him back to their honeymoon. "You'd think you'd never spent an evening with a celebrity before. Or is it just French actresses that make you nervous?"

This one French actress, B.C. thought and turned to his wife. She'd always been lovely, not the breath-catching beauty Monique had been, but lovely with the kind of quiet looks that remain lovely through the years. Her pure, rich brunette hair was liberally streaked with gray, but styled in such a way that the contrasting colors enhanced her looks.

Lillian had always had style. She'd been his partner, always, had stood up to him, stood by him. A strong woman. He'd needed a strong woman. She was the best damn first mate a man could ask for. He put his hands on her shoulders and kissed her, quite tenderly.

"I love you, Lily." When she touched his cheek and smiled, he took her hand, feeling like the condemned man walking his last mile. "We'd better go. We'll be late."

Blake hung up the phone in disgust. He was certain Summer would be back that evening. But though he'd called her apartment off and on for over an hour, there'd been no answer. He was out of patience, and in no mood to go down and be sociable in Monique's suite. Much like his father had done, he tugged on his tie.

When all this was over, when she was back, he was going to find a way to convince her to go away with him. He'd find that damn island in the Pacific if that's what it took. He'd *buy* the damn island and set up housekeeping. Build a chain of pizza parlors or fast-food restaurants. Maybe that would satisfy the woman.

Feeling unreasonable, and just a little mean, he strode out of the apartment.

Monique surveyed the suite and nodded. The flowers were a nice touch—not too many, just a few buds here and there to give the rooms a whiff of a garden. A touch—only a touch of romance. The wine was chilling, the glasses sparkling in the subdued lighting. And Max had outdone himself with the hors d'oeuvres, she decided. A little caviar, a little pâté, some miniature quiches—very elegant. She must remember to pay a visit to the kitchen.

As for herself—Monique touched a hand to the chignon at the base of her neck. Not her usual style, but she wanted to add the air of dignity. She felt the evening might call for it. But the black silk pants and off-the-shoulder blouse were sexy and chic. She simply couldn't resist the urge to dress with a bit of flair for the part.

The scene was set, she decided. Now it was only a matter for the players…

The knock came. With a slow smile, Monique went toward the door. Act one was about to begin.

"B.C.!" Her smile was brilliant, her hands thrown out to him. "How wonderful to see you again after all this time."

Her beauty was as stunning as ever. There was no resisting that smile. Though he'd been determined to be very aloof and very polite, his voice warmed. "Monique, you don't look a minute older."

"Always the charmer." She laughed, then kissed his cheek before she turned to the woman beside him. "And you are Lillian. How lovely that we meet at last. B.C. has told me so much of you, I feel we're old friends."

Lillian measured the woman across the threshold and lifted a brow. "Oh?"

No fool, this one, Monique decided instantly, and liked her. "Of course, that was all so long ago, so we must get to know each other all over again. Now please come in. B.C., you'd be kind enough to open a bottle of champagne."

A bundle of nerves, B.C. crossed the room to comply. A drink would be an excellent idea. He'd have preferred bourbon, straight up.

"Of course, I've seen you many times," Lillian began. "I'm sure you haven't made a movie I've missed, Ms. Dubois."

"Monique, please." In a simple, gracious gesture, she plucked a rosebud from a vase and handed it to Lillian. "And I'm flattered. From time to time I would retire, this last occasion has been the longest. But always, going back to the film is like going back to an old lover."

The cork blew out of the bottle like a missile and bounced off the ceiling. Calmly Monique slipped an arm through Lillian's. Inside she was giggling like a girl. "Such an exciting sound, is it not? It always makes me happy to hear champagne being opened. We must have a toast, *n'est-ce pas*?"

She lifted a glass with a flourish, and looked, to Lillian's thinking, just like the character she'd played in *Yesterday's Dream.*

"To fate, I think," Monique decided. "And the strange way it twists us all together." She clinked her glass against B.C.'s, then his wife's, before drinking. "So tell me, you are still enchanted with sailing, B.C.?"

He cleared his throat, no longer certain if he should watch his wife or Monique. Both of them were definitely watching him. "Ah, yes. As a matter of fact, Lillian and I just got back from Tahiti."

"How charming. A perfect place for lovers, *oui*?"

Lillian sipped her wine. "Perfect."

"Et voilà," Monique said when the knock sounded. "The next guest. Please help yourself." It was now Act Two. Having the time of her life, Monique went to answer. "Blake, so kind of you to come, and how charming you look."

"Monique." He took the hand she extended and brought it to his lips even as he calculated just how long it would be before he could make his escape. "Welcome back."

"I must be certain not to wear out the welcome. You'll be surprised by my other guests, I think." With this she gestured inside.

The last two people he'd expected to see in Monique's suite were his parents. He crossed the room and bent to kiss his mother. "Very surprised. I didn't know you were in town."

"We only got in a little while ago." Lillian handed her son a glass of champagne. "We did call your suite, but the phone was busy." Just what stage is this woman setting? Lillian wondered as Monique joined them.

"Families," she said grandly, helping herself to some caviar. "I have a great fondness for them. I must tell you both how I admire your son. The young Cocharan carries on the tradition, is it not so?"

For an instant, only an instant, Lillian's eyes narrowed. She wanted to know just what tradition the French actress referred to.

"We're both very proud of Blake," B.C. said with some relief. "He's not only maintained the Cocharan standard, but expanded it. The Hamilton chain was an excellent move." He toasted his son. "Excellent. How's the turnover in the kitchen going?"

"Very smoothly." And it was the last thing he wanted to discuss. "We start serving from the new menu tomorrow."

"Then we timed our visit well," Lillian put in. "We'll have a chance to test it firsthand."

"Do you know the coincidence?" Monique asked Lillian as she offered the tray of quiches.

"Coincidence?"

"But it is amusing. It is my daughter who now manages your son's kitchen."

"Your daughter." Lillian glanced at her husband. "No, it wasn't mentioned to me."

"She is a superb chef. You would agree, Blake? She often cooks for him," she added with a deliberate smile before he could make any comment.

Lillian held the rosebud under her nose. Interesting. "Really?"

"A charming girl," B.C. put in. "She has your looks, Monique, though I could hardly credit that you had a grown daughter."

"And I was just as surprised when I first met your son." She smiled at him. "Isn't it strange where the years go?"

B.C. cleared his throat and poured more wine.

Weeks before, Blake had wondered what messages had passed between Summer and his father. Now he had no trouble recognizing what wasn't being said between B.C. and Monique. He looked at his mother first and saw her calmly drinking champagne.

His father and Summer's mother? When? he wondered as he tried to digest it. For as long as he could remember, his parents had been devoted, almost inseparable. No—abruptly he remembered a short, turbulent time during his early teens. The house had been full of tension, arguments in undertones. Then B.C. had been gone for two weeks—three? A business trip, his mother had told him, but even then he'd known better. But it had been over so quickly, he'd rarely thought of it since. Now…now he had a definite idea where his father had spent at least some of that time away from home. And with whom.

He caught his father's eye—the uncomfortable, half-defiant look. The man, Blake mused, was certainly paying for a slip in fidelity that was two decades old. He saw Monique smile, slowly. Just what the hell was she trying to stir up?

Almost before the anger could fully form, she laid a hand on his arm. It was a gesture that asked him to wait, to be patient. Then came another knock. "Ah, excuse me. You would pour another glass?" Monique asked B.C. "We have one more guest tonight."

When she opened the door, Monique couldn't have been more pleased with her daughter. The simple jade silk dress was soft, narrow and subtly sexy. It made her slight pallor very romantic. "*Chérie,* so good of you not to disappoint me."

"I can't stay long, Mother, I have to get some sleep." She held out a pink-ribboned box. "But I wanted to bring you a wedding gift."

"So sweet." Monique brushed her lips over Summer's cheek. "And I have something for you. Something I hope you'll always treasure." Stepping aside, she drew Summer in.

Not like this, Summer thought desperately when the first shock of seeing Blake again rippled through her. She'd wanted to be prepared, rested, confident. She didn't want to see him here, now. And his parents— one look at the woman beside Blake and she knew she had to be B.C.'s wife. Nothing else made sense— Monique's kind of sense.

"Your game isn't amusing, Mother," she murmured in French.

"On the contrary, it might be the most important thing I've ever done. B.C.," she said in gay tones, "you've met my daughter, *oui*?"

"Yes, indeed." With a smile, he handed Summer a glass of champagne. "Nice to see you again."

"And Blake's mother," Monique continued. "Lillian, may I present my only child, Summer."

"I'm very pleased to meet you." Lillian took her hand warmly. She wasn't blind and had seen the stunned look that had passed between her son and the actress's daughter. There'd been surprise, longing and uncertainty. If Monique had set the stage for this, Lilian would do her best to help. "I've just been hearing that you're a chef and responsible for the new menu we'll be boasting of tomorrow."

"Yes." She searched for something to say. "Did you enjoy your sailing? Tahiti, wasn't it?"

"We had a marvelous time, even though B.C. tends to become Captain Bligh if you don't watch him."

"Nonsense." He slipped his arm around his wife's shoulders. "This is the only woman I'd ever trust at the wheel of one of my ships."

They adore each other. Summer realized it and found it surprised her. Their marriage was nearing its fortieth year, and obviously hadn't been without storms… yet they adored each other.

"It's rather beautiful, is it not, when a husband and wife can share an interest and yet be—separate people?" Monique beamed at them, then looked at Blake. "You would agree that such things keep a man and woman together, even when they have to struggle through hard times and misunderstandings?"

"I would." He looked directly at Summer. "It's a matter of love, and of respect and perhaps of...optimism."

"Optimism!" Monique clearly found the word perfect. "Yes, this I like. I, of course, am always so— perhaps too much. I've had four husbands, clearly too optimistic." She laughed at herself. "But then, I think I looked always first, and perhaps only, for romance. Would you say, Lillian, that it's a mistake not to look beyond that?"

"We all look for romance, love, passion." She touched her husband's arm lightly, in a gesture so natural neither of them noticed it. "Then of course respect. I suppose I'd have to add two things to that." She looked up at her husband. "Tolerance and tenacity. Marriage needs them all."

She knew. As B.C. saw the look in his wife's eyes he realized she'd always known. For twenty years, she'd known.

"Excellent." Rather pleased with herself, Monique set her gift on the table. "This is the perfect time then to open a gift celebrating my marriage. This time I intend to put all those things into it."

She wanted to leave. Summer told herself it was only a matter of turning around and walking to the door. She stood rooted, with her eyes locked on Blake's.

"Oh, but it's beautiful." Reverently, Monique lifted the tiny hand-crafted merry-go-round from the bed of tissue. The horses were ivory, trimmed in gilt—each one perfect, each one unique. At the turn of the base, it played a romantic Chopin Prelude. "But, darling, how perfect. A carousel to celebrate a marriage. The horses should be named romance, love, tenacity and so forth. I shall treasure it."

"I—" Summer looked at her mother, and suddenly none of the practicalities, none of the mistakes mattered. "Be happy, *ma mére.*"

Monique touched her cheek with a fingertip, then brushed it with her lips. "And you, *mignonne.*"

B.C. leaned down to whisper in his wife's ear. "You know, don't you?"

Amused, she lifted her glass. "Of course," she answered in an undertone. "You've never been able to keep secrets from me."

"But—"

"I knew then and hated you for almost a day. Do you remember whose fault it was? I don't anymore."

"God, Lily, if you'd known how guilty I was. Tonight, I was nearly suffocating with—"

"Good," she said simply. "Now, you old fool, let's get out of here so these children can iron things out.

Monique—" She held out her hand, and as hands met, eyes met, things passed between them that would never have to be said. "Thank you for a lovely evening, and my best wishes to you and your husband."

"And mine to you." With a smile reminiscent of the past, she held out her arms to B.C. *"Au revoir, mon ami."*

He accepted the embrace, feeling like a man who'd just been granted amnesty. He wanted nothing more than to go up to his own suite and show his wife how much he loved her. "Perhaps we'll have lunch tomorrow," he said absently to the room at large. "Good night."

Monique began to giggle as the door shut behind him. "Love, it will always make me laugh. So—" Briskly, she began to rewrap her gift and box it. "My bags are being held for me downstairs and my plane leaves in one hour."

"An hour?" Summer began. "But—"

"My business is done." Tucking the box under her arm, she rose on her toes to kiss Blake. "You have the good fortune of possessing excellent parents." Then she kissed Summer. "And so, my sweet, do you, though they weren't suited to remain husband and wife. The suite is paid for through the night, the champagne's still cold." She glided for the door leaving a trail of Paris in her wake. Pausing in the doorway, she looked back. *"Bon appétit, mes enfants."* Monique considered it one of her very finest exits.

When the door closed, Summer stood where she was, unsure if she wanted to applaud or throw something.

"Quite a performance," Blake commented. "More wine?"

She could be as urbane and casual as he. "All right."

"And how was Rome?"

"Hot."

"And your cake?"

"Magnificent." Lifting her freshly filled glass, she took two steps away. It was always better to talk of the unimportant when so many urgent needs were pressing. "Things running smoothly here?"

"Amazingly so. Though I think everyone'll be relieved that you're here for the first run tomorrow. Tell me—" he sipped his own wine, approving it "—when did you first know that my father and your mother had had an affair?"

That was blunt enough, she thought. Well, she would be equally blunt. "When it was happening. I was only a child, but children are astute. You could say I suspected it then. I was sure of it when I first mentioned my mother's name to your father."

He nodded, remembering the meeting in his office. "Just how much have you let that bother you?"

"It was awkward." Restlessly she moved her shoulders.

"And you were determined not to let history repeat itself."

His perception was too often killingly accurate. "Perhaps."

"But then, in a matter of speaking, it did."

With another attempt at casualness, she spread some caviar on a cracker. "But then, neither of us was married."

As if it were only general cocktail talk, Blake chose a quiche. "You know why your mother did this tonight."

Summer shook her head when he offered the tray. "Monique could never resist a scene of any kind. She set the stage, brought in the players, to show me, I think, that while marriage might not be perfect, it can be durable."

"Was she successful?" When she didn't speak, Blake set down his glass. It was time they stopped hedging, time they stopped speaking in generalities. "There hasn't been an hour since the last time I saw you that I haven't thought of you."

Her eyes met his. Helplessly she shook her head. "Blake, I don't think you should—"

"Damn it, you're going to hear me out. We're good for each other. You can't tell me you don't believe that. Maybe you were right before about the way I planned out my…courtship," he decided for a lack of a better word. "Maybe I was too smug about it, too sure that if I waited for just the right moment, I'd have exactly what I wanted with the least amount of trouble. I had to be sure or I'd've gone insane trying to give you enough time to see just what we could have together."

"I was too hard that night." She wrapped her arms around herself then dropped them to her sides. "I said things because you frightened me. I didn't mean them, not all of them."

"Summer." He touched her cheek. "I meant everything I said that night. I want you now as much as I wanted you the first time."

"I'm here." She stepped closer. "We're alone."

The need twisted inside him. "I want to make love with you, but not until I know what it is you want from me. Do you want only a few nights, a few memories, like our parents had together?"

She turned away then. "I don't know how to explain."

"Tell me how you feel."

She took a moment to steady herself. "All right. When I cook, I take this ingredient and that. I have my own hands, my own skill, and putting these together, I make something perfect. If I don't find it perfect, I toss it out. There's little patience in me." She paused a moment, wondering if he could possibly understand this kind of analogy. "I've thought that if I ever decided to become involved in a relationship, there would be this ingredient and that, and again I'd put them together. But I knew it would never be perfect. So..." She let out a long breath. "I wondered if that too would be something to toss out."

"A relationship isn't something that has to be created in a day, or perfected in a day. Part of the game is to keep working on it. Fifty years still isn't long enough."

"A long time to work on something that'll always be just a little flawed."

"Too much of a challenge?"

She whirled, then stopped. "You know me too well," she murmured. "Too well for my own good. Maybe too well for your own."

"You're wrong," he said quietly. "You are my own good."

Her mouth trembled open, then closed. "Please," she managed, "I want to finish this. When I was in Rome, I tried to tell myself that this was what I wanted—to go back to flying here, there, without anyone to worry about but myself and the next dish I would create. When I was in Rome," she added with a sigh, "I was more miserable than I've ever been in my life."

He couldn't prevent the grin. "Sorry to hear it."

"No, I think you're not." Turning away, she ran her fingertip around and around the rim of a champagne glass. Since she would only explain once, she wanted to be certain she explained well. "On the plane, I told myself that when I came back, we would talk, reasonably, logically. We'd work the situation out in the best manner. In my head, I thought that would be a continuation of our relationship as it was. Intimacy without strings, which is perhaps not intimacy at all." She lifted the glass and sipped some of the cold, frothy wine. "When I walked in here tonight and saw you, I knew that would be impossible. We can't see each other as we have been. In the end, that would damage us both."

"You're not walking out of my life."

Turning back, she stood toe-to-toe with him. "I would, if I could. And damn it, you're not the one who's stopping me. It's me! None of your planning, none of your logic could've changed what was inside me. Only I could change it, only what I feel could change it."

She took his hands. She took a deep breath. "I want to ride that merry-go-round with you, and I want my shot at the brass ring."

His hands slid up her arms, into her hair. "Why? Just tell me why."

"Because sometime between the moment you walked in my front door and now, I fell in love with you. No matter how foolish it is, I want to take a chance on that."

"We're going to win." His mouth sought hers, and when she trembled he knew it was as much from nerves as passion. Soon they'd face the passion, now he would soothe the nerves. "If you like, we'll take a trial period." He began to roam her face with kisses. "We can even put it in contract form—more practical."

"Trial?" She started to draw away from him, but he held her close.

"Yes, and if during the trial period either of us wants

a divorce, they simply have to wait until the end of the contract term."

Her brows came together. Could he speak of business now? Would he dare? Her chin tilted challengingly. "How long is the contract term?"

"Fifty years."

Laughing, she threw her arms around his neck. "Deal. I want it drawn up tomorrow, in triplicate. But tonight—" she began to nibble on his lips as she ran her hands beneath his jacket "—tonight we're only lovers. Truly lovers now. And the suite is ours till morning."

The kiss was long—it was slow—it was lingering.

"Remind me to send Monique a case of champagne," Blake said as he lifted Summer into his arms.

"Speaking of it…" Leaning over—a bit precariously—she lifted the two half-full glasses from the table. "We shouldn't let it get flat. And later," she continued as he carried her toward the bedroom, "much later, perhaps we can send out for pizza."

* * * * *

Don't miss the next enticing release from
New York Times Bestselling author
NORA ROBERTS,
For Now, Forever,
which is available in December 2017!

Continue reading to see a glimpse of how
Daniel and Anna MacGregor's love story began...

Chapter 1

An empire. At the time he'd turned fifteen, Daniel MacGregor had promised himself he'd have one, build one, rule one. He always kept his word.

He was thirty years old and working on his second million with the same drive that had earned him his first. As he always had, he used his back, his brains and pure guile in whatever order worked best. When he'd come to America five years before, Daniel had had the money he'd saved by working his way up from miner to head bookkeeper for Hamus McGuire. He'd also brought a shrewd brain and towering ambition.

He could have passed for a king. He topped six-four with a build bold enough to suit his height. His size alone had kept him out of a number of fights, just as his size had seduced some men into challenging him. Either way was fine with Daniel. He was reputed to have a temper, but he considered himself a mild sort of person. Daniel didn't think he'd broken more than his share of noses in his day. He didn't consider himself handsome, either. His jaw was long and square, and running along its right edge was a scar that he'd gotten when a loose beam had toppled down on him in the mines. As a sop to his vanity, he'd grown a beard in his teens. A dozen years later it remained, deep red and well trimmed around his face, blending with a mane of hair that was too long for fashion. The combination made him look both fierce and royal, which pleased him. His cheekbones rose high and wide, and his mouth appeared surprisingly soft in its cushion of wild red hair. His eyes were a deep brilliant blue that lit with humor and goodwill when he smiled and meant it, just as they cooled to frost when he smiled and didn't.

Imposing. That was one adjective used to describe him. Ruthless was another. Daniel didn't care how he was described as long as he didn't go unnoticed. He was a gambler who played the odds boldly. Real estate was his wheel, and the stock market was his game table. When Daniel gambled, he played to win. The chances he'd taken had paid off. And when they had, he'd taken more. He never intended to play it too safe, because with safety came boredom.

Though he'd been born poor, Daniel MacGregor

didn't worship money. He used it, wielded it, played with it. Money equaled power, and power was a weapon.

In America he found himself in a vast arena of wheeling and dealing. There was New York with its fast pace and hungry streets. A man with brains and nerve could build a fortune there. There was Los Angeles with its glamour and high stakes. A man with imagination could fashion an empire. Daniel had spent time in both, dabbled in business on either coast, but he chose Boston as his base and as his home. It wasn't simply money or power he sought, but style. Boston with its old-world charm, its stubborn dignity and its unapologetic snobbishness suited Daniel perfectly.

He'd come from a long line of warriors who had lived as much by wit as by the sword. His pride in his line was fierce, as fierce as his ambition. Daniel intended to see his line continue with strong sons and daughters. As a man of vision, he had no trouble seeing his grandchildren taking what he'd molded and building on it. There could be no empire without family to share it. To begin one, he needed the proper wife. Acquiring one, to Daniel, was as challenging and as logical as acquiring a prime piece of real estate. He'd come to the Donahues' summer ball to speculate on both.

He hated the tight collar and strangulating tie. When a man was built like a bull, he liked his neck free. His clothes were made in Boston by a tailor on Newbury Street. Daniel used him as much because his size demanded it as for the prestige. Ambition had put him in a suit, but he didn't have to like it. Another man dressed in the elegant black dinner suit and pleated silk shirt would have looked distinguished. Daniel, in either tartan or dress blacks, looked flamboyant. He preferred it that way.

Cathleen Donahue, Maxwell Donahue's eldest daughter, preferred it, as well.

"Mr. MacGregor." Fresh out of finishing school in Switzerland, Cathleen knew how to serve tea, embroider silk and flirt elegantly. "I hope you're enjoying our little party."

She had a face like porcelain and hair like flax. Daniel thought it a pity her shoulders were so thin, but he, too, knew how to flirt. "I'm enjoying it more now, Miss Donahue."

Knowing most men were put off by giggles, Cathleen kept her laugh low and smooth. Her taffeta skirts whispered as she positioned herself beside him at the end of the long buffet table. Now, whoever stopped for a taste of truffles or salmon mousse would see them together. If she turned her head just a fraction, she could catch a glimpse of their reflection in one of the long narrow mirrors that lined the wall. She decided she liked what she saw.

"My father tells me you're interested in buying a little piece of cliff he owns in Hyannis Port." She fluttered her lashes twice. "I hope you didn't come here tonight to discuss business."

Daniel slipped two glasses from the tray of a passing waiter. He'd have preferred Scotch in a sturdy glass to champagne in crystal, but a man who didn't adjust in certain areas broke in others. As he drank, he studied Cathleen's face. He knew Maxwell Donahue would no more have discussed business with his daughter than he would have discussed fashion with her, but Daniel didn't fault her for lying. Rather he gave her credit for knowing how to dig out information. But while he admired her for it, it was precisely the reason he didn't consider her proper wife material. His wife would be too busy raising babies to worry about business.

"Business comes second to a lovely woman. Have you been to the cliffs?"

"Of course." She tilted her head so that the diamond flowers in her ears caught the light. "I do prefer the city. Are you attending the Ditmeyers' dinner party next week?"

"If I'm in town."

"So much traveling." Cathleen smiled before she sipped her champagne. She'd be very comfortable with a husband who traveled. "It must be exciting."

"It's business," he said. Then he added, "But you've just returned from Paris yourself."

Flattered that he'd been aware of her absence, Cathleen almost beamed. "Three weeks wasn't enough.

Shopping alone took nearly every moment I had. You can't imagine how many tedious hours I spent in fittings for this gown."

He swept his gaze down and up as she'd expected. "I can only say it was well worth it."

"Why, thank you." As she stood, posing, his mind began to drift. He knew women were supposed to be interested mainly in dresses and hairstyles, but he'd have preferred a more stimulating conversation. Sensing she was losing his attention, Cathleen touched his arm. "You've been to Paris, Mr. MacGregor?"

He'd been to Paris and had seen what war could do to beauty. The pretty blonde smiling up at him would never be touched by war. Why should she be? Still, vaguely dissatisfied, Daniel sipped the dry bubbling wine. "Some years ago." He glanced around at the glitter of jewels, the sparkle of crystal. There was a scent in the air that could only be described as wealth. In five years he'd become accustomed to it, but he hadn't forgotten the smell of coal dust. He never intended to forget it. "I've come to prefer America to Europe. Your father knows how to throw a party."

"I'm glad you approve. You're enjoying the music?"

He still missed the wail of bagpipes. The twelve-piece orchestra in white tie was a bit stiff for his taste, but he smiled. "Very much."

"I thought perhaps you weren't." She sent him a

slow, melting look from under her lashes. "You aren't dancing."

In a courtly gesture, Daniel took the champagne from Cathleen and set both their glasses down. "Oh, but I am, Miss Donahue," he corrected, and swept her onto the dance floor.

"Cathleen Donahue continues to be obvious." Myra Lornbridge nibbled pâté and sniffed.

"Keep your claws sheathed, Myra." The voice was low and smooth, by nature rather than design.

"I don't mind when a person's rude or calculating or even a bit stupid—" with a sigh, Myra finished off the cracker "—but I do detest it when one is obvious."

"Myra."

"All right, all right." Myra poked at the salmon mousse. "By the way, Anna, I love your dress."

Anna glanced down at the rose-colored silk. "You picked it out."

"I told you I loved it." Myra gave a self-satisfied smile at the way the folds draped over Anna's hips. Very chic. "If you'd pay half the attention to your wardrobe as you do your books, you'd put Cathleen Donahue's nose out of joint."

Anna only smiled and watched the dancers. "I'm not interested in Cathleen's nose."

"Well, it isn't very interesting. How about the man she's dancing with?"

"The red-haired giant?"

"So you noticed."

"I'm not blind." She wondered how soon she could make a dignified exit. She really wanted to go home and read the medical journal Dr. Hewitt had sent her.

"Know who he is?"

"Who?"

"Anna." Patience was a virtue Myra extended only to her closest friends. "Fe fi fo fum."

With a laugh, Anna sipped her wine. "All right, who is he?"

"Daniel Duncan MacGregor." Myra paused a bit, hoping to pique Anna's interest. At twenty-four, Myra was rich and attractive. Beautiful, no. Even at her best, Myra knew she'd never be beautiful. She understood beauty was one route to power. Brains were another. Myra used her brains. "He's Boston's current boy wonder. If you'd pay more attention to who's who in our cozy little society, you'd recognize the name."

Society, with its games and restrictions, didn't interest Anna in the least. "Why should I? You'll tell me."

"Serve you right if I didn't."

But Anna only smiled and drank again.

"All right, I'll tell you." Gossip was one temptation Myra found impossible to resist. "He's a Scot, which is obvious I suppose from his looks and his name. You should hear him talk, it's like cutting through fog."

At that moment, Daniel let out a big, booming laugh

that raised Anna's eyebrows. "That sounds as though it would cut through anything."

"He's a bit rough around the edges, but some people—" she cast a meaningful look at Cathleen Donahue "—believe that a million dollars or so smooths out anything."

Realizing that the man was being weighed and judged by the size of his bank balance, Anna felt a twinge of sympathy. "I hope he knows he's dancing with a viper," Anna murmured.

"He doesn't look stupid. He bought Old Line Savings and Loan six months ago."

"Really." She shrugged. Business only interested Anna when it involved a hospital budget. Sensing the movement to her left, she turned to smile at Herbert Ditmeyer standing with an unfamiliar gentleman. "How are you?"

"Glad to see you." He was only a few inches taller than Anna and had the lean, ascetic face of a scholar, with dark hair that promised to thin in a matter of years. But there was a strength around his mouth that Anna respected, and he had a sense of humor it took a sharp wit to understand. "You're looking lovely." He gestured to the man beside him. "My cousin, Mark. Anna Whitfield and Myra Lornbridge." Herbert's gaze lingered just a moment longer on Myra, but as the orchestra began a new waltz, he lost his nerve and took Anna's arm. "You should be dancing."

Anna matched her steps to his naturally. She loved to dance, but preferred to do so with someone she knew. Herbert was comfortable. "I heard congratulations are in order—" she smiled up into his dependable face "—Mr. District Attorney."

He grinned. He was young for the position but had no intention of stopping there. If he hadn't considered it bad form, he might have told Anna of his ambitions. "I wasn't sure Boston news traveled as far as Connecticut." He glanced to where Myra was dancing with his cousin. "I suppose I should have known better."

Anna laughed as they twirled around another couple. "Just because I've been out of town doesn't mean I don't want to keep up with what's happening here in Boston. You must be very proud."

"It's a beginning," Herbert said lightly. "And you—one more year and we'll have to call you Dr. Whitfield."

"One more year," Anna murmured. "Sometimes it seems like forever."

"Impatient, Anna? That's not like you."

Yes, it was, but she'd always managed to conceal it so successfully. "I want it to be official. It's no secret that my parents disapprove."

"They might disapprove," Herbert added, "but your mother doesn't have any trouble mentioning you're in the top ten percent of your class for the third year running."

"Really?" Surprised, Anna thought it over. Her mother

had always been more apt to praise her hairstyle than her grades. "I'll have to be grateful for that then, though she still harbors the hope that some man will come along and make me forget about operating rooms and bedpans."

As she spoke, Herbert turned her. Anna found herself looking directly into Daniel MacGregor's eyes. She felt her stomach muscles tighten. Nerves? Ridiculous. She felt the quick chill that raced down her spine and up again. Fear? Absurd.

Though he still danced with Cathleen, he stared at Anna. Stared at her in a way that was designed to make a young woman's cheeks flush. Anna stared back coolly while her heart raced. Perhaps it was a mistake. He seemed to take it as a challenge and smiled very slowly.

With a detached admiration, she watched him maneuver. Catching the eye of another man on the edge of the dance floor, Daniel gave a quick, almost imperceptible signal. Within moments, Cathleen found herself dancing in the arms of another man. Anna braced herself for the next step.

With the ease of experience, Daniel weaved through the dancers. He'd noticed Anna the moment she'd begun to dance. Noticed, then watched, then calculated. As soon as she'd glanced over and had given him that coolly appraising stare, he'd been hooked. She didn't have the stature of Cathleen, but seemed small and delicate. Her hair was dark and looked as warm and soft as sable. Her eyes matched it. The rose hue of her dress set off her creamy skin and smooth shoulders. She looked like a woman who would fit easily into a man's arms.

With the confidence he carried everywhere, Daniel tapped Herbert's shoulder. "May I cut in?"

Daniel waited only until Herbert had relinquished his hold before he clasped Anna and swirled her back into the dance. "That was very clever, Mr. MacGregor."

It pleased him that she knew his name. It pleased him as well that he'd been right about the way she'd fit into his arms. She smelled like moonbeams, soft and quiet. "Thank you, Miss…?"

"Whitfield. Anna Whitfield. It was also very rude."

He stared a moment because the stern voice didn't fit the quietly lovely face. Always one to appreciate a surprise, Daniel laughed until heads turned. "Aye, but I go with what works. I don't believe I've seen you before, Miss Anna Whitfield, but I know your parents."

"That's very possible." The hand holding hers was huge, hard as rock and incredibly gentle. Her palm began to itch. "Are you new to Boston, Mr. Mac-Gregor?"

"I'll have to say yes because I've lived here only two years, not two generations."

She tilted her head a bit farther so that she could keep her eyes on his. "You have to go back at least three not to be new."

"Or you have to be clever." He twirled her in three quick circles.

Pleasantly surprised that for his size he was light on his feet, Anna relaxed just a little. It would be a shame to waste the music. "I've been told you are."

"You'll be told so again." He didn't bother to keep his voice low, though the dance floor was crowded. Power, not propriety, was his forte.

"Will I?" Anna cocked a brow. "How odd."

"Only if you don't understand the system," he corrected her, unsinged. "If you can't have the generations behind you, you need money in front."

Though she knew it was true, Anna disliked both forms of snobbery. "How fortunate for you society has such flexible standards."

Her dry, disinterested voice made him smile. She wasn't a fool this Anna Whitfield, nor was she a silk-coated barracuda like Cathleen Donahue. "You've a face like the cameo my grandmother wore around her neck."

Anna lifted a brow and nearly smiled at him. The look made him realize he'd said no more than the truth. "Thank you, Mr. MacGregor, but you'd be better off saving your flattery for Cathleen. She's more susceptible."

A frown clouded his eyes, and he looked fierce and formidable, but it cleared quickly, before Anna could gauge her reaction. "You've a cool tongue in your head, lassie. I admire a woman who speaks her mind…to a point."

Feeling aggressive for no reason she could name, Anna kept her gaze directly on his. "What point is that, Mr. MacGregor?"

"To the point where it becomes unfeminine."

Before she'd anticipated his move, Daniel swung her through the terrace doors. Until that moment she hadn't realized just how hot and stuffy the ballroom had become. Regardless of that, Anna's normal reaction with a man she didn't know would have been to excuse herself firmly and finally and walk back inside. Instead, she found herself stopping just where she was, with Daniel's arms still around her, the moonlight pouring over the flagstones and warm roses scenting the air.

"I'm sure you have your own definition of femininity, Mr. MacGregor, but I wonder if you keep it in tune with the fact that we're in the twentieth century."

He enjoyed the way she stood in his arms and subtly insulted him. "I've always considered femininity a constant thing, Miss Whitfield, not something that changes with years or fashion."

"I see." His arms seemed to fit around her a bit too easily. She drew herself away to stroll to the edge of the terrace nearest the gardens. The air was sweeter there, the moonlight dimmer. The music became more romantic with distance.

It occurred to her that she was having a private conversation, one that might have been approaching an argument, with a man she'd only just met. Yet she didn't feel any urge to cut it short. She'd taught herself to be comfortable around men. She'd had to. As the only woman in her graduating class, Anna had learned how to deal with men on their own level and how to do so without constantly rubbing against their egos. She'd gotten through the first year of criticism and innuendos by staying calm and concentrating on her studies. Now she was about to enter her last year of medical school, and for the most part, Anna was accepted by her colleagues. She was perfectly aware, however, of what she would face when she began her internship. The stigma of being labeled unfeminine still stung a bit, but she was long resigned to it.

"I'm sure your views on femininity are fascinating, Mr. MacGregor." The hem of her dress skimmed the flagstone as she turned. "But I don't think it's something I care to discuss. Tell me, what is it exactly that you do in Boston?"

He hadn't heard her. He hadn't heard anything from the moment she'd turned back to face him. Her hair swung softly just at her white, smooth shoulders. In the thin rose-colored silk, her body looked as delicate as fine china. The moonlight filtered over her face so that her skin was like marble and her eyes as dark as midnight. A man hears nothing but the thunder when he's struck by lightning.

"Mr. MacGregor?" For the first time since they'd stepped outside, Anna's nerves began to hum. He was huge, a stranger, and he was looking at her as though he'd lost his senses. She straightened her shoulders and reminded herself she could handle any situation that came along. "Mr. MacGregor?"

"Aye." Daniel pulled himself out of his fantasy and stepped closer. Oddly Anna relaxed. He didn't seem as dangerous when he stood beside her. And his eyes were beautiful. True, there was a very simple genetic reason for their shade. She could have written a paper on it. But they were beautiful.

"You do work in Boston, don't you?"

"I do." Perhaps it had been a trick of the light that had made her look so perfect, so ethereal and seductive. "I buy." He took her hand because personal contact was vital to him. He took it because part of him wanted to be assured she was real. "I sell."

His hand was warm and as gentle as it had been when they'd danced. Anna drew hers away. "How interesting. What do you buy?"

"Whatever I want." Smiling, he stepped a bit closer. "Whatever."

Her pulse accelerated, her skin heated. Anna knew there were emotional as well as physical causes for such things. Though she couldn't think of them at the moment, she didn't back away. "I'm sure that's very satisfying. That leads me to believe you sell whatever you no longer want."

"In a nutshell, Miss Whitfield. And at a profit."

Conceited ox, she thought mildly and tilted her head. "Some might consider that arrogance, Mr. MacGregor."

She made him laugh with the cool, calm way she spoke, the cool, calm way she looked even when he could see traces of passion in her eyes. She was a woman, he thought, who could make a man wait on the doorstep with bouquets and heart-shaped boxes of candy. "When a poor man's arrogant it's crude, Miss Whitfield. When a man of means is arrogant, it's called style. I've been both."

She felt there was some truth in his words but wasn't willing to give an inch. "Strange, I've never felt arrogance changes with years or with fashion."

He took out a cigar as he watched her. "Your point." His lighter flared, highlighting his eyes for one brief instant. In that moment, Anna realized he was dangerous after all.

"Then perhaps we should call it a draw." Pride prevented her from stepping back. Dignity prevented her from continuing what was, despite logic, becoming interesting. "Now, if you'll excuse me, Mr. MacGregor, I really must get back inside."

He took her arm in a way that was both abrupt and proprietary. Anna didn't jerk away, and she didn't freeze; she merely looked at him as a duchess might look at a dust-covered commoner. Faced with that serene disapproval, most men would have dropped their hand and mumbled apologies. Daniel grinned at her. *Now here's a lass,* he thought, *who'd make a man's knees tremble.* "I'll see you again, Miss Anna Whitfield."

"Perhaps."

"I'll see you again." He lifted her hand to his lips. She felt the soft, surprising brush of his beard across her knuckles, and for a moment, the trace of passion he'd seen in her eyes flared full blown. "And again."

"I doubt we'll have much occasion to socialize, as I'll only be in Boston for a couple of months. Now, if you'll excuse me—"

"Why?"

He didn't release her hand, which troubled her more than she could permit to show. "Why what, Mr. Mac-Gregor?"

"Why will you only be in Boston for a couple of months?" If she were running off to get married it might change things. Daniel looked at her again and decided he wouldn't allow it to change anything.

"I go back to Connecticut at the end of August for my last year in medical school."

"Medical school?" His brows drew together. "You're not going to be a nurse?" His voice carried the vague puzzlement of a man who had no understanding of, and little tolerance for, professional women.

"No." She waited until she felt him relax. "A surgeon. Thank you for the dance."

But he had her arm again before she could reach the door. "You're going to cut people open?" For the second time she heard his laughter boom out. "You're joking."

Though she bristled, she managed to make it appear she was simply bored. "I promise you I'm much more amusing when I joke. Good night, Mr. MacGregor."

"Being a doctor's a man's job."

"I appreciate your opinion. I happen to believe there is no such thing as a man's job if a woman is capable of doing it."

He snorted, puffed on his cigar and muttered, "Pack of nonsense."

"Succinctly put, Mr. MacGregor, and again, rude. You are consistent." She walked through the terrace doors without looking back. But she did think of him. Brash, crude, flamboyant and foolish.

He thought of her as he watched her slip into the crowd. Cool, opinionated, blunt and ridiculous.

They were both fascinated.